Peng
ZAYNI BARAKAT

Gamal al-Ghitani was born in 1945 and educated in Cairo. As a war reporter he has covered the Arab–Israeli conflicts, the Lebanon and the Iran–Iraq war. He has published six collections of short stories and is widely regarded as the most important living Egyptian novelist.

Farouk Abdel Wahab is based at the Center for Middle Eastern Studies at the University of Chicago.

Edward Said is Parr Professor of English at Columbia University and is the author of many books, including *Orientalism* (Penguin 1985).

90p

Gamal al-Ghitani

ZAYNI BARAKAT

TRANSLATED FROM THE ARABIC BY
FAROUK ABDEL WAHAB

PENGUIN BOOKS

PENGUIN BOOKS

Published by the Penguin Group
27 Wrights Lane, London w8 5tz, England
Viking Penguin Inc., 40 West 23rd Street, New York, New York 10010, USA
Penguin Books Australia Ltd, Ringwood, Victoria, Australia
Penguin Books Canada Ltd, 2801 John Street, Markham, Ontario, Canada l3r 1b4
Penguin Books (NZ) Ltd, 182–190 Wairau Road, Auckland 10, New Zealand

Penguin Books Ltd, Registered Offices: Harmondsworth, Middlesex, England

First published by the Ministry of Culture, Damascus, 1971
This translation first published in Great Britain by Viking 1988
Published in Penguin Books 1990
1 3 5 7 9 10 8 6 4 2

Printed and bound in Great Britain by
Richard Clay Ltd, Bungay, Suffolk
Filmset in Photina

Contents

Foreword

First published in Damascus in 1971, *Zayni Barakat* is the work of a remarkable Egyptian novelist, Gamal al-Ghitani. Originally a designer of rugs, he published two short-story collections before *Zayni* appeared, when he was only twenty-nine. Since that time al-Ghitani has written several more novels and collections of short stories, each of which has added stature to his considerable reputation. In addition, he has continued to work in journalism, first as a correspondent (covering the major Arab conflagrations, including the siege of Beirut), then as a commentator and essayist.

But it is as a novelist of vision and daring that al-Ghitani is best appreciated, and *Zayni Barakat* is a particularly good place to see him at work. It is set in early sixteenth-century Cairo, just at the time when Mamluk reign (which had begun in the mid thirteenth century) is about to be defeated by the invading Ottomans. A Venetian traveller, Visconti Gianti, tells of events during this troubled unpleasant period in Egypt's history, on the threshold of the long Ottoman epoch, which lasted until the early twentieth century and caused major changes, not only in Egyptian history, but in Middle Eastern history as a whole. Yet Gianti's narrations are intermittent. Other narrators, medieval native Muslims all, participate in the telling of the tale: the rise and enigmatic, deeply problematic career of Zayni Barakat ibn Musa, a man whose austere, almost evangelical, attitude to public morality places him at the pinnacle of Cairo's civil society. The nature of his rule and power furnishes the novel with its central intrigue and its major themes.

These are, of course, historical, but they have an urgent connection with the present, that is modern, post-independent, post-revolutionary Egypt. In his return to the world of medieval chronicles, al-Ghitani has important predecessors in Egyptian fiction, though his particular modes as a contemporary novelist distinguish him from other practising novelists today. An earlier generation of writers, Girgi Zeidan most prominent among them, used fiction as a sort of adjunct to nationalism, much as Walter Scott did a century before; the history of the Arabs as narrated by Zeidan gives texture and historical breadth to the struggle for nationhood during the last years of European tutelage. The result was to have been, in Benedict Anderson's phrase, an imagined community of unified Arabs, a prospective goal for the present based upon a fully presented national story in the past. Some of this is ironically relevant to *Zayni Barakat*, whose crux is the defeat of an indigenous order by a newly powerful outside force. In his obsession with purity of life, with honesty, with reform, as well as puritanical and retributive justice, Zayni corresponds with Gamal Abdel Nasser, also a popular figure, genuine reformer, ambitious patriot, whose pan-Arab plans for Egypt collapsed ignominiously in 1967. Al-Ghitani's disenchanted reflections upon the past directly associate Zayni's rule with the murky atmosphere of intrigue, conspiracy and multiple schemes that characterized Abdel Nasser's rule during the 1960s, a time, according to Ghitani, spent on futile efforts to control and improve the moral standard of Egyptian life, even as Israel (the Ottomans) prepared for invasion and regional dominance. An even more damning indictment of Zayni and the nationalism he represents is that he is able to survive the Ottomans' victory and to re-emerge as ruler under their wing.

Yet al-Ghitani is still a nationalist whose appreciation of the great figure criticized so profoundly in the novel none the less answers very exactly to Egyptian needs, past and present. Zayni is no roguish adventurer, no mere conspirator, no corrupt deceiver and unacceptable outsider. He is the brightest and best of Egypt's sons, and if he errs it is partly out of zeal, partly because of the illusions of power. But here Ghitani's narrative techniques tell the story brilliantly. Unlike his immediate fictional predecessors (the early and middle Naguib Mahfouz, principally), al-Ghitani is not a social realist, influenced by Balzac, Gogol and Dickens. His reality is less stable, more tricky, less amenable to definition and representation, just as post-revolutionary Egypt is a world dominated not only by American and Israeli power, but by 'the consciousness industry', by subtle techniques of surveillance and political intelligence, by overlapping brigades of state security forces. Therefore Zayni's story is told by multiple narrators, each of whom complements and, to some extent, contradicts the others. Like Conrad, James and Ford, al-Ghitani multiplies, but does not confine, reality; his style, with its assured use of antique sources, its unerring depiction of character in pursuit of interest, its unique power to convey the wonderful flavours, sights, sounds of the city of Cairo (whose Arabic name *al-Qahira* means the 'city triumphant'), accomplishes the paradoxical feat of complicating reality in the process of rendering it.

Even though some of its scenes are full of rococo grisliness (the tortures of various delinquents are reminiscent of de Sade and Foucault) and ornate evasions, *Zayni Barakat* is a gripping, unforgettable work of prose fiction. It displays its author's originality of conception and execution at every step. The beauty of it, moreover, is that, as a novel in Arabic written in and about contemporary Egypt, *Zayni Barakat* also attains to the status of world literature, a position made possible for the novel by Farouk Mustafa's elegant and perspicaciously sensitive English translation.

Translator's Note

The events depicted in *Zayni Barakat* take place over the last ten years or so of Mamluk rule in Egypt. The Ottoman conquest in AD 1517 put an end to a dynasty that had ruled Egypt and most of the Near East for 267 years. In what follows I shall outline the salient features of that dynasty and the conditions of Egyptian society under the Mamluks. I shall also comment briefly on the uses the author has made of his main Egyptian historical source and show how the fictional world of *Zayni Barakat* corresponds to, or diverges from, the factual accounts given in that source. To make the text more accessible and readable, I have omitted diacritical marks where appropriate.

The word *mamluk* is Arabic, the passive participle of the verb *malaka*, meaning 'to own'. It thus means 'one who is owned' or 'a slave' and refers to the origin of the members of the dynasty: they were slaves, mainly Turks and Mongols and, later on, Circassians, who were purchased and raised as warriors to form the private army of a prince or a ruler. The practice of importing slaves for such a purpose was neither new nor peculiar to Egypt. Sir William Muir in *The Mameluke or Slave Dynasty of Egypt* (London, 1896, p. 3) writes:

For several generations the Caliphs of Bagdad had fallen into the dangerous habit of attracting to their capital thousands of slaves ... from Turcoman and Mongol hordes. These they used both as bodyguards and also as contingents to countervail the overweening influence of the Arab soldiery, whom in the end they superseded altogether. From the bondmen, they became the masters of the Court, fomented riots and rebellion, and hastened the fall of the effete Caliphate. The same habit, with the same eventual result, was followed by the Fatimide Caliphs; and after them likewise by the Eyyubite dynasty who, being strangers in the land, were glad of the support of foreign myrmidons. Conquered tribes in Central

Asia were nothing loth to sell their children to the slave-dealer who promised them prosperity in the West; and the tidings which spread from time to time of fortune to be gained in Egypt, made his task an easy one. It was thus that not only prisoners of war, but children of the Eastern hordes, kept streaming to the West, where they were eagerly bought, sometimes at enormous prices, both by Sultans and Emirs.

The Mamluks of Egypt stand out, however, because they maintained their hold on the Near East for such a long time and because, although they were a military ruling elite, they made major unwarlike contributions to learning and more especially to art and architecture.

The Mamluk rulers have traditionally been divided into two dynasties: the *Bahri* Mamluks (1250–1390), so named because they were settled in barracks on an island in the Nile (*bahr* is Arabic for 'sea' and is also used colloquially for 'river'); and *Burji* Mamluks (1382–1517), so named because they were housed in the towers of the Citadel (*burj* is Arabic for 'tower'). The foundation for the first dynasty was laid in 1250 when Shajar al-Durr. widow of the Ayyubid king al-Salih, one of the last descendants of Salah al-Din (Saladin) to rule Egypt, reigned as sultana for a few weeks after the murder of her stepson. Rather than suffer the ridicule of the whole Muslim world for being ruled by a woman, the late king's warrior-slaves elected one of their own, Izz al-Din Aybak, to be sultan. Shajar al-Durr married the new sultan, who spent most of his time during the following few years trying to subdue the remnants of the Ayyubids still reigning in parts of Syria and Palestine. When she heard that Aybak was considering taking another wife, Shajar al-Durr arranged for him to be murdered in his bath. Soon after she herself was killed by the slave women of Aybak's first wife. Another Mamluk, Qutuz (1259–60), stepped in, first as regent and then, after deposing Aybak's son, as sultan. Qutuz not only repulsed Syrian Ayyubid attacks against Egypt, but, together with his fellow Mamluks, achieved a far greater feat by stopping the Mongol hordes, which had already devastated Baghdad, overthrown the Abbasid caliphate and ravaged Syria with unparalleled cruelty. By delivering a crushing blow to the Mongol army at Ayn Jalut, Qutuz saved Egypt from a fate similar to that of her neighbours. On the way back from Ayn Jalut, Qutuz was murdered by one of his generals, a fellow Mamluk by the name of Baybars.

Assuming the title 'al-Malik al-Zahir', Baybars (1260–77) succeeded to the throne of Egypt. He is generally considered to be the real founder of the dynasty. In addition to his military exploits against both the Mongols and the Crusaders, which elevated him to the status of a folk hero almost rivalling that of Antara, Baybars is credited with reinstating, though only in name, the institution of the Abbasid caliphate in Cairo to lend legitimacy to his rule and that of subsequent sultans. This institution continued until the very end of the second Mamluk dynasty in 1517, when the Ottoman sultan Salim took away with him the last caliph from Cairo to Istanbul. Much later the caliphate, no longer Abbasid, was briefly assumed by the Ottoman sultans themselves, until it was finally abolished in 1924.

Baybars's reign, a relatively long one by Mamluk standards, was also characterized by interest in public works, among them canals and bridges, charitable and religious endowments, monumental architecture, such as mosques and schools, and the development of a swift postal service that connected Egypt and Syria. Baybars was also the first ruler to appoint four *qadis* (chief judges), who represented the four Sunni, or orthodox rites. These concerns, initiated or encouraged by Baybars, were shared and furthered, in varying degrees, by subsequent Mamluk sultans.

Of the forty-seven Mamluk sultans (twenty-four *Bahris* and twenty-three *Burjis*) only a few are notable for their achievements, either in war or peace or in both. Of these we have already mentioned al-Zahir Baybars. Al-Mansur Sayf al-Din Qalawun (1279–90) should be counted among the outstanding Mamluk sultans, if only because the importation of Circassian Mamluks, who later constituted the *Burji* dynasty, started during his reign and because fifteen out of the twenty-four *Bahri* Mamluk sultans were his sons, grandsons and great-grandsons. Indeed, the very last of the *Bahris*, al-Salih Hajji, was his great-grandson. One of Qalawun's sons, al-Nasir, ruled three times: 1293–4, 1298–1308 and 1309–40, for a total of about forty-two years, the longest of the dynasty. During al-Nasir's reign, Mamluk art and culture reached their peak.

The *Burji* Mamluks, all Circassian except for two who were Greek, had far less regard for hereditary succession to the throne. Not that dying sultans did not name their sons as successors; almost invariably, the strongest or the least controversial Mamluk took over and immediately began to get rid of his predecessor's supporters and other potential rivals. Of the twenty-three *Burji* Mamluks, perhaps only three are worthy of mention: Barsbay (1422–38), for his conquest of Cyprus; Qait Bey (1468–95), for his long reign and for being victorious in two limited encounters with Ottoman armies; and Qansawh al-Ghawri or, more commonly, al-Ghuri (1500–16), who, despite his defeat at the hands of the Ottoman sultan Salim at Marj Dabiq, near Aleppo, is remembered for his contributions to the architectural splendour of Cairo.

The whole period of Mamluk rule, especially the second dynasty, was characterized by great political, social and economic turmoil. For one thing, the question of legitimacy was never really addressed, despite the Abbasid puppet caliphate inaugurated by Baybars. Everyone, including the Caliph, knew who wielded the real power, and it was never the Caliph. Indeed, several caliphs were dismissed from office by the very sultans they themselves had installed on the throne. Succession to the throne was achieved, more often than not, by means of assassination, actual or threatened, or by open rebellion, which often developed into factional wars on a small-to-medium scale. Once one of the factions emerged victorious, that group would then elect the new sultan. Installing a sultan with the blessing of the Caliph and oaths of fealty from the other emirs never really settled the matter, however; the vanquished emir or emirs, unless they had already been killed, would be waiting for the next available opportunity to try their luck again. Such a state of affairs meant, of course, that each emir, and not just the sultan, maintained his own private army of Mamluks who owed their allegiance to him alone. The presence of so many distinct groups of warriors in one location often led to bloody friction, even when there was no contention for the throne.

Other factors besides ethnic origin and allegiance further divided the Mamluks who belonged to the same sultan or emir. One such factor was whether a Mamluk was one of the veteran *qaranisah* or the newly imported *julban*, a division based on a system of seniority with different rates of pay and assignments. The two groups were treated differently by different masters and by the same master on different occasions. Further distinctions were made on the basis of whether a Mamluk served in the sultan's bodyguard or the standing army. Sons of Mamluks, free men at birth, constituted yet another distinct group.

The Mamluks also remained separate from the local populations they ruled, which in turn were divided along ethnic, occupational and confessional lines. In Egypt, for instance, there was the indigenous population, which was augmented by the Arabs who had settled there over a long time. These were largely peasants, merchants, craftsmen, scholars and civil servants, who lived in the countryside as well as the cities. The Bedouin Arabs constituted a discrete group; they led a nomadic life, often raided villages and cities and were constantly fighting with the Mamluks.

All these regular and irregular armies were maintained by taxes levied against the local populations and by income derived from fiefs distributed among the emirs, the ranking Mamluks and their regular soldiers. Judging by the accounts in contemporary chronicles, the income of the Mamluks and the taxes that provided for this were poorly synchronized. Time after time we read in these chronicles that Mamluks or certain groups of them would ride to the Citadel and often besiege it because their pay was months in arrears. After long negotiations and threats, the sultan would pay part of the money owed and promise to pay the rest at some future date. This kind of haggling over pay and rations was so common that, even in the face of the clear and imminent danger of the Ottoman sultan Salim's invasion and while his army was only miles away from Cairo, the Mamluks under Sultan Tuman Bey, the last of the dynasty, would not move until they were each paid 130 dinars. They finally settled for 25 dinars each when they saw how dangerous the situation was. Whenever the sultan or emir faced such pressure to pay his men, he would summon his top officials and demand that they raise the money needed through taxation or any other means – or else they themselves would pay dearly.

Another source of income for the sultan was the sale of public offices: a man who wanted to become a judge, for example, had to pay the sultan a certain sum of money and would normally be expected to recoup his investment by assessing fees and collecting fines for himself. A tax collector would pay in advance or pledge an amount of money to the sultan and then would go out and collect as much money as he could. Adding to the economic turmoil and sense of insecurity experienced by people under that system was the fact that estate taxes were quite often literally confiscatory. If a wealthy Mamluk official or emir had not tied up his estate in a *waqf* (trust or endowment), the sultan would simply inherit the estate of the deceased, only sometimes granting the man's wives and children an allowance. Occasionally the confiscation of the 'estate' took place while a person, especially an official or a Mamluk who was out of favour, was still alive. That person might then be gaoled and tortured in a most brutal manner until he died or led the sultan's men to where he had hidden the money.

Conditions in the market-place were no less chaotic: pricing by merchants themselves or by the *muhtasib* (markets inspector) was, for the most part, quite arbitrary. Inflation and serious shortages were rampant and were caused by several factors. The prices of agricultural commodities, for instance, depended not only on the level of the Nile water and weather conditions in general, but also on the fact that some of those commodities and even some food staples were monopolies of the sultan or of the high-ranking emirs. Often when the sultan needed more money, he would order the *muhtasib* to impose weekly and monthly taxes on the merchants, who in turn would raise the prices of their goods. Markets were also frequently the targets of pillaging by brigands or Mamluks who were disconcerted because they had not been paid. To make matters even worse, the price of money or the rates of exchange between silver and gold fluctuated wildly, and the *muhtasib*'s men would go round announcing the new prices whenever there was a change. This practice was a common occurrence and more often than not was to the advantage of the sultan.

This, however, should not be taken to mean that all aspects of life in Egypt under the Mamluks were dismal. That the Mamluk sultans made significant contributions to art and architecture has already been mentioned. To this may be added their passion for parades and spectacles, which must have provided entertainment for the dwellers in big cities, at least. The sultans also showed great interest in religious institutions and pious foundations, especially in times of hardship, for example during plagues or when the water level of the Nile was low, or at times of war and other calamities. It was in such periods that religious figures, whether they were leaders of Sufi orders or shaykhs who had developed a reputation for piety, were shown great veneration.

The main source for the historical components of *Zayni Barakat* is the chronicle by the historian Muhammad ibn Iyas (b. June 1448; d. after November 1522), entitled *Bada'i al-Zuhur fi Waqa'i al-Duhur*. Ibn Iyas was an eyewitness to the historical events depicted in al-Ghitani's novel and was quite well acquainted with its main character, the historical figure Zayni Barakat ibn Musa.

The most striking impression of the historical Zayni Barakat conveyed by ibn Iyas is that he is a survivor. As in the novel, we hear of him for the first time as the successor to Ali ibn Abi al-Jud as *bardadar* (bailiff) of the Sultan Qansawh al-Ghawri in A D 1503. We are told that his father was an Arab (a Bedouin), that his mother's name was Anqa, that he had started out as a *bazdar* (falconer). In that first reference to him we are also told that he was going to become one of the prominent notables and great chiefs of Egypt. Less than two years later, we come across him supervising the punishment – really a very gruesome torture scene – of a former judge (not Ali ibn Abi al-Jud, who had been hanged a few weeks after his arrest). Less than two months after that, in A D 1505, Zayni Barakat ibn Musa was appointed *muhtasib* of Cairo – a post that he held for about twenty years with only a few interruptions – and was also given numerous honours and other posts. The historical *muhtasib* Barakat ibn Musa survived the last two Mamluk sultans, al-Ghawri and Tuman Bey, and Salim, the first Ottoman sultan to rule Egypt. We do not know how long he continued in his post, because the very last words in the last part of ibn Iyas's chronicle to reach us, which is the entry for the last day of 928 A H (19 November, A D 1522), tell us that it was announced that Barakat ibn Musa had been confirmed once again as *muhtasib*, 'and most people rejoiced'.

The image of Zayni Barakat ibn Musa that we get from reading ibn Iyas is, on the whole, a positive one. He is shown to be ambitious but fair, efficient and well liked by the people, as well as by the Mamluk and, later on, the Ottoman rulers. He apparently knew how to give sumptuous banquets, for we read about many that he gave, especially to the first sultan under whom he served. He was dismissed from the post of *muhtasib* five times and was placed under sequestration and gaoled twice. He was arrested, beaten and detained by Shaykh Abu al-Su'ud of Kom al-Jarih, who planned to expose him in disgrace and then to hang him. But he survived that too. It was perhaps this propensity for getting out of the most difficult situations that gave the novelist Gamal al-Ghitani the idea of portraying Barakat ibn Musa as the quintessential opportunist and sinister manipulator.

Apart from the character of Zayni Barakat, which has been modified to fit the new construct that is the novel, only three other characters, similarly modified, are borrowed from or inspired by ibn Iyas's factual account. They are Ali ibn Abi al-Jud, Shaykh Abu al-Su'ud of Kom al-Jarih and Abu al-Khayr al-Murafi'. In the case of Ali ibn Abi al-Jud, the historical and the fictional converge only up to the point where he is placed in Zayni Barakat's custody. According to ibn Iyas, it is the Sultan and then the Governor of Cairo who have Ali tortured and hanged. All the rest of Ali's story – his imprisonment, interrogation, torture and death by dancing – is fictitious.

Shaykh Abu al-Su'ud is mentioned on three different occasions in ibn Iyas's chronicle. The first is when Sultan al-Ghawri visits him in Kom al-Jarih. The second is when the emirs try to convince a most reluctant Tuman Bey to become sultan; they all go to the Shaykh, who produces a Quran and makes them swear on it that if they make him sultan, they would not betray him or intrigue against him, but would cheerfully accept whatever he says and does. The Shaykh then lectures them all on good government and makes them repent before God for their acts of oppression. The third occasion has to do with Zayni Barakat. The following excerpts are taken from ibn Iyas's account, as translated by Lieut.-Col. W. H. Salmon in *An Account of the Ottoman Conquest of Egypt in the Year AH 922* (London, 1921, pp. 79–81):

On Tuesday, the 9th, a quarrel occurred between al-Zeini Berekat Ibn Musa and Sheikh Abu al-Su'ud, which arose thus. A certain tanner and dealer in skins named Damrawi agreed about the sale of some skins; Ibn Musa acted wrongfully towards him and a quarrel was started between them. Ibn Musa determined to arrest him. Then Damrawi went to Sheikh Abu al-Su'ud and implored his protection . . .

Then the Sheikh summoned Ibn Musa, and on his appearing before him at Kaum al-Jarih the Sheikh reproved him sharply, saying: 'You dog, how you do oppress the Faithful!' This infuriated Ibn Musa, who left his presence in anger. So the Sheikh ordered his head to be uncovered, and that he be beaten with shoes on the head and body till he nearly died. Then after securing him he sent for Amir Allan, the Chief Dawadar, and said to him, 'Put him in irons and go and consult the Sultan about him, and inform him that the man is injuring the Faithful.' The Sultan on hearing the case sent to Sheikh Abu Su'ud, telling him to act as he thought fit in the matter. The latter ordered Ibn Musa to be publicly exposed in Cairo and then hung at the Zawilah Gate . . . He desired to sign his death-warrant by hanging or drowning, but the people pointed out to the Sheikh that he owed the Sultan money, and that if he were hung the Sultan would forfeit it. So the Sheikh repealed the death-sentence, and Ibn Musa remained in irons at Amir Allan's residence . . . As to Sheikh Abu al-Su'ud, a storm of indignation arose against him, on account of his treatment of Ibn Musa, and the poor people and others found fault with him saying, 'What business has the Sheikh to interfere in the Sultan's affairs.'

. . . On Friday, the 19th, it was reported that Sheikh Abu al-Su'ud had sent and released Ibn Musa from irons, and showed that he had pardoned him, and he began to interfere in political matters, and the people disapproved of this.

Abu al-Khayr al-Murafi' is mentioned twice by ibn Iyas. He tries to convince Sultan al-Ghawri to hand over to him an unnamed person so that he may extract 250,000 dinars from him. The Sultan, we are told, is tempted, but some emirs convince him not to agree with this scheme. On the second occasion we are told that the Sultan changed his mind about Abu al-Khayr and delivered him to Zayni Barakat, who took him from the Citadel in irons. As they were going through Cairo, the populace almost stoned him and voices rang out with praise for Zayni Barakat for having caused his arrest. Zayni had him beaten and banished.

All the other characters in *Zayni Barakat* – the Venetian traveller Visconti Gianti, Said al-Juhayni, Amr ibn al-Adawi, Shaykh Rihan and Zakariyya ibn Radi – are fictitious. Much of what is attributed to Zayni and the other characters drawn from, or inspired by, ibn Iyas's chronicle is also fictitious. Ibn Iyas is quoted directly several times, even though he is acknowledged only once. But Ghitani's indebtedness to him is not confined to the historical material, the characters or the passages that are quoted. By attempting to reproduce ibn Iyas's cadences and turns of phrase and his deceptively spontaneous casualness, the novelist is neither trying to emulate the historian nor to write an historical novel; rather he is using authenticating devices to create a chronicle of another era in Egypt's history.

Acknowledgements

I would like to thank the following friends and colleagues for help with various aspects of the translation: Colleen Beadling, Palmira Brummett, Fred Donner, Boyd Johnson, John Perry, Ayse Turkseven and John Woods (University of Chicago); John Rodenbeck (American University of Cairo); John Michael McDougal (*Cairo Today*); and Helen Jeffrey (Penguin Books).

Glossary

ardeb: a unit of capacity for dry measure, about 5.5 bushels

balaliq: dolls made of sugar

basbusa: a type of pastry

bashmaqdar: a slipper-bearer

bassass (pl. *bassassin*): informer or spy (literally 'peeker')

bilila: stewed wheat used as a hot cereal with milk and sugar

al-Bukhari: compendium of the *hadith* held in great veneration by Muslims

fatwa: judicial decision

fedawi: assassin willing to sacrifice his own life

galabiyya: a loose-fitting gown worn by men or women in Egypt

hadith: saying or sayings of the Prophet Muhammad

imam: the man who leads the Muslims in prayer and delivers the Friday sermon

julban: newly imported Mamluks

kantar: a unit of weight corresponding to the hundredweight

mashrabiyya: a window with elaborate wooden lattice-work, which allows one to look out without being seen from the outside

mughat: a nourishing concoction, traditionally given to women after childbirth

muhtasib: markets inspector. In addition to overseeing prices and ensuring the quality of products, a *muhtasib* was charged also with safeguarding public morals and 'enjoining what is right and forbidding what is wrong'. It thus combined religious with temporal concerns

mulukhiyya: Jew's mallow (*corchorus olitorius*) chopped and made into a thick, green soup

qaranisah: veteran Mamluks

rababa: single-string musical instrument, played with a horsehair bow, used to accompany heroic tales and love songs

riwaq: living and working quarters of students at al-Azhar

Rumi: Turkish or Greek

saqanqur: powder of a type of lizard, used medicinally

shaykh: Muslim religious scholar

tablakhanah: a band of drummers, which only emirs of a certain rank or standing were entitled to have

ulema: plural of *alim,* a Muslim religious scholar, traditionally a graduate of al-Azhar or a similar institution

'To every first, there is a last
and to every beginning an end.'

Excerpt A from the observations of the Venetian traveller Visconti Gianti, who visited Cairo more than once in the sixteenth century AD in the course of his travels around the world.

These observations describe the situation in Cairo in August/September AD 1516/Rajab 922 AH.

The land of Egypt is in a state of turmoil these days. The face of Cairo is that of a stranger, one that I hadn't encountered on my previous travels here. I know the language of the city and its dialects, but the people seem to be speaking a different language. I see the city as a sick man on the point of tears, a terrified woman afraid of being raped at the end of the night. Even the clear blue of the sky is thin, with clouds laden with an alien fog that has come from distant lands. I remember the small villages of India as the plague descends upon them: the air grows heavy with a thick moisture. Tonight, the houses are waiting for something that tomorrow might bring. I listen to the thudding sound of hooves as they hit the stones of the road, moving farther and farther away. I look out of the *mashrabiyya* careful not to be seen by anyone. I look out as the dark envelops the houses. I do not see the minaret of the new mosque of Sultan al-Ghuri, built only a few years ago. I didn't see it when I came here the last time, before my long voyage in the Orient. I had heard of preparations under way for its construction and the erection of the huge dome facing it. I stick my head out a little way, afraid lest the darkness should suddenly reveal the faces of the cruel-hearted guards. If they were to find out that I am Frankish, they would put me to death with no trial, no interrogation, not even a question about who I am or where I came from. I would have no chance to tell them, convince them, that I know the Governor, Emir Kurt Bey, personally. I have even had audience, twice, with the *Muhtasib* of Cairo, Zayni Barakat ibn Musa, who holds several other offices and is responsible for pre-serving law and order. If he saw me, he would remember me. I know that he doesn't forget a face that he has seen casually but once, even ten years later. Anyway, I shall stay here tonight, otherwise I would certainly not be safe from the police, the brigands or the Mamluks. All the houses in the city are locked, trembling, wishing to hide, to be transported where they might find some precious security. The candles in my house are out; I fear the dance of the light in the pupils of spying eyes.

Early in the afternoon I had walked from Husayniyya; my heart was filled with the yearning that came over me every time I arrived in a country or came to a town I had visited before. Normally I would spend days before getting in touch with my acquaintances, wandering all over, seeking news of those I knew, mourning the loss of those who had departed. I would see in my mind's eye the day on which one of them had departed this life and I'd ask myself where I was at that time, in which city. Sometimes I would meet one of my acquaintances by chance and I would open my arms wide, as local custom dictated. I would kiss his shoulder as he kissed mine. I would stand back the better to observe him, then once again embrace him. I would tell him how he hadn't changed at all (if he was advanced in years) and that he looked very healthy. He would mumble something in praise of God and thank Him and would insist and swear by God that I go with him to his house. We would sit in the guest-room, its decorative windows overlooking a small garden with sweet basil and Arabian jasmine, in the middle of which there would be a small fountain, its basin inlaid with beautiful coloured marble, turned on only when a guest had arrived.

Today, however, I didn't meet any of my old friends. Perhaps they've changed. I heard people on the street saying that many of the notables and the shaykhs had moved their valuables to faraway, unknown places, sent their children to the countryside and left their own homes to live in shrines or cemeteries. I heard that the place was rife with rumours; everybody was saying whatever he wanted; everybody was talking, whether it was his business or not.

Some people called for the intervention of the Interim Viceroy, Emir Tuman Bey, to silence these tongues. Others said that that would be impossible, that the lack of news meant something terrible, something no one dared think had happened. Someone said, 'Could that which we dare not think actually happen?' 'That's impossible! The Sultan's army has in its ranks the heroes and champions of Islam, each of whom is worth a thousand Ottomans. And, just as al-Ashraf Qait Bey had beaten them, they would be defeated by al-Ghuri.'

Another man said, 'If that were true, how come we haven't caught even one whiff of the good news? There has been no joyous music; no bands have played. How can we believe that nothing has happened?'

Even here in the coffee-house things were in a state of confusion; a man adjusted his turban and asked, 'Has any of you seen Zayni Barakat ibn Musa since the day before yesterday?'

A cautious hush fell upon the gathering. I put back the bowl of hot wine; I had only one sip of fenugreek. What has happened to Zayni Barakat ibn Musa? If nothing had happened to him, why were rumours being spread about him? Everyone looked at the man who had asked the question. My guess is that he probably works in a mosque or sells old books. Perhaps he is a student at al-Azhar. The tone of his voice and his demeanour suggest such an occupation. Whenever I see a man I don't know, I ask myself what he does. Where has he lived: in China, India or the deserts of the Hejaz?

There was a long silence, then someone said, 'That's true. We haven't seen him in three days.'

Another said, 'Five days.'

Each one was now knitting his brow, trying to remember. Even I told myself that I hadn't seen Zayni all the days I'd spent here. Zayni is usually seen by the people of Cairo at least once every day. The *tablakhanah* would march, playing in front of him, and his retinue of aides would follow. Zayni constantly checked the prices of commodities and went after the wrongdoers. He set down and enforced strict rules for walking in the street. Sometimes he prohibited women from wearing certain styles of dress or forbade them to go out in the street altogether if the Mamluks were more mischievous than usual. Last time I visited Egypt, I saw Zayni strong and healthy. I don't know what has become of him. Three years can really change a man. I have seen Zayni go down to the markets himself, arguing with the vendors of pastries, cheese and eggs, standing along with the peasant women who sold chicken, geese, rabbits and ducks. He set the prices himself and had the violators publicly exposed and disgraced. I know that the people are pleased with him, that they love him. I remember what I wrote about him after I had met him for the first time.

I have seen many men: Berbers, Indians, Italians, princes from Gaul, Abyssinia and the northernmost parts of the world. But I haven't seen anything like his gleaming eyes, which narrow as he speaks as if they were the eyes of a cat in the dark. His eyes were created to pierce the dark fog of the countries of the North, to penetrate their total silence. He doesn't see one's face or features; rather he penetrates to the very bottom of the skull, to the ribs of the chest, uncovering one's hidden hopes and true feelings. His features radiate with a brilliant intelligence, while a momentary closing of his eyes shows a kindness, a tenderness that makes one want to be close to him even while one is still in awe of him. He asked me about countries I had visited, how I liked my stay there and how I got on with the people. He asked me about the freedom of women in Frankish lands. He inquired about justice among the subjects and about postal routes in India. He mentioned names of shaykhs in Jedda and Mecca, and notables from Damascus. I told him I hadn't been to Jedda, but that I had visited Mecca and stayed in Damascus. He wrote down for me names of some people and I promised him to inquire about them.

At that time I heard of an interesting incident, which he himself had resolved. It happened that a white Rumi slave girl sent him a plea for help. It was said that she was no older than fifteen, that she had been purchased from the slave market by a gluttonous, lecherous, old rose-water distiller. After he purchased the virgin Rumi slave girl, he forsook everything and devoted himself full-time to her. He abandoned his distilling plant and stayed at home. He didn't even leave the house to go to prayers. He had intercourse with her several times every day and every night, as if he were a twenty-year-old man. Some people even claimed (but I think it's one of those exaggerations that common folk are given to) that her screams were heard clearly by passers-by outside the house.

These screams would start high-pitched, then running footsteps would be heard, then a silence would fall, but one that didn't last long. Then the screaming would begin again, and so on and so forth. The neighbours attested to that and felt sorry for her. They wondered among themselves when the girl got any sleep, since her screaming didn't stop day or night. (That was said by a man who was envious.) The neighbours didn't take their eyes off the door of the house, which hadn't been opened once in a whole week. Young men kept their eyes trained on the *mashrabiyyas* and, as the girl's screams got louder, they laughed and winked and pulled each other's hair. A water-carrier who delivered water to the house – Zayni later called him as a witness – said that he had heard with his own ears the girl's screaming in the harem quarters. He said that he had seen her once watching from the *mashrabiyya* that overlooked the inner courtyard, her hair dishevelled, and that he had left that day, shaking his head in amazement at what he had seen.

Anyway, when the slave girl sought Zayni Barakat's help, by sending him a young servant, Zayni moved immediately. He sought the counsel of the *ulema* and deliberated with them, and their chief gave him a *fatwa* to the effect that what Zayni intended to do was right. Then Zayni went to the house of the man – his name was Attar, if I remember correctly – and he raided the house. The man got angry and began to shout, 'What business does the *Muhtasib* have with people's affairs inside their homes?'

Zayni arrested him and ordered him to be thrown down on the floor. Then they uncovered him and it was said that they were terrified at the sight of it. The Shaykh of the Hanafi rite swore that he had never in his life seen anything like it. Zayni said, 'The girl is forty years younger than you are. Have you no pity that you so hurt her? And with *that* too?'

He had him caned fifty times, then ordered him to manumit her. The man indeed freed her against his will, but he never forgot what Zayni had done to him. He was heartbroken over his separation from the girl and began to roam the alleys with wandering eyes, tattered clothes, drooling at the mouth, looking for what he had lost. He never mentioned her name, but kept crying out for something without being explicit. Whenever he appeared in a place, the crowds shouted at him, beat him on his private parts, laughed and made fun of him. All the while, his eyes kept wandering, looking for the dear thing he had lost.

I heard from someone whom I trusted that the old man Attar had not touched a woman in his life before that girl, that he had not married and that all his life he had supported his mother and sisters. When his youngest sister got married, he was left all by himself. He had saved the price of the slave girl over many years. He had a definite picture of a slave girl with a specific figure etched clearly in his mind: she was as white as a silver platter, her breasts were two globes of Turkish delight and as soft as silk. He dreamt of her for many years until he found her. His joy wasn't long-lived; they took her away from him, snatched her. It was, as the common people of Egypt would say, 'a joy cut short'.

People differed over Zayni Barakat's disposition of the matter. Many thought he did the right thing, especially since the girl had appealed to him for help when she was close to dying. Another group was of the opinion that he had invaded people's innermost privacy and that no one was safe in his house and with his family any more, especially after a stronger rumour had started, denying that the girl had ever appealed to Zayni Barakat for help. According to this rumour, Zayni was able to learn of the matter thanks to amazing methods, which enabled him to detect the most intimate goings-on inside houses and behind walls. It was also said that Attar had been wronged, that he was not a violent man. The men wondered whether the woman existed who could hate a man as equipped as Attar was. They said, 'The girl is loose. She must have fallen out of love with him and appealed to Zayni Barakat to help her to fly the coop for reasons she alone knew.'

People were left with a deep-seated feeling of fear. They marvelled at the skill of the *Muhtasib* and his unique ability to learn the most intimate, the most private particulars of what went on behind closed doors. It was said that there was a special team of veteran *bassassin* who answered directly to him. None of those men was known to anyone and nobody knew where they lived or how they went about their business. That team, it was said, had no connection with the team of *bassassin* headed by a certain well-known fierce man.

Anyway, I heard of the Attar incident one year after it had taken place. I have seen him roaming the alleys, stopping every now and then in the open spaces, shouting obscenities at a person whose name he never mentioned. It was said that he made little paper dolls, which he burned after reciting certain charms every night before going to sleep. He remained in that condition until events, which we shall recount in due time, overtook him.

Back to the men in the coffee-house. They asked the reason for Zayni's disappearance. Each of them wondered how he had failed to notice it. Zayni's disappearance was an extraordinary event. It must be due to the turbulent times in which a person was likely to forget even his own affairs. Hadn't a good shaykh declared in last Friday's sermon that it was time for the wind that would blow before the Day of Judgement and that would sweep away every-thing? It was a south wind sent by God Almighty from Yemen, softer than silk and more fragrant than musk, that would leave no single atom of belief in God or truth or justice in anyone's heart. It would alienate father from son and brother from brother. People would spend a hundred years showing no regard for this world or the next. These would be God's most evil creatures and it was on them that the Day of Judgement would break. The men in the mosque had cried and embraced each other. When they got out of the mosque they thought they smelled the fragrant scent of musk. They declared loudly that the evil times were upon them and they were afraid. On such days one would be heedless of such rare and weighty matters as a whole day passing without Zayni Barakat ibn Musa appearing on the streets of Cairo and nobody noticing. The Azhar student – as I surmised him to be – said, 'I know that Zayni is hiding in a place that only a very few persons know about . . .' He fell silent, as if to imply that he was one of those few persons.

Those present asked, 'Where, Said?'

'He is sending his followers throughout Egypt to call upon the bedouin chiefs to send their men to Cairo.' They pricked up their ears. In my mind's eye, I saw Zayni sitting in a secret place, inspired by the momentous events of the day, with deputies coming and others going, sent by him to the various towns and strongholds of the bedouins in the desert.

One of those present wondered aloud, 'How can the country be without a *Muhtasib* while we are in a state of war?'

'Whenever Zayni left for a week and as soon as he stepped outside Cairo, prices went up and everybody did what they liked. What is going to happen now that he's disappeared?'

Said said, 'Absolutely nothing. Zayni's eyes are watching everybody, despite his disappearance. And don't forget Shihab Zakariyya.'

They fell silent. In their eyes was a mute hope, deep down in their souls a fear. Out in the street, at a painfully slow pace, marched a column of peasant prisoners, with iron chains round their necks. They seemed to be heading for one prison or another. A child stuck out his tongue several times. There was a distant drumbeat. Perhaps the peasants were going to depart this life shortly. I strolled near them. Their eyes were wandering and they looked as if they wished they could take in anything they came across. I had seen the same thing in Tangier: a column of men passing before the walls of the white city, chained to each other by the bonds of eternal perdition. They had in their eyes the same look. So did that man being led to his execution in a small island in the Indian Ocean. He begged the people to reconsider his case, prayed that one of those roc birds would catch up with him and carry him away. For a man to know that after a number of steps, after a certain period of time, he would not open his eyes ever again, that he would lose all sight and sensation! I might die the next instant, but I don't know for a fact. But to know exactly that I'd be departing this life at a specific moment! That was the look stamped on the faces, a look of knowing that one was going out to a world of which one knew nothing and from which there was no rescue, no miracle to be hoped for. Seeing the men going to their deaths reminded me of my going from one country to another, my constant travel. I remembered those who had gone ahead of me, men who had left Venice to begin a journey that might last thirty years. A man might die in a country thousands of miles away from home.

I walked on, afraid. Everything I saw was the very embodiment of fear. Cairo was being driven to an uncertain destiny; it was being banished from its houses. I walked cautiously. Yesterday the Mamluks descended from the Citadel, went to Khan al-Khalili and almost burned it all down to the ground. They had caught a Rumi merchant gathering intelligence and corresponding with the Ottomans about the conditions here. When they caught him, the masses almost tore him to pieces, but the *bassassin* who worked under Zakariyya ibn Radi, Zayni's deputy, took him in custody, sparing his life so that he might be interrogated and made to tell on his accomplices. I heard someone saying that Governor Kurt Bey had been secretly executed in the Jubb dungeon at the Citadel. That, however, was not confirmed. People were shaken when rumours started that a messenger had arrived in Cairo from Syria, having crossed the mazes of the desert; that he had gone up to the Citadel, met the Interim Viceroy and conveyed to him the terrifying news that the Sultan's army had been defeated somewhere near Aleppo. Details were not known.

They say that the most interesting moments remembered by travellers later on are those moments when things undergo change, when they observe great events and watch their impact on faces, houses and cities. I would say, years after the event, after I had seen the outbreak of a war or a plague, that I saw what happened.

At sunset I continued on my way; huge hands were pulling people and throwing them inside their houses and tenements. I smelt a kind of air that I had known only in Hyderabad in India, when a virulent epidemic had killed and destroyed many and where I was kept a prisoner by the odious plague for a whole year, during which I was born again several times every day.

I see Cairo now as a blindfolded, supine man awaiting a mysterious fate. I feel the breath of the men inside their houses, bringing their heads closer to each other, whispering about what they've heard. The calls are undecipherable. Time passes and does not pass. I cannot go upstairs to observe the stars. Maybe it will be dawn soon, but I haven't heard a single cock crow.

FIRST PAVILION

What happened to Ali ibn Abi al-Jud and the
first appearance of Zayni Barakat ibn Musa
(Shawwal, 912 AH)

Daybreak

AT daybreak the houses are deeply sunken in a soft sleep. The sun is late in arriving at the alleys of Husayniyya, Batiniyya, Jamaliyya and al-Utuf, but it can be seen clearly over the walls and towers of the Citadel of the Mountain. The band of Mamluks going through Hadarat al-Baqara has not come from the Citadel but rather from the house of Emir Qani Bey al-Rammah, Master of the Horse. The horsemen have crossed the canal and slowly made their way to Bab al-Luq, brandishing their swords in the face of the approaching day. The water-carriers – the first to rise in the city to bring water to the houses – encountered them near Bab al-Luq, but knew nothing of the horsemen's destination. The hooves of the horses stir up little eddies of dust as the pace of the camels, heavily laden with brown water-skins, quickens. The whispers of the water-carriers grow softer. In their minds is left a faint impression, like the stroke of an oar on the calm water of a small canal. The Mamluks slip away at the break of day. The houses appear as they usually do on the days following Eid al-Fitr and other festivals: languorous.

Ali ibn Abi al-Jud never wakes up until three hours after daybreak. He always sleeps late. Every night after he returns from the Citadel, his deputies arrive, and together they review what has been accomplished that day. Towards dawn he dismisses them and stays by himself for about an hour. Then he goes to one of his four wives or sixty-seven concubines. A month ago their number reached sixty-seven after the acquisition of one Abyssinian and one Rumi slave girl. Ali ibn Abi al-Jud never misses his mark in reaching the woman he has chosen to spend the last part of the night with. He would let her know hours ahead of time and when he goes to her his nose is greeted by a perfume: the fragrance of clothes blending with the scent of a female. Every step he takes on the short staircase at which the corridors suddenly end distances him gradually from the hubbub of the departing day and from the things he has heard, the things he has added to his ledgers and books, the rumours that have reached him, what is being said about him personally, things that the emirs and the common people say.

Tonight, when he entered the room of Salma, his third wife, she began to take his clothes off: a black embroidered cloak with a gold brocade border and a big yellow turban bound with white muslin, which only emirs of a thousand were permitted to wear. He was given permission to wear it a year ago and since then he has worn it when he bowed in front of the Sultan, sat with the notables or rode in processions. And, as was well known, big turbans were not created for just anybody; nobody dared wear one in the presence of people of higher rank and distinction. The sight of the turban on his head has aroused the malice of the envious, awakened slander and inspired secret machinations. But Ali ibn Abi al-Jud didn't care. He deliberately donned it when he went on his tours. Not only that, but he kept touching it, adjusting it backwards and pushing it forwards, especially when talking to high-ranking emirs. Some of his friends warned him not to flaunt his turban or to strut in the presence of those princes, but he did not concern himself with them. He concerned himself very much with learning what they said about him. If he found in what they said anything worth conveying to the Sultan, he would immediately go to the Citadel and would add a few things to what had been said and make a few changes that would stoke the ire of the Sultan against the person who had made those comments or remarks. Besides, he didn't keep what he had done to himself, but talked about it freely, embellishing it and elaborating on how the Sultan listened to him, how he patted him on the shoulder and was so very kind to him.

Tonight, apparently, the deputies of Ali ibn Abi al-Jud made a mistake. They made no mention of anything taking place. Later on, some people claimed that they had known of what had happened, specifically in the house of Emir Qani Bey, Master of the Horse. The common people hinted and some of them even said outright that Zakariyya ibn Radi, one of the deputies of Ali ibn Abi al-Jud and the Head of the *Bassassin* of the Sultanate, had not conveyed what he had learned to Ali ibn Abi al-Jud, who slept contented, clinging to his third wife, Salma. Salma was awakened by sounds of movement: footsteps scurrying, doors opening, muffled cries the harem. The sounds arrived here disembodied, unclea mixed up: a water-wheel raising water, its old wooden squeaking; raindrops falling on dry ground; waves lapping at a boat; hooves galloping.

What, exactly, is happening? To awaken him before he is ready is difficult.

'Master Ali! Master Ali!'

He turns. Some vessels fall to the floor. Her heartbeats are now racing as she listens. Something has happened. What is it? She doesn't know. Suddenly her blood rushes through veins trembling with terror. She is unaware of his sudden awakening, his listening and the drying up of his mouth. The door is pushed open by a foot wearing a black leather Mamluk horseman's boot with the trouser-leg tucked in.

From the gate of Emir Qani Bey al-Rammah, Master of the Horse, emerged a crier with a deep voice familiar to the people. At the very same moment, another herald came out of his house near the palace of Emir Qusun al-Dawadar, the Executive Secretary, near Birjuwan, heading for Utuf, Husayniyya and the Rum al-Juwwaniyya Alley. A pleasant light breeze carried to the ears the beating of a drum and the voices of other criers, shouting news that awakened those still sleeping and parted their eyelids. The workers in the baths and those in the neighbouring bath-ovens came out. The vendors of milk and those who sold fava beans stopped, pricking up their ears. The women shouted, calling out to each other. A woman selling *bilila* on Mida Alley, which had opened its gate a little while ago, suddenly stopped hawking her *bilila* and instead shouted the news in her shrill voice. Heads looked out from the small doors of the small rooms inside the huge tenements. Little children held the hems of their *galabiyyas* between their teeth and ran. Where to exactly? Nobody knew. A shrill, trilling ululation of joy, let loose by a woman from one of the highest windows, pierced the air and was soon answered by another, then more ululations followed. Barefoot women came out from Utuf, Judariyya and Suk-kariyya, carrying their babies on their shoulders, clapping and facing the new day with a new-born joy.

Said al-Juhayni

FROM the *riwaq* of the Southern Egyptian students at al-Azhar Mosque, Said listened to the din outside. The upper window of the *riwaq* overlooked the entrance to Batiniyya. The voices were getting nearer and nearer. At last! They've caught Ali ibn Abi al-Jud, arrested him! Only yesterday, just before sunset, the crowds watched him in procession. Did anyone dare to imagine at that time that the same streets were going to see him exposed in disgrace on the back of a tailless donkey? The people were now jamming the streets like swarms of locusts. Anger had been building up in their hearts and when it saw a chance it exploded. Said was now seeing Ali in his mind's eye. There he was, riding a horse with a golden saddle, passing in front of the houses of the shaykhs and the emirs, preceded by drums more powerful than any *tablakhanah* that led the procession of any emir as a symbol of rank. And there again he was, walking in the street, surrounded by an escort of tough guards. When he persuaded the Sultan to impose a tax on salt, he did great harm to the Muslims, and salt became a very rare commodity. When Ali ibn Abi al-Jud walked, no one dared raise his eyes to look him in the face. His turban dazzled the eyes. Then, in just a few hours! Look at him riding a donkey backwards, utterly humiliated. Young and old alike were now slapping him, the women spitting in his face.

The *riwaq* is now completely empty; everybody has left. There is the smell of dampness in the air and dry bread is piled in the corners of the long rectangular room with straight perpendicular walls. Said slipped his feet into his old pair of shoes. He must go to his master, Shaykh Abu al-Su'ud in Kom al-Jarih, to talk to him and listen to what he thinks of what has happened. The large courtyard of the mosque is buzzing with al-Azhar students and scholars. Yes, indeed, he must go to his master, Abu al-Su'ud. But now he is sitting next to the large marble column close to the Chapel of the Blind, tracing lines on the floor with a straw. Said is watching developments cautiously. He is not hiding his joy at the fall of that repugnant man. But what do the coming days have in store? What does *today* have in store? Perhaps things will lead to strife among the emirs, in which heads would roll, the blood of perfectly innocent bystanders would be shed, houses would be boarded up or burned down and mosques, great and small, would be destroyed. Who knows? Perhaps someone mightier and more cruel would succeed him. At that point Said snapped the straw and dusted his hands. The dismissal of Ali ibn Abi al-Jud was an act of mercy to the people.

The noise grew louder suddenly. Said was now hearing what one of the students was saying in this place three months ago. Amr ibn al-Adawi had then bent over to tell him what he thought: he had had it up to there with what Ali ibn Abi al-Jud was doing to the people, with all those fresh acts of injustice. Amr knew exactly what that evil man did: he stayed up all alone for two hours every night thinking up new methods of oppression, inventing new techniques of torture for his victims. It was even rumoured that he had asked Zakariyya ibn Radi, may God be displeased and angry with him, to find new ways and means to make prisoners talk – ways that no one could even dream of. Amr said that he had arrested a pregnant woman, who was poor and unprotected by anyone, and had her beaten with cudgels in his presence. He then had her limbs burned with tar until she had a miscarriage and dropped the six-month-old male foetus that she was bearing. 'Ali ibn Abi al-Jud didn't think that was enough. He had her hanged at the Gate of Zuwayla. Why? Do you know why, Said? Because Zakariyya's men caught her selling a few melons. As you know, he has a monopoly on melons.' Amr bent over, whispering, 'I intend to kill him.'

Said had trembled. He had looked in the dim light of the sunset at his colleague's gleaming eyes. His mouth had gone dry. He bowed his head and looked again at his colleague. Amr had repeated, 'I will kill him to rid the people of him.'

That very night Shaykh Abu al-Su'ud had spat, then washed his mouth with fresh water. Said listened to the serene silence, which flowed like rose-water throughout the small mosque. The Shaykh praised God that Said had listened in silence to what Amr ibn al-Adawi had said.

'Should I avoid him, Master?'

'No. I didn't mean it that way. But you should be careful. Someone who wants to kill a man like Ali ibn Abi al-Jud doesn't announce his intent.'

In the *riwaq* Said kept watching his colleague. During lessons he looked at him discreetly, trying to find in his actions or behaviour a confirmation of what Shaykh Abu al-Su'ud had hinted at. When he talked to him, Said chose his words carefully, avoiding criticism of any emir or notable. Said could visualize Amr heading for that house near Muqattam. He saw him having a private meeting with Zakariyya ibn Radi. No, not Zakariyya himself; maybe one of his deputies. A poor student like him would not sit with Zakariyya, the mere mention of whose name makes grown men tremble. Amr would repeat what has been said. The following days would bring forth strangers, asking secretly about Said. Some of Zakariyya's lackeys would be following him around. He wouldn't know them, but they would know him. They would follow his every step, keep track of the alleys he entered, his every laugh, the moments of his private agony, his joy and his delight. At an appointed moment they would descend upon him like a disaster, like the first thunder of winter surprising a peaceful town. One of them would reach out with his hand and touch him on the shoulder, saying just one word. He would then be led to Zakariyya ibn Radi's gaol. They would inflict different varieties of torture on him and throw him in a big gaol: al-Arqana, al-Jubb, or al-Maqshara, where his days would evaporate and news of him or his having ever existed would disappear without a trace.

Said seems dejected. He hears of a slave being hanged, a thief's hand being cut off, the public exposure in disgrace of a woman caught stealing a loaf of bread; her left hand would be cut off or, if that has already been done, then her right hand. As he hears of these things, Said's heart quivers like a wet little bird. Why is all this happening? Why? The questions rise and then they fall upon him as if they were drumsticks beating a drum or thick links in a red-hot chain burning his nerves, draining his very marrow and drying up the water of life. If only he could shout from the top of the minaret of Ashraf Qait Bey at al-Azhar to awaken the houses of the common, poor people, as well as those of the emirs. The walls of the Citadel of the Mountain pierce his eyes. He would raise his hands and let loose a long relentless call to prayer in which he would denounce every evil oppressor. He would see with his eyes Zakariyya ibn Radi impaled next to the Gate of al-Wazir. Said can only visualize himself going among the people screaming, causing them to shudder, warning them of what is yet to come. In Kom al-Jarih he is calmed down by Shaykh Abu al-Su'ud, the good, pious, noble, generous, learned scholar who has travelled all over the world, stayed for some time in Hejaz and Yemen, learned the language of the Indians and the tongue of the Abyssinians, handled the affairs of the Muslims in Persia, debated the *ulema* in Anatolia and has seen, with his very eyes, the waters of the great ocean at the western edge of the world. Said listens to him and forgets the moment that has been constantly living in his imagination: the moment when one of the lackeys or the spies puts his hand on his shoulder, laughing and revealing two rows of yellow teeth, saying, 'Please come with us.'

Now Ali ibn Abi al-Jud himself is in chains. Said will allow himself a little joy. After he goes to his master, he will go to Shaykh Rihan to talk for a while with him. Undoubtedly Shaykh Rihan would say that he had heard the news several days ago. Maybe he would even go so far as to bend over him and whisper to him that Qusun and Qani Bey had not moved before consulting him. Said would hide his smile and wait. Maybe he would catch a glimpse of Samah, Shaykh Rihan's daughter. Perhaps he would hear her laughter or the rustling of her dress. She might come into the room where her father is sitting, covering her face, but Shaykh Rihan would invite her to stay, saying that Said is no stranger, that he also has come from Juhayna and that, had his birth been delayed by a few years, the two of them would have spent some time playing together. Perhaps he would be reasonably lucky and smell the aroma of food that she herself had cooked. He might even partake of the food. His heart would surely be shaken and his soul would soar high. He would go back to the *riwaq*, staying by himself all night, drawing sustenance from that moment, reliving it a thousand times.

Now a clamour has arisen among the students. One of them is asserting that it would be impossible to have one new man assume all the posts of Ali ibn Abi al-Jud: Agent of the Exchequer, Controller of Sharqiyya and, his most important post, *Muhtasib*, in addition to his original profession, which he hasn't been practising the last few years, namely being the *Bashmaqdar* of the Sultan – the Official Bearer of the Sultan's Slippers at prayer time. To that job he was no stranger, since earlier he had been the little *Bashmaqdar* of Emir Tuman Bey. When he got on in the world, when his star shone and he reached the zenith of his fortune, however, he turned his back on being a *bashmaqdar*, even though that was the very source of his fortune.

'Who, then?'

'The names are many, but none of them is unknown to us: Emir Mamai, Tughluq, Tutuq, Qushtimur . . .'

'Well, count your sheep, Juha!' (And Juha said, 'One is asleep, the other awake.')

'But it is impossible for one emir to assume all the posts!'

'Plans have been under way for a long time to get rid of Ali. Do you think the Sultan would kick him out to get another one person to control everything?'

'Who, then? Who will it be?'

Everyone is trying to foretell the future. Schemes are now being laid, whispers exchanged on cushions and behind closed doors at the Citadel, in the houses of the emirs and the judges. Ali ibn al-Jud is waiting, chained in a dark cellar filled with a rotten odour, seeing his days as an illusion, a dream that is lost and forgotten.

'Perhaps we'll get someone whose name hasn't occurred to us at all.'

'Count your sheep, Juha. I told you. Juha, count your sheep.'

Classes have been suspended. Things can't go on like that much longer. It is impossible that these posts should remain unfilled for long. The departing rays of the sun are now filling the main court-yard of the mosque. The bread that is given to the students daily as a stipend has been arranged in rows since the morning to dry and so to keep longer. The conversation is droning on and on, endlessly. Said sees Amr ibn al-Adawi like a buzzing bee that has lost its way to its hive, going from one circle to another, listening, participating in the conversations, getting angry or happy as the occasion requires. He would give an opinion that sounds casual and spontaneous but which pushes the conversation in a direction that would please Zakariyya. Amr doesn't get close to the Syrian, Afghan or Moroccan students. They do not interest him since they are always uninterested in what happens around them. In the evening Amr would report what he had seen and heard. But, this evening in particular, to whom is he going to report? Who will listen to him? Said smiles as the question floats around in his mind. Would Zakariyya's eyes and ears be as wide open as usual? Does he or his deputies find the time to listen? Perhaps at this very moment he is thinking of what must be done now that his benefactor Ali ibn Abi al-Jud is gone. For it was he who appointed him as the Head of the Spies of the Sultanate and as his own deputy. To whom will Amr ibn al-Adawi go tonight? Said bites his lower lip. How is Amr going to be punished on the Day of Judgement? He may have caused a head to roll by saying one word or condemned a whole family to death with one little piece of paper. He may have killed hope in the heart of an old father awaiting the return of his son, the chaplain, to lead the prayers in the village. If only Said could go now, grab him by the neck, get to the depths of his soul with a look as sharp as a knife plunged between the shoulders! The main courtyard of the mosque is now silent. Said is cautious; he chooses his words carefully. Amr's bedding and his ration bag are separated from his own by only three students. If he were to turn in his sleep at night or to go out to perform his ablutions just before dawn, his eyes would undoubtedly catch him. Perhaps his master is mistaken. God forbid! His master doesn't think ill of anyone.

Said turns slowly. The smell of the old mat . . . The square outside the mosque is filled with passers-by. Some donkeys are tied to a nearby wall. The town crier is not tired of repeating the news: the unjust, the tyrant, the oppressor Ali ibn Abi al-Jud has been caught; his belongings, his granaries, his moneys, his harem and his slave girls have been impounded. He has been incarcerated in the Jubb dungeon at the Citadel, pending further investigation of his affairs. A woman tosses a coin to the crier as a tip for his good news. A joy creeps into Said's soul, slowly, as if it were water flowing into narrow cracks. He sees Samah. If only she were with him now, watching the people with him! He hears her footsteps. He doesn't know to whom they belong, but when he is there, sitting at Shaykh Rihan's house with the Shaykh, he is certain that the footsteps are hers and nobody else's. The joy of the people fills him with warmth. He would tip the crier if only he had a coin to spare. The bitter taste in his mouth has begun to dissolve. From Batiniyya, boys who work in the dye-house of Khidr, Head of the Dyers' Guild, have painted their faces red and green and have come out dancing and chanting:

> Grieve, grieve, envious one:
> Ali ibn Abi al-Jud is gone.

A Sublime Decree

In the name of God, the Most Gracious, Most Merciful.

'Let there arise out of you a band of people inviting to all that is good, enjoining what is right and forbidding what is wrong.'

'Help ye one another in righteousness and piety, but help ye not one another in sin and rancour', as the Glorious Book tells us.

Now then: praise to God who has guided us to unmask the evil ones amongst us and to find the righteous ones for the comfort of the people and for the preservation of law and order throughout the land. After our apprehension of the transgressor Ali ibn Abi al-Jud, and having applied to him what God has ruled, we have decided to fill his posts and ranks. And in order to be even more equitable – for each of us is being watched by the vigilant Almighty – we have decided to divide these posts among those with learning and skill, for they are a heavy burden unless shared by many hands. We have commenced with the Markets Inspectorship since it most directly affects the life and the livelihood of the people and cannot be left vacant. And, having looked into the conditions of the people to determine who amongst them would bring them comfort and spare them hardship; and having read the histories and the chronicles of bygone eras and epochs; and having learned the lessons of the past and delved deep into the truth of the matter; and after long thinking and deliberation, we have decided that Barakat ibn Musa shall assume the Markets Inspectorship in view of what we have determined, by means of the process mentioned above, of his virtue and integrity, his honesty and righteousness, his strength and firmness, his revered respectability, his showing no favouritism to the high and the mighty, his piety; and of how, in matters of right and wrong, he makes no distinction between rich and poor. For these reasons we have conferred upon him the title 'al-Zayni', to be attached to his name henceforth and for the rest of his days.

We have charged him with inspecting weights and measures, with warning against the adulteration of foods and drinks and with regulating prices. We have further charged him with the making of inquiries and the gathering of news and of what is being said by people in every street and alley, in every home and market-place, unbeknown to them. We have also charged him with appointing deputies to look into the affairs of the Muslims, provided that said deputies be honest, faithful and trustworthy. Moreover, he has been charged with preventing apothecaries from selling strange drugs, preventing anyone from cheating people out of their possessions and taking upon himself the enjoining of what is right and the forbidding of what is wrong and the banning of debauchery. We have also charged him with looking into the affairs of poor scholars and female singers and entertainers and providing them with protection, appointing as deputies over them only such men as are known for their honesty, integrity, chastity and freedom from cupidity and wrong. We have, moreover, charged him with observing God Almighty in word and deed, seeking His pleasure, unconcerned in his Inspectorship with people's displeasure, resentment or contentment with him. We have also instructed him to be meticulous in observing the *Sunna*, which is the way of the Prophet, in the cutting of the moustache, the removal of the hair in the armpits, the shaving off of the pubic hair, the paring of the nails, the cleanliness of the clothing and the use of musk.

This is what we have decided and commanded. Peace be upon the noblest of God's creations, the Master of Messengers, Muhammad ibn Abd Allah, God's prayers and peace be upon him.

Citadel of the Mountain
8 Shawwal

Zakariyya ibn Radi

HAS he ever failed to understand what is going on anywhere? Has anything ever prevented him from getting to the bottom of things, be they small or great? At this moment in particular he is trying to understand the reasons why. He is puzzled by what is happening. Earlier in the evening he had gone down to the little gaol deep below the house, preceded by the torch-bearer and executioner, Mabruk. They hardly ever went down to the gaol. Only a few times had he crossed the dark, narrow walkway that led to the small cavities in the damp, sticky walls. Each of the cavities was hardly big enough for a man; a prisoner had to bow down as he stood so as not to hit the uneven ceiling with his head. He couldn't turn his face or turn around or sit or lie down because the place was too small and because of the water, which Mabruk, the mute, poured several times a day to maintain it at a constant level on the sticky floor. Zakariyya didn't meet the prisoners here. He stayed on the other side of the house. Mabruk would come, unchain the prisoner in question, blindfold him and poke him in the ribs with a short spear. Ultimately the prisoner would stand before Zakariyya. The silence would remain absolute, adding to the terror of the prisoner, who had no way of knowing where the blow would come from. After a few moments, short or long, Zakariyya would stretch out his hand and touch the prisoner's shoulder. Most of the time his touch was gentle, soft and slow. Many couldn't stand the surprise, which was as soft and smooth as a viper's belly, and they fainted. The blindfold would be removed and at first there would be a calm smile like a fire about to die down. Some time would pass, then there would be shouts and screams of pain. The wheels of the water-wheel raising the water from the deep well would squeak. Sometimes Zakariyya ordered the drums of the *tablakhanah* to beat, especially at night, in the midst of the total quiet. As the sound of the drum came from a distance, only a very few persons who worked closely with Zakariyya knew the meaning of those drumbeats coming from the foot of the Muqattam hills.

This evening Zakariyya himself went down to the damp, dark gaol. Before the end of the day he had told Mabruk to empty the cavities of the gaol completely. Nobody knew anything about the prisoners; no arrest warrants had been issued for any of them. Zakariyya did not know what the next few hours would bring. He never trusted anyone, no matter how secure everything was and no matter what anyone else thought. Zakariyya didn't under-estimate the narrowest breach or the slightest possibility of one. Who knows? Perhaps an emir would send a letter to the Sultan to tell him about the prisoners here, some of whom even Zakariyya himself had completely forgotten about since they were brought here so long ago. Perhaps Sultan al-Ghuri's own Mamluks, be they the newly imported *julban* or the veteran *qaranisah*, would come and scale the walls or force the doors and pour through the halls and corridors and catch him and disgrace him. Then they would look for the gaol. They would look for Sha'ban. Yes, Sha'ban. Months ago he had disappeared and nobody knew anything about him; Sha'ban, the Sultan's favourite boy, his constant companion, both when he was alone and when he entertained; Sha'ban, who sat to the right of the Sultan, where the Emir Dawadar (Executive Secretary) should sit, and close to the places of the Master of Arms, the Master of the Horse and all the Masters of the Sword and the Pen. Sha'ban looked like the very twin of the silver moon. His lips were two rubies. His eyes were cat's eyes. His mouth was as fragrant as musk, his cheek smoother than silk and his hand softer than dough. He wasn't a day over twenty.

When Zakariyya decided to kidnap Sha'ban, he had not been put up to it by anyone, either emir or vizier. He had decided to find out for himself the true nature of the relationship between Sha'ban and Sultan al-Ghuri. A burning question was keeping him sleepless at night and searing his eyes: 'Does the Sultan like boys? Does he prefer them to women?' Such a matter should never elude Zakar-iyya. So the truth had to be found out, especially since circum-stantial evidence almost confirmed his suspicions; ever since his accession to the throne, he was not reported to have deflowered any virgin or added new acquisitions to his harem, with the exception of ten slave girls sent to him as a gift from the King of Venice when he sent an ambassador to him months ago. Zakariyya knew about them. He had their names and their descriptions and had learned from his own sources that the Sultan had not touched any of them and that they spent their nights tossing and turning from desire. Had it not been the case that only eunuchs were allowed in their quarters, they would have done such things as would have been talked about for generations to come. Besides, al-Ghuri had only two wives. So, was there a liaison between the Sultan and Sha'ban? Nobody but Sha'ban himself would answer the question.

For three full months, Mabruk staked him out, noting the times of his going up to the Citadel and coming down from it, until he became thoroughly familiar with his daily routine, the places he frequented, the turns on his route, the number of houses on either side of it and the open spaces along it. At a specific moment, on a night with no moon and no stars, a number of masked men lay in ambush on both sides of the sandy road leading to the street of the Citadel. On the same night he was delivered at Zakariyya's place. Zakariyya looked a long time at his lips, marvelled at his appearance and his face and his tenderness. He touched with his hands the softness of his complexion and his long hair. He was struck by the whiteness of his teeth, his sweet smell and his delicate tongue. Oh, God, could such a person be born a man? He took off the boy's clothes, one piece at a time, while the boy was still unconscious. Zakariyya dismissed his men, then suddenly bent down and kissed the boy. He said to himself that the kiss would feel better after he awoke.

In the morning Zakariyya saw his beautiful face, which looked like roses adorned with dewdrops. He was worried, but the boy appeared calm and confident. He talked to him without stating his purpose explicitly. He listened to the description of countries that Sha'ban had seen and he wondered afterwards if he was really under twenty. Sha'ban had seen China, visited Persia and danced in the mountains of Anatolia. He was fluent in the Frankish languages as well as the dialects of the Berbers who inhabited the mountains of the Maghrib. How did he learn all that? When did he have the time to do that at such a tender age? It was as if Zakariyya were sitting with an old man who had experienced the world and held the keys to its secrets. This beautiful mouth was reciting the sweetest, most tender poetry, relating the quintessence of wisdom. When did he listen to all that? Why didn't he ask what it was that was wanted of him? There were many times when Zakariyya was certain that the boy had other names, that Sha'ban was just one of those names.

Three months passed and Zakariyya almost forgot the original purpose, almost lost sight of the need to learn the true relationship between the Sultan and Sha'ban. At the beginning he hinted and beat around the bush and Sha'ban denied it. Casually during the conversation Zakariyya would pose the vicious question and the boy would ignore it. Zakariyya's patience was running out like grains of sand falling through his fingers. One night he couldn't stand it any longer. He went down to the cellar, bound the boy, undressed him and kissed him on the lips. He saw the beautiful face and ears turn white. He felt the soft, smooth neck. The boy groaned and bit Zakariyya's hand. Zakariyya threw him to the floor and spoiled the virgin land. He crossed unknown passages, which heretofore nobody had ever penetrated, and stood over a chasm never before revealed to a male. He didn't look at the boy's face, but left him. Zakariyya was annoyed and sad. Why? He didn't know. The reason was not his failure to find out the true relationship between the boy and the Sultan. Three days later he went down to the cellar and there saw a face that had changed, hardened and aged dozens of years. At first he thought the boy had been switched. Where had the beauty of his face or the tenderness of his youth gone? He called his name. Sha'ban did not answer, not one syllable did he utter. The bloom of youth was gone, the stem of the rose broken. The boy forgot the countries he had visited, the villages he had seen, the white snows he had spoken about so eloquently. Zakariyya was puzzled and left the cellar quickly. He went back several times, secretly, and was horrified at what he saw. The boy had wasted away and was on the verge of death. If only Zakariyya had time, just a little time, he might figure out the secret of what had taken place; he might put his finger on the beginnings of things; he might find out the true relationship between the Sultan and his boy, Sha'ban.

Tonight, however, Zakariyya was grieved and vexed. Regretfully he decided to choke Sha'ban and bury him alive. He watched the strangulation himself. Mabruk alone did the whole job and the muted blows of his pickaxe were still clinging to his ears. The night, the strangeness of the affair and the departure of the boy made it all sound so gloomy and frightening, but what he had ordered must be carried out. Maybe they would come and kidnap Sha'ban alive and take him up to the Sultan. They would say, 'My lord, here is your beloved boy. We found him at the place of Zakariyya ibn Radi, Head of the Spies and deputy of Ali ibn Abi al-Jud. Zakariyya, my lord, has betrayed you and abducted the person you love most; he has violated the person closest to you and changed him totally and for ever. The very same Head of the Spies whom one day you had sent for and in front of whom you almost revealed your weakness and asked, with a broken heart, to send forth his men, his spies, to find Sha'ban, your love, your most favoured. This Zakariyya who . . .'

At that point there was bound to be a great perdition, absolute annihilation. He wouldn't be cut into two halves; he wouldn't be impaled; hanging would be too much of a blessing to be hoped for; death by strangulation would be an unattainable dream. As for poisoning, that would be a paradise, which the likes of him couldn't even aspire to enter. The Sultan would order him to be roasted alive over a slow fire. He had already spitted three men just because it was said that they had been seen several times in the boy's company. He didn't wait to find out who they were or where they had come from. What did the three wretches have in common with Sha'ban? Zakariyya himself didn't know. The boy didn't tell him about them or the reason for their meetings. Anyway, if things went well tonight, tomorrow or the day after, he would send some of his ablest, veteran spies to try to find out everything they could about those three and the boy. Who knows? Maybe he would learn more about him dead than he did when he was alive. Maybe the investigation would uncover things that would never occur to anyone; fires usually started from the slightest spark. Indeed, it wouldn't be safe to keep Sha'ban alive, nor the other prisoners, for that matter. Anyone who stayed here, whether low-born or of unknown lineage or even identity, even if he were a small-time crook or thief, would all of a sudden become important. Everybody, high and low, would make the most hideous accusations and would say very nasty things about him: 'Zakariyya gaols God's creatures!

Zakariyya has a gaol underneath his house! One wonders how many people Zakariyya has killed or what methods he has used to torture bodies created by God!'

At that time those who hated him – the emirs, the sons of Mamluks, the well-to-do, the shaykhs of Sufi orders and the students and scholars of al-Azhar – they would all think of the prisoners and all those caught by Zakariyya as poor innocent wretches who had done no wrong, had not conspired, stolen or uttered insults against an emir or a notable in a public thoroughfare.

Zakariyya was now inspecting the gaol himself. He took the torch from Mabruk and with his own eyes was examining the cavities of the gaol. The smell of rot was rising to his nostrils; the rot was sticky. But he had to endure it; he must be patient. He was satisfied with what he was doing right now. So, these cavities would be without moans and groans for a few nights. There would be no hoarse exchanges as the prisoners asked each other about their names, their villages or towns and the reasons they were there. When Zakariyya saw the prisoners, he was amazed to see faces whose names he didn't remember, as if they had come without his knowledge. He had forgotten them as the years passed and his worries increased. Now Zakariyya was satisfied. He would go out in the cool breeze coming from the top of the Muqattam hills. Now he could be by himself. Mabruk knew exactly what his master wanted and he moved away, vanishing in the dark. Zakariyya felt the handle of his short dagger with the poisoned blade and crossed the big courtyard in long strides; his cloak made a rustling sound. A laugh, smooth as a thread of silk or the cocoon of a butterfly, came from upstairs. Some of the women were spending the night in pleasant conversation in the harem quarters. He wasn't going to be with any of them tonight, nor would he see his son, Yasin.

Zakariyya pushes open a certain spot in the wall, then closes it. He climbs narrow stairs, which lead to the top storey in the office building adjacent to his house. Someone with sharp eyes, looking from a distance, might be able to see a little light escaping from the lattice-work in the *mashrabiyya*. But, no matter how clever a person might be, no matter how talented or able, he would never guess what was on the top floor. Zakariyya doesn't come here except in times of turmoil and uncertainty, when the very foundations are in danger and when quick changes threaten to sweep everything away. Before starting to work, he leans against a soft cushion to shield his back from the cold, red and black marble wall. He closes his eyes. What is the meaning of what has happened? His bewilderment now is greater than it was the moment he first received the news. Around him the long walls are lined with wooden cases divided into compartments and pigeon-holes, each of which contains a number of books and registers in different colours and sizes. Here the land of Egypt is summed up. Zakariyya always tells his closest aides, 'Whenever I want to go to any town or village in Egypt, I don't journey far from home. I come here. There is a section for each town, village, hamlet, estate or fief in the land of Egypt from one end to the other. Each register contains the description of the place, what it is famous for, its most important personages and everything known about them. The section on Cairo contains its alleys, the layout of its quarters and its mosques; its men, old men, women, boys, slave girls, houses of sin, policemen, guards and scholars; its baths, markets and inns; its guilds, its singers and its places of pleasure; the names of the Rumis residing, arriving and departing; the names of the Franks in transit and those Egyptians who get in touch with them or visit them. Everything, big or small, is here. As for the emirs, notables and illustrious persons, everything that has to do with them, their temperaments and habits, their likes and dislikes, their joys and sorrows – everything is here.'

Zakariyya would sometimes brag, saying, 'This department of the Bureau is a source of pride for the Sultan and a prized jewel in the crown of the Sultanate. Nothing like this has ever before been done by a *bassass*, Egyptian or Frankish. And, if God, the All-Knowing, Ever-Present, wills, there will come a day when every human being will have a section devoted to him alone, summing him up from the first cry at birth to the last tremor of death.'

Now Zakariyya is looking among the registers: there it is, exactly what he wants – a red, clothbound register. Herein lie the government officials, functionaries and members of the smaller guilds. At the end is an appendix containing the names of those who are thought likely one day to assume posts and the offices they are likely to assume. He doesn't remember what is written about Barakat ibn Musa. Shihab al-Halabi, the controller of the Bureau, added his name about two years ago. Zakariyya hasn't requested his sheet to read. He doesn't know if Shihab al-Halabi has added new information on him. It is late now; the night is almost gone. Had it not been for the confidential nature of the matter, Zakariyya would have sent for Shihab al-Halabi to gather all the scattered information about Zayni. But in order to send for him he would have to go through closed alleys and streets and to elude the night-watchmen as well as Zakariyya's own spies. Perhaps summoning Shihab now would look suspicious. No need to do that.

Zakariyya was annoyed. He was taken by surprise when the news was announced. He didn't keep all his men at the Bureau and had not implemented the plan he had proposed some time ago to facilitate communications between him and his deputies and aides and men. This must be looked into and implemented tomorrow. Had he not taken pains to know everything in the Bureau, the way the registers, reports and papers were arranged and classified, he would have been lost now. He didn't let any of his deputies keep anything to himself, no matter how small or insignificant. He must be familiar with all the work procedures and circumstances, methods and difficulties, so that none of his men would ever play games with him or deceive him. But, oh, how he needed Shihab al-Halabi, in particular, now! Shihab al-Halabi didn't bother to look up anything; he had a fantastic memory and knew thousands of persons and whatever had anything to do with them. He forgot nothing, even after years had passed. He remembered what reports or documents were exchanged, what information and lines were added in which year.

Zakariyya is now turning the pages of the register, holding the coloured ribbon marking the pages. The As don't interest him. It's an unimportant letter. Some of these entries may be dead already. Some of them should be transferred to other registers since their status has changed or is uncertain. Take this one, for instance: Ahmad ibn Umar, janitor of the Sidi Suwaydan Mosque. Now he has become the imam of the mosque, reads the *hadith* and the Quran and leads the prayers. He has married an Abyssinian woman. He is rumoured to favour Abyssinian women. And yet his name and title are still in the category of 'servants'. All his women are here: one of them, the mother of his children, one of whom is a student at al-Azhar, is a peasant woman from the village of Osim. No! Shihab al-Halabi must be told about this. Perhaps someone would say, 'What is the importance of this?' No! No! Everything must be written down and noted; something that nobody knows about yet might come of it. There it is, the B, exactly 'Barakat'. Yes! Barakat ibn Musa. At the top of the page in the left corner is just one word, seven letters in all. The ink is black and the handwriting is fine.

'Barakat.'

If an innocent person were to look at the page, he would think it had nothing on it at all except the name. And what did one word mean on a blank, white page, gleaming under the candles in the holders on the walls lined with wood and marble and shelves that were heavy with books and registers? Zakariyya wipes the page with a small transparent object, a substance the composition of which is known only to a few. Little by little, the shapes of letters begin to reveal themselves as if an invisible hand were writing the words. Zakariyya wipes the page several times with the substance, then he blows: only four lines! Four? He takes refuge in God, the Almighty, who inspires mankind, reveals secrets and knows the unknown. Why is it that nothing but bewilderment comes from the direction of this man? All that Shihab al-Halabi has written is just four, short lines: 'Barakat ibn Musa: has ability to read the stars; mother's name: Anqa.'

Zakariyya closes the register. Any low-born person, any of those trouble-making students of al-Azhar, any courtesan or vendor of fried cheese or meat pies has an entry at least half a page long, and this man here is worth a mere four lines! He closes his eyes. The night is quiet; all secrets are safe and secure. He knows that people are staying up this very minute, whispering, saying what they think of the new *Muhtasib* and what they expect of him. When will the day come when a spy will learn what is being said thousands of villages and towns away? God is capable of everything! If Zakariyya had not been confident of what had been conveyed to him after sunset, he wouldn't have believed it now. More than one source, more than one spy, each unaware of the others, conveyed to him the details of Barakat ibn Musa's efforts to obtain the post of *Muhtasib*: his going daily to Emir Qani Bey, staying with him, talking to him, and then the sum of three thousand dinars, which he handed to Emir Qani Bey on the twenty-eighth of the holy month of Ramadan after the evening prayers. Three thousand dinars bought Barakat the post of *Muhtasib*. Zakariyya is now blowing hot air from his mouth. He had thought, had been certain, that the post would undoubtedly go to Emir Tughluq. His hands tighten their grip on the edges of the register. Earlier in the evening he had heard the puzzling news, something that made him utter a word that he hated: 'Why?' But how can that be? What mettle is this Barakat made of? Has the Antichrist come, in disguise? Has he managed to slip into this world unbeknown to Zakariyya? How? After the Sublime Decree of the Sultan had been issued, after Barakat ibn Musa had been praised, after the title of Zayni had been conferred upon him for life, after Barakat had paid three thousand dinars to buy the post, after the herald had repeated the announcement for a whole day, he went out of his house at Birkat al-Ratli, going through side-streets, with no *tablakhanah*, no cymbals, no noise; his very first ride! Incognito, he went up to the Citadel, prostrated himself in front of all the emirs and shed real, absolutely genuine tears and spoke words that have made Zakariyya continue pacing up and down until now. He didn't go to see his only son or any of the women in his harem. The night weighed heavily upon him. He couldn't care less about the execution of Ali ibn Abi al-Jud. He wouldn't bat an eyelid if Sultan al-Ghuri stayed in power or if he was deposed and replaced by the lowest of God's creatures. All he cared about was finding an explanation for what Zayni Barakat ibn Musa did at the Citadel. And in front of whom? The whole State! Things that would totally stun whoever witnessed them. His leg was getting numb, as if a line of tiny ants were marching under his skin. He clasps his hands behind his back. Maybe he didn't pay three thousand. No, no, that couldn't be. Zakariyya is all by himself now. He shakes his head vigorously. He is absolutely certain of the veracity of the reports of the spies assigned exclusively to Qani Bey. He knows full well that one thousand dinars have been deposited in Emir Qani Bey's treasury the very day he received the bribe from Barakat ibn Musa. He did not receive any revenues from anywhere else that day. As for the remaining two thousand dinars, they went up to the Citadel. If only the Sultan would make up his mind tonight! Then Zakariyya would be at ease. But the Sultan told Zayni to await his decision. Zakariyya holds the register and once again opens the page.

'Barakat.'

As of tonight, Zakariyya himself is going to take care of Barakat ibn Musa. Let Shihab al-Halabi add whatever information he likes to his anaemic four lines! Zakariyya bends over a small cabinet, from which he takes a register bound in green silk. The night around him is a blindfolded mute. He takes out of his pocket a bundle of scraps of paper he received from the Citadel, which recount everything that took place at the Baisariyya Hall: Barakat ibn Musa kissed the marble floor of the hall, washed it with his tears. That has never happened in the history of any sultan. From now on, he himself is going to read and convey everything that has to do with this Zanyi from near or far; his own eyes are going to take care of him whenever occasion permits. From a small cavity draped by a small curtain he takes out a clay pot and dips a fine-pointed wooden pen in a coloured vessel.

The First Page

10 Shawwal 912 AH

In full view of the emirs and in the presence of a great crowd, Zayni Barakat requested, in a voice overcome with emotion, that his lord relieve him of the Markets Inspectorship. He said in a trembling voice, 'The Inspectorship, my lord, is a post the holder of which is entrusted with the affairs of the people. God forbid that I find it in me to be capable of handling that. I am a poor servant who cannot bear the thought of being in charge of a single human being. All I hope for is to pass my days in peace and quiet, away from matters of government and rulers. All I want is to sleep peacefully, undisturbed by anyone's curses or the resentment of a wronged person whom I have overlooked or whose right I failed to exact from his oppressor.'

Kom al-Jarih

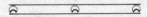

THEY are great in number, but no loud voice disturbed the quiet house. On an old mattress covered with the remnants of a rug, which has retained its bright colours despite the passage of time, sits the Master, Shaykh Abu al-Su'ud. He listens long. He knows them all. Some of them have memorized the Quran under his tutelage, as he spent part of his life near a marble pillar at the Mosque of Sidi Suwaydan or the Mosque of Sidi Ismail al-Imbabi, teaching the foundations of jurisprudence, explicating texts, explaining the *hadith* of the Prophet and the verses of the Quran and relating histories. Here they are in the latter years of their lives, at that time when one knows that one will live fewer years than one has lived already. Here are assembled the oldest and most distinguished heads of the guilds – the blacksmiths, the butchers, the marble-workers, the masons and the storytellers – as well as heads of alleys, notables and sons of Mamluks. Said brings a big plate filled with washed dried dates, which he places in front of them. Shaykh Ridwan, Head of the Coal-dealers' Guild and the oldest of those present bends forwards, saying, 'No one will convince him but you. No one.'

The words remain suspended in mid-air inside the house. A sweet calm flows noiselessly like a flock of sparrows flying very high in the sky. At the same time the alley is filling with large crowds. All voices outside the walls of the house die down. A scent that does not belong to any known plant species or perfume, almost like a blend of sweet basil and rose-water, permeated by the essence of iris, pervades the air. Each is lost in his thoughts; the air gets darker, filling hearts with reverence and awe. The beads of the rosary roll audibly, matching the rhythm of the thoughts of Shaykh Abu al-Su'ud as he ponders what he hears and what he sees on the men's faces.

'We haven't heard of any man like him and we accept no other!'

A light smile appeared, like tiny rays of light coming through the narrow lattice-work of a *mashrabiyya*, fleeting like lightning in the midst of clouds.

'Do you know him?'

Shaykh al-Qasabi, Head of Zuwayla Alley says, 'His turning down the post is his best recommendation, Master.'

Said doesn't say a word, in order to let the guests speak. Earlier in the evening, his usual time to call on the Shaykh, he had talked to him more than all of these men combined. At the end of the day it is only Said who visits him after his classes at al-Azhar. The disciples come in the morning: they recite the Quran and *hadith*. Some would clean the house and make the Shaykh his meal of buttermilk and hot, soft bread. The highest ambition for each of them is one word of approval from the Shaykh. Said does not hesitate to express irritation or anger in front of the Master. Even things that he would be afraid to say, explicitly or implicitly, among the crowds or in al-Azhar, he would say here, however daring they might be. The Master would look at him, his eyes quickly penetrating to his very soul. Neither Said nor any of those present can say exactly how old the Shaykh is. The wrinkles show signs of many decades; he may be over a hundred years old. His voice and his stature have the strength of a palm-tree trunk. He hates solitude. Said knows what passionate joy he feels as he listens to thunder. He would say that that was the sound of the world, the voice of the universe, which only the Omniscient, Most Merciful could understand and interpret. No one has actually seen him as he listened to the thunder or witnessed his joy at the first raindrops, the first tears shed by the sky every winter. Said hears the thunder every year at the *riwaq* or the coffee-house or the street. At the times when he would be vaguely wondering what Samah was doing at a specific moment, he would pause, knowing full well that the Shaykh was listening, standing at the exact centre of the courtyard, his eyes shining with a joy not of this world. His soul would be dancing with gaiety in another universe, conversing with the saints, remembering in sorrow what happened at Karbala, asking God's mercy for the members of the Prophet's house whom neither decay nor extinction would touch. He usually receives the first whispers of the rain with his head bare and turbanless, hands outstretched.

Now it is getting colder as the night, confident and black, takes over the sky.

Shaykh Bahjury, Head of the Marble-workers' Guild, leans over. 'It has never happened before, Master, that a man, with or without a turban, no matter what rank or status, has been offered a post and turned it down. Everybody, the students of al-Azhar and the members of the guilds, ever since they heard the news, has been speaking of nothing but Zayni Barakat, Zayni Barakat!'

'Who spread the word, my son?'

The face of the winter is expressionless, its glances indifferent, the cold quite forceful. The truth is, none of those present had a ready answer. Said doesn't know how the news has been leaked from Baisariyya Hall in the Citadel. Perhaps it was the servants at the Citadel or some Mamluk? Each of those around the Shaykh has heard a different version of the news. The common people in Husayniyya asserted that Zayni didn't bow his head before the Sultan; he didn't tremble and had no fear. He said in front of all the emirs, 'I do not accept the Markets Inspectorship because I do not want to see injustice and look the other way.'

As for people in Judariyya, al-Rum al-Juwwaniyya Alley and Batniyya, they categorically denied that he had gone up to the Citadel at all. They said that he had sent the Sultan a letter in which he politely but firmly declined to accept the post since corruption was rampant, people were oppressed on all sides and justice was banished from the land. This, he said, went against his nature and everything he believed in. The responsibility was too great and nobody would help him. Rather the Sultan was going to demand that he impose new taxes on the Muslims. Zayni Barakat ibn Musa would never accept that. In Bulaq in the public baths, especially the women's baths, it was said that he stood in front of the Sultan as a paragon of manliness, chivalry and courage, that he poked the Sultan gently but firmly in the chest – something that has never been done before by any human being – and said, 'You will order me to be unfair to the subjects, but I will never comply because I fear that I will be held accountable for the injustice. How could I meet my Maker on the Day of Reckoning?'

'The truth, Master, is that we don't know how the news got out, but such matters cannot be kept hidden for a long time.'

The Shaykh's eyes are two springs of serenity. Who would be

better suited to the post? Who but him would establish justice among the people? He is a God-fearing man, without hypocrisy or affectation. He speaks his mind in front of the Sultan himself and in the presence of the mightiest and most cruel-hearted emirs. Some said they had seen him enter the palace of Emir Qani Bey and that he hadn't come out yet. The Sultan himself has not yet made up his mind.

Said was now seeing al-Azhar Mosque; Amr ibn al-Adawi was moving among the students and scholars, going to the nearby cafés and pastry shops, listening to what the people were saying among themselves. If only Said had a chance to get close to that Zayni. He had never seen him before. Whenever he thought that the world was devoid of courage, time proved him wrong. Shaykh Abu al-Su'ud always listened to him recounting the atrocities being committed in the city. Said memorized the names of everyone who had been unjustly hanged: the peasant who was impaled because he had stolen a cucumber; the woman who was cut into two halves because she cursed a profligate Mamluk who had abducted her virgin daughter. On the same day Said would come to his master, name the victim and ask in a broken voice how all of that was going on; how a man could be disposed of at the cheapest price, without blood-money being paid and without anyone inquiring about him. The spectre of a smile, like the scent of mint, would stir gently on the Shaykh's tender lips. Sometimes he would whisper, 'May the grace of God soften the blows of Fate!'

On the pupils of the Shaykh's eyes have been imprinted momentous events: travelling all over God's world, reaching the end of the earth, crossing completely barren deserts, climbing mountains that reach up to the very heavens, visiting poor villages in the regions of Syria, the deserts of Hejaz, Najd, Hadramaut and the valleys of Yemen. Said has never seen the snow. Sometimes, very rarely, hail fell in Cairo, making a thudding noise as if it were rocks, but that was not the same as snow in vast open fields, radiant with vapour frozen in space, extending in a silence that sent fear deep down into the souls: space and time with no beginning and no end. The Master says, 'The world appears to be without end, without horizons: intangible and inexhaustible.' The Shaykh has seen seas with waves as high as the mountains, where the land appeared as a faraway dream, an elusive delusion. It was at such moments that strange forces would well up deep within his soul and he would let loose a cry in the face of the endless and the infinite, a cry that reached the Qaf mountain, creating an earth-quake, freezing the ocean: 'God lives! God lives! God is here!'

His friends, and they are many, would let loose the same cry wherever they are. He would meet them once every year when he arrived at the Holy Mosque. They would express their affection for each other, recount what they had seen and what they had done to further the cause of Islam, to keep alive the memory of the Prophet's family and the blood of al-Husayn, still fresh after so many cen-turies. At the Kaaba they would mourn those who hadn't turned up, those who had departed where no man alive could go. After the pilgrimage, the meetings and the circumambulation, each of them would head in a different direction. The body would not lie down two nights in the same place. The cry 'God lives!' would extend across time and stretch across the earth. Years ago, Shaykh Abu al-Su'ud came back to his birthplace, to Egypt. Since then he hasn't gone anywhere. Now he lives in Kom al-Jarih, visited by travelling dervishes and the heads of Sufi orders at all hours of the day and the night. No visitor or guest went back without seeing the Shaykh and telling him what he had come to tell him. The only times when that was not possible were prayer times. Often he would interrupt his meditations and his reflections on long-gone eras to listen to someone with a request. Then he would answer him explicitly or in an indirect manner.

Once again, Said would very much like to take part in the conversa-tions with the shaykhs. If Amr ibn al-Adawi were to come to him tonight to ask him what he thought, trying to provoke him, he would fear no prying eyes or eavesdropping ears or reports written about him. He wouldn't even fear Zakariyya ibn Radi himself, whose name and reputation alone were enough to spread terror throughout the whole country.

Shaykh al-Qasabi says, 'I swear by God, Master, if they don't appoint Zayni, we would come to no good!'

The Head of the Coal-dealers' Guild says, 'I swear by God that I've never heard of him. I do not know him and have never seen him.'

The Master leans forwards. Shaykh Qasabi stops. 'How has the Sultan selected him when he doesn't hold any high office, when he is unknown to the people?' The Shaykh's question stirs up other questions.

'How do we know, Master? Perhaps he overlooked the evil wrongdoers whom he knew and God guided him to choose Zayni Barakat.'

'Only you, blessed Master, can convince him he should accept the Markets Inspectorship.'

Shaykh Abu al-Su'ud leans forwards, whispering, 'May God place us in the hands of those who are good, not those who are evil, among us!'

Wednesday, 10 Shawwal

'WHEN I heard that Zayni Barakat was going to the Azhar Mosque to address the people, I swore not to miss seeing him in person. I thought I was alone, but, when I went, I couldn't find a spot to stand in. It was like the Day of Judgement. I said to myself, "Where have these people come from?"'

Safadi, the perfumer in Hamzawi and the best at extracting the essence of lilies, leans forwards, placing his hand on his chest. 'I saw him.' They all look at him. 'What piety! What goodness! Everything he said could have come only from a real man. A man such as he was not created to bow before potentate or sultan!'

Mahmud, the milkman, asks, 'Is he short and dark? I heard it said that he was dark, with a long beard . . .'

'No. His face is just like that of any of us.'

Master Murshidi laughs, 'God forbid! You mean his face looks like your face, your ugly face?' Then, earnestly, he adds, 'I saw him riding the *Muhtasib*'s mule on the street, but I couldn't tell whether he was tall or short. I didn't see him on the pulpit of al-Azhar.'

At this point Amr ibn al-Adawi says, as the beads of his rosary follow each other at great speed, 'You said that the heart didn't dislike him . . .'

'Yes, by God, Shaykh Amr.'

Master Safadi's apprentice comes in carrying a tray filled with cups of carob drink. Amr holds the clay mug with his fingers as the aroma of the drink seeps into the cold air. Safadi is used to drinking tamarind and carob drinks and lemonade in the middle of winter, saying they open the paths of the heart and fill one with cheer. Amr's lips murmur some prayers before drinking his drink. His eyes remain fixed on the faces for a few moments then retreat quickly behind his closed eyelids. He doesn't talk much but rather listens. With such people he is not afraid of a slip-up that might give him away; they speak their minds freely. He doesn't have to make a comment that would sound casual and spontaneous but which is meant to steer the conversation in a certain direction. He feels the cold carob drink permeating his body. It has been a difficult day; nobody had slept the night before. The shops were open all night with the owners sitting in front. The emirs locked their houses. The *tablakhanahs* played their drums longer than usual after the evening prayer, shaking the whole city. News came and went like huge waves breaking on the rocks on the shore, then receding: 'Zayni came down from the Citadel!'; 'Zayni is now going up to Duhaisha Hall in the Citadel!'; 'Not at all, Zayni hasn't left the house of Emir Qani Bey!'

At dawn the news was all over the city: Shaykh Abu al-Su'ud sent for Zayni Barakat. A young scholar from al-Azhar went to him and accompanied him to Kom al-Jarih, where Zayni Barakat met the old Shaykh. Amr didn't have a single quiet moment. He was not going to miss anything, no matter how slight. He was going to monitor every glance, every strange-sounding laugh, every joke told by any of those louts who do nothing under such circumstances except sit on the floor next to the drinking-water fountains or in front of the pastry shops, laughing and jeering. Amr knew that he was not alone, that there were others besides him, watching the people and watching him and sending in reports about him to the Head Spy of Cairo. When the Head *Bassas* himself told him that, he couldn't rest a moment. He wondered who they were and tried to find out one of them. He had his suspicions, but he couldn't be certain and decided to give up the idea. But no matter how well he managed that, it was always there, lurking. If anyone should report something that happened in front of Amr that he hadn't reported, he would lay himself open to blame, would be accused of negligence, of playing favourites, of not being honest about what he reported, what he heard.

The Head Spy, summoning him, would yell, 'You have no idea what I have to go through because of your negligence! The Sultan would be gravely alarmed, wouldn't be able to sleep for a whole night if one of you neglected to report just one incident. Are you not his eyes, his ears? If an eye is blinded or an ear turned deaf, how would he know the affairs of the people? How would he administer justice among his subjects? A little incident, which you overlook, might appear insignificant to a negligent person. But you don't know, you cannot appreciate what consequences it might have. During the reign of the late Sultan Ashraf Qait Bey some leaders plotted against him. Do you know how they conspired? They feared the Sultan's eyes. The Chief of Spies at that time was so efficient and capable that he uncovered every plot or conspiracy against the Sultan. How do you think Sultan Qait Bey was able to stay on the throne for thirty long years? His spies were resourceful, alert and hard-working. The emirs resorted to a new trick. Each would leave Cairo as if on a ride for fresh air at Birkat al-Ratli or Bulaq or in the middle of the trees at Azbakiyya. At exactly the same time – one agreed upon in advance – each emir would start moving from the opposite end and they would spot each other and shout as if they hadn't seen each other for a long time. Then they would exchange a very brief conversation in the course of which they would agree on matters of great moment, then they would part company. Who would have the slightest suspicion or give the matter a second thought? But it didn't escape Shihab Jaafar ibn Abd al-Jawwad, the smartest *Muhtasib* in the history of these kings and sultans, surpassed only by Shihab Zakariyya ibn Radi. The late Jaafar realized what was taking place thanks to an eighty-year-old woman. That is how old she appeared; in reality she wasn't a day over forty. Jaafar was the one to start the practice of recruiting old women as spies and teaching them to be beggars and to sit in public places, next to drinking-water fountains and tombs or in front of houses, asking for alms and charity but in reality monitoring the slightest detail. Anyway, this particular spy grasped the significance of what was taking place in front of her every two days: the way the two emirs met, each saying upon seeing the other, 'I haven't seen you in ages . . .' It is said, but only God, who uncovers the unknown, knows, that that spy was blind and that she had grasped the whole situation by ear alone. As a result of that little detail, the conspirators were caught. They were arrested by Shihab Jaafar the night before their planned attack against Ashraf Qait Bey, God have mercy on his soul. Read the histories, men! You are the very eyes of justice! You are justice itself! How can you be negligent? How can you let anything slip by you? How?'

Master Safadi gets up. 'God be praised; everything went as we had hoped.'

Shaykh Qasabi looks for his cane. 'Tonight at the bath, if God wills. Let's soak in the hot water to purify ourselves so that we might meet the new *Muhtasib* pure and sinless when he makes his rounds.'

Mahmud, the milkman, says, 'You want to regain your vigour and get rid of the cold!'

The beards shake with gentle laughter. The dark night approaches, enveloping the departing day. They say goodbye.

'Maybe I'll come. I long for the bath tank.'

'The bath tank and the masseur, Shaykh Amr!'

Amr laughs a quick laugh. His fingers shake. Only once before had he listened to the Head Spy of Cairo, who chastised him for neglecting to report a conversation among three Syrian immigrants. From that moment on he realized that he was being watched by vigilant eyes. Maybe it is one of these men: Master Safadi, the milkman, perhaps even Shaykh al-Qasabi himself. It doesn't matter; he is not going to worry about them. Why is he wondering who is watching him? The Head will summon him and will ask him why at such and such a time he was thinking who might be watching him. He is not going to worry about that. Things always change. After they had summoned him the first time, he walked about town filled with satisfaction. The Head had praised him for his piety. Many an Azharite has gone bad! He told him that he knew everything about him. He knew that he was totally dependent on the stipend he received from al-Azhar, that he didn't get a single dirham from his village, that he was desperate for a few dirhams to send to his old mother. That day the Head Spy told him his mother's name, something that Amr himself occasionally forgot and had never mentioned to anyone. Not only that, but the Head told him how old she was, even though she herself didn't know what year she had come into the world. Amr was flabbergasted as he listened to how her husband, whom she had married after Amr's father's passing, beat her. She was now living in a reed hut that might be washed away by rain or the Nile waters and she would be drowned. Perhaps she would die of exposure. Months would pass without any news of Amr's mother. The Head told him that once every week he would furnish him with reports about how she was faring to put him at ease. He could give him a daily report about her most intimate affairs, but that would only worry him. The Head Spy told him of the number of times he had recited verses from the Quran, in the morning, in the dead of winter when he went to the house of a well-off merchant and how the man sent him a plate with some cottage cheese, a handful of fava beans, a cup of goat's milk and half a dirham.

'Reciting the Quran in the houses of notables, Amr, does not become an Azhar scholar. It is a craft for the blind. I personally do not approve of it for you. I am not comfortable with it. It bothers me a great deal. Believe me, Amr, it upsets me that you, an Azhar student, one who might one day, God, the One, the Almighty, willing, become a great judge, dispensing justice to the very people who send you goat's milk and fava beans to stop your hunger in the morning. We will, if God wills, help you become a judge, a head of a department, a man of substance and dignity. But let's think of you now. Are you comfortable doing that? No, no, I didn't think you were. No, no, Amr, please, consider me your brother. Don't conceal anything from me, even your personal, your very personal problems. Confide in me and I, I alone, will help you solve them. Trust me. Trust me, please.'

Next to the third marble pillar to the right of the old wall at al-Azhar – the pillar under which Azharites claim a buried talisman kept sparrows, snakes and scorpions away from the mosque – he sat many times, holding imaginary conversations with his mother. His mother made her living digging out radishes and sweet potatoes in the fields of Benha and neighbouring villages, lighting ovens, carrying firewood, bundling reeds or mowing grass. She hardly ever had any rest or joy. Some time ago he heard that the Shaykh of the Chapel of the Blind was going on a trip to Benha, that he had made his plans, got his provisions ready and packed his mule. At that time Amr did not have a dirham to his name. The Shaykh was going to the very town where Amr's mother lived. People would learn of that and his mother would know that a man had come from Cairo, from al-Azhar specifically, and that her son had not sent with him some sugar or a piece of black cloth in which to wrap herself for a whole year. Perhaps she would think that he had died under the hooves of Mamluk horses or in a plague. For a whole night, Amr could get no sleep at all; he felt cornered, as if a rock the size of the Muqattam hill was slowly, steadily moving towards him. He made the rounds of his friends in the *riwaq*, sat with them, talked for a while and laughed with those who laughed, but when the time came for him to ask, he was tongue-tied, his voice trembled and the letters and words refused to come out and he told himself that it was unseemly or that he would find somebody else. Then he crossed the main courtyard of the mosque, telling himself that he wasn't going to beat around the bush, but, as soon as he sat down, sweat collected on his brow, things got confused, words failed him and he was completely overcome by shame. He remembered that time now with bitterness and grief like a dust storm blowing from the mountain, clouding a clear day. At that time he hadn't got to know any of the businessmen or the patrons of the baths with whom he sat now, listening to what they said and conveying it. Back then he was shy and retiring. He didn't dare borrow a few dirhams to send his mother what she needed. He carried his ration of dried bread and went far away from al-Azhar Mosque, where the students stood during the day, selling their rations or exchanging them for some other food. A passer-by gave him a piece of aged cheese for two loaves of bread. At Megharbilin, Sanadiqiyya, Attarin, Fahhamin, the people of Judariyya, the Sharabshiyyin, passers-by on Saliba Street and the loiterers at Bab al-Wazir all shook their heads or said, 'May God provide.' As nightfall approached, its darkness crept to the heart and he felt that rock moving in closer on him. The air stumbled and fell in his chest. He sat squat on an old stone near al-Hakim Mosque, raised his hand to his ear and his voice rang out, chanting the blessed verses of the Quran. The cold of the night penetrated his innards. As he saw his mother's eyes, his bones almost lit the whole place with the burning worry that permeated them. As the daylight approached, he heard the squeaking noises of alley gates opening. When the sun rose he had collected eleven dirhams, tossed by unknown passers-by who didn't see his face. He bought some sugar and some boiled sweets. At the Chapel of the Blind a heavy dagger split his heart.

'The Shaykh left at dawn, Amr.'

And here was the Head Spy of Cairo telling him, 'This is unacceptable, Amr. It's beneath you.'

At first the Head Spy appeared gentle. Oh! Amr shakes his head. To every first there is a last. His being ashamed of being different from others: where is it now? His aloofness from people: why has it withered away? What he fears now is the wrath of the Head Spy. After the first slip-up, he forgave him. A second mistake, and who knows what will happen? A severed head? That's too easy. Perhaps they would bury him alive for the rest of his life, making of him a moving, breathing scandal, with fingers pointing at him and the shaykhs kicking him out. To this moment, God be praised, no one has given him an accusing look or uttered a single innuendo. Now that the day is departing, people like to talk, let off steam in front of pastry shops and tailors' shops. At the Chapel of Sidi Halwaji, a group of men from Qasr al-Shawq stay up after the evening prayer, interpreting verses of the Quran and their dreams. No stranger could penetrate the group. Amr had been repeatedly visiting the Chapel, performing his prayers, politely listening to them in silence, constantly nodding his head to concur with whatever they said, acting as if he were a pupil anxious to benefit from men who have experienced and gained knowledge, all of which brought him so close to them that if he missed a night they would ask about him. The Head Spy praises him for his success in penetrating that circle. Tonight they are speaking more softly than usual. His ears are about to hear something new, something different from what he usually reports. Perhaps this time it will even reach the Sultan himself, bring him closer to the Head, who will express his satisfaction and praise him. Amr has not been able to see him for quite some time; his reports have been received by his Abyssinian deputy. Amr wonders whether he is angry with him, whether he is planning something for him.

Master Halim is now making a sceptical gesture with his lips. 'By God, my good men, all this joy that the people are feeling leaves me cold.'

Amr murmurs, 'Yes, by God! Yes, by God!'

'The days have taught me to be cautious. We haven't seen him doing anything, good or bad. Why then this elation? Besides . . .' The eyes turn to him. 'I didn't like what he did today.'

Amr's words come rushing out. 'Why, Shaykh Halim al-Din?' Ah! Why the haste? Did his question sound suspicious? One of them was about to ask the same question. He is not supposed to ask directly. He is still a little too rash. Had the crowd been bigger, someone who knew him but whom he didn't know would have noted the slip. But who knows? Perhaps the walls are listening.

Perhaps someone is watching him, reading his lips with no need to hear his voice. He knows that such spies exist. Hasn't the Head Spy told him, 'We have methods of knowing the truth that would never occur to humans or demons, even if that truth were whispered by somebody on the other side of the Qaf mountain'?

One must be careful and calmly watch their reactions.

Wednesday Evening, 10 Shawwal

MABRUK finally arrives, carrying a bundle of papers that Zakariyya has been waiting for for a long time. In the morning, Mabruk had given him an urgent report, prepared by the Head Spy of Cairo, detailing Zayni Barakat's movements: he had left his house at dawn in the company of an Azhar student for Kom al-Jarih, spent some time with Shaykh Abu al-Su'ud, after which he left the house. As the sun reached the alleys and side-streets, a new herald, whom nobody had heard before (said to be one of Zayni's own servants), went round telling the people of Zayni Barakat's intention of going to al-Azhar and that Zayni had things to say to them. A new herald whom Zakariyya didn't know? It is true that the *Muhtasib* has the right to employ a special herald to convey to the people his wishes and regulations – that's what the rules say – but reality belies that. It has become customary, since the time of Shihab Jaafar, Chief Spy of Ashraf Qait Bey, that all heralds be under the chief spy to whom all texts of the announcements would be sent, since the way an incident or news item is announced may have very serious consequences. The chief spy sometimes might give directives that the criers show enthusiasm in announcing one particular item or feign sadness or indifference in announcing other items. These are all important factors that influence people. There are certain areas and sectors in the city that heralds should not enter. How come then that a crier, unknown to Zakariyya, has appeared? How come he doesn't review the text of his announcement? Besides, Zayni has not yet assumed the Inspectorship; how does he give himself the right to speak to the people directly and without supervision? Is that a way to begin an administration: wreaking havoc and making a mockery of established procedure?

At the beginning of the day Zakariyya was exhausted, having spent the previous night away from his harem, away from the young slave girl, Wasila, who has been in his house no more than four days. He tried to pierce the veil of the days to see what was in store. This Zayni is up to no good. Ever since he heard his name, nothing but strange things have come from his direction. Shortly before dawn he had sent a message to the Head Spy of Cairo, telling him to undertake three tasks: firstly, to gather as much information as possible on Zayni Barakat and send that to him immediately; secondly, to mobilize all the spies in Cairo, so that they open their eyes to everything, no matter how slight, that takes place whenever people assemble and to how the people receive Zayni; thirdly, to raise the number of reports sent to his headquarters to twenty-four – one every hour – rather than the customary single report at each of the five times of prayer, then a detailed report after the evening prayer, covering the villages and towns.

The thing that drove the remnants of sleep away from Zakariyya's eyes, the thing that made him eat in a hurry and not think of Wasila, the sixteen-year-old Syrian girl, the thing that made him neglect to groom his beard and forgo drinking his sugar-sweetened fresh milk, were his persistent questions about Zayni Barakat. What is he up to? What is he going to tell the populace? What language is he going to speak? Is there a precedent for what he is about to do? No, none whatsoever. Zakariyya knows his history and is familiar with recent events. No *Muhtasib* has ever addressed an assembly of people. This has never been done, even by an emir, be he great or small. When the great address the populace directly, it costs them their respect. The awe of rule and rulers would be lost; the populace would be emboldened and would grow impudent. If the *Muhtasib* talks to them, then how come the emirs do not? Hasn't anybody thought of that?

Earlier in the day Zakariyya had gone into the wardrobe room, a long, narrow room containing every imaginable kind of clothing: sultan's turbans, other turbans that only emirs of a thousand are entitled to wear, cloaks, fur coats, Syrian trousers, bedouin *galabiyyas*, frocks of Azhar shaykhs, caftans and cheap *galabiyyas* of pastry vendors, butchers and fruit grocers. Zakariyya knew what he was looking for. He picked out a dirty white overcoat and a small green turban with a red scarf wound round it and grabbed a stick made of a palm-tree frond. He went out of the rear of the house as a dervish, a follower of Sidi Marzuq, the disciple of Sayyidi

Ahmad al-Badawi. He walked slowly, stopping every now and then, letting loose a loud cry: 'God lives! God lives! *Help.*' Slowly he proceeded, followed by Jubran, the mute, one of his stalwarts who always travelled with him to protect him from the perils of the road, the secret hate that might be translated into a dagger, stealthily trying to find its way to his heart. In spite of his worries, he felt joy, as he usually did when he found himself moving among the people, unrecognized even by those closest to him. Should the Head Spy of Cairo himself run into him, he wouldn't recognize him. All of these people were at his disposal. Wasn't he the Sultan's eyes and ears? Thousands of men, women and children who did not know one another were working for him, reporting whispers and gestures from homes and tenements all over the city. If one man's breathing was different from that of the others, he would know about it thanks to all these people.

When Zakariyya entered al-Azhar, he was truly alarmed; he had never seen such crowds. He felt dejected. How can the Sultan allow that? Do they realize the consequences of people assembling in such numbers? What is happening is a terrible mistake. One must warn the leaders and the Sultan himself. To condone the matter might lead to its getting out of hand. That is something he will not tolerate. This is a precedent that forebodes consequences of which the ignorant are unaware.

Zakariyya was now untying the bundle that Mabruk had brought him: the reports of the Head Spy of Cairo, in which he had gathered and summarized the reports he had received from his men and monitors all day long.

On the old pulpit of al-Azhar he stood. The mosque was overflowing with people of all colours and walks of life. They shouted and the pillars shook and the minarets almost leaned. It appeared that nothing on earth could quiet them, but Zayni raised his right hand, fingers outstretched (it was a normal, five-finger hand), and it was as if a magical force flowed from him and silence shut the people's mouths. It was said later on that he had the ability to make people fall silent and that if he wanted people to shed tears, he would make them do that. His voice flowed quietly among the people. This, in effect, is what he said:

Firstly, he would never have accepted the Inspectorship had he not informed the emirs of the conditions that his soul had laid down for the comfort of the people. Besides, had it not been for the Shaykh, learned in the foundations and the various branches of knowledge, the ascetic hermit, the friend of God, Shaykh Abu al-Su'ud, he would never have accepted. (At this point the clamour of the people rose, saying, 'We want nobody but you!', 'No one would do but you!', and such slogans that expressed the same idea in different words and phrases. Once again, his hand gestured calmly. The people's clamour subsided and they listened.)

Secondly, he fears nobody but God. How could he face God if one of his deputies oppressed even one of His creatures without his knowledge? That was unbearable and he would not hear of it. Hence, should an act of injustice be committed against anyone, poor or rich, near or far, he should immediately go to his deputy and he would surely right the wrong and punish the transgressor, after the case was heard and the truth established.

Thirdly, he is not going to stay in Cairo all the time. Rather he is going to travel throughout the provinces of Upper and Lower Egypt, for on this very day the Inspectorship of the Markets of Giza has been added to his duties. He will make the rounds, openly sometimes and in disguise at others, to see firsthand how people are doing. As for his house in Cairo, it is open, day and night, to anyone in need. There shall be nothing to stand between him and the people, great and humble, and should any wrong befall anyone, let that be righted publicly, in front of everyone.

Fourthly (and this is very serious), in every alley, street, village, town and fief, he will have agents monitoring, policing and staking out inequities wherever they occur; and these agents will inform him.

After going out of al-Azhar, he made his way with difficulty atop a high mule with a modest saddle and plain saddle-cloth (this pleased the people; they said, 'Look, that is how justice and just rulers should be!'). His procession continued until he reached the Sharabshiyyin market where singers welcomed him, dancing and playing reed flutes and tambourines. The women greeted him with shrill trills of joy from the windows. In front of him walked three of his new deputies, whom nobody had seen before (their backgrounds are being investigated). One of them carried a sword, another a scale and weights, while the third waved a large Quran, which he kissed from time to time. Behind the procession walked Abd al-Azim al-Sayrafi. As for Zayni, he kept nodding his head slowly, with a pious and righteous look on his face.

First remark: all our men are agreed as to the existence of an Azhar student who remained throughout the procession close to Zayni Barakat. He appeared to be enthusiastic. Upon investigation it turned out that it was the same subject who had accompanied him from his house to the Chapel of Shaykh Abu al-Su'ud at Kom al-Jarih. Subject's name: Said al-Juhayni.

Second remark: as the procession approached al-Hakim Mosque, a short distance before Bab al-Futuh Gate, where a passer-by might see the walls of al-Maqshara Prison and its upper entrance, a fat woman, advanced in years, clad in black with an old shawl wrapped around her head, made her way with difficulty until she stopped in front of Zayni's mule. She let out a great scream, gaining everyone's attention, whereupon, as in a seizure, she kept repeating, 'You bastard son of a bitch!' By the time people realized what she was saying and tried to pounce on her, she had disappeared without a trace. A search for her and an investigation as to where she is from and what she is about are being conducted.

Third remark: we have assigned an expert spy to Zayni to draw a precise profile of him. We shall submit same to you as soon as it is finished, for your information and for taking necessary measures.

Zakariyya is now looking out of the small window in the *mashrabiyya*. The winter is cloaked in a dark, cold night. A light is shining on the opposite side. Wasila is up; she is afraid he might come to her suddenly. Tonight he is not going to hold her breasts, the likes of which he has never seen before in his life: firm and soft, tender and hard; fear and ecstasy, approach and flight, getting closer and moving away; two globes of smooth dough, pliable in his hands. He loves breasts that have not been touched by human hands. That is how he puts it to Arif, the chief slave merchant. Arif is one of his most faithful agents. When he got Wasila, he was overjoyed. He made sure first that she had actually come from Turkey. Perhaps she has been planted by one emir or another for an unknown purpose. He spent his first night with her sailing in oceans uncharted by a man or a demon, watching the first pleasurable pain, a slight tremor stirring gently in two wide eyes. He thought of staying home from work for a few days to watch her, sucking the first nectar of her youth. Then this Zayni came out of the blue, kept him away from that moan and the delicious tremor. Here, he is facing a new situation. He has to be careful and firm. It will be remembered later on that he acted wisely and firmly. What he does now will be seen by his successors. They will be guided and enlightened.

A short while ago he had sent for Shihab al-Halabi, who would bring the pen and the ink that dried up after a specific interval, enough time for the letter to reach its destination and to be read. Then the ink would vanish and the paper would be totally blank again. Two days later the paper itself would disappear, evaporate, like the mist of a morning burned away by a strong sun. Once, during the reign of Sultan Faraj ibn Barquq, a single letter cost the Chief Spy his head. Now no adversary could confront Zakariyya with one written word. He had discussed this matter at great length with the Chief Spy of Shah Ismail al-Sufi. The man, an outstanding veteran spy, said that it was best that a spy go directly to the emirs and convey matters orally. Zakariyya disagreed. Words stay in the mind; a group of men might testify against you and blow you away. But, what if there existed some kind of ink that would vanish after the letter had done its job? He didn't tell the Shah's Chief Spy that he actually had the ink in his possession – that method was his alone and he wasn't about to give it up easily. The Chief Spy of the Shah denied the existence of such methods, saying that the time when such an ink would be available was still far off in the future. Tonight however, letters from him will reach the emirs Qunbuq, Qani Bey, Qusun, Tuman Bey and other key figures of the State. He is going to list in detail the reprehensible things Zayni has perpetrated that fly in the face of accepted Inspectorship practices, things that have infringed his own functions, especially after Zayni's reference to his deploying his own agents and aides. Was he going to introduce a new system for spies? Blood was now racing in vexation in Zakariyya's veins. Maybe the bastard is familiar with the system adopted by the Indian Maharaja who thinks one team of spies is not enough. So he appointed three deputies, each of whom presided over a special team of spies. This way he guarantees that things will not get out of hand, that no single spy has the run of the whole place to himself. Zakariyya likes this arrangement; it shows that the Maharaja is quite clever. He thinks of going to India to familiarize himself with the system or of sending one of his trusted deputies to bring back details of it. But such a trip by his deputy would arouse suspicions. The Sultan might get wind of the system and might want to adopt it in the Sultanate, in which case Zakariyya would lose his unique position. But how does Zayni obtain such information? Zakariyya is filled with vexation; until now he hasn't received sufficient information on Zayni. The Head Spy of Cairo may have difficulty gathering the necessary intelligence; perhaps the fool doesn't appreciate the importance of this request. One must learn everything about Zayni's habits, his time of sleep, his women, the countries he has visited, the languages he speaks, his preferences in bed. That fat woman must be found and arrested, no matter what. Also that young Azhar student; it seems he is close to Abu al-Su'ud. But that's another story, which Zakariyya will take care of.

Zakariyya is now standing right in the middle of the room, holding a bowl filled with hot milk sweetened with sugar, which he very much likes to drink after he gets up and early at night. He says, 'I face my day with creamy milk and let come what may, then I end my day with it also.' He is not as gluttonous as the others: Emir Qunbuq gulps down a pitcher filled with the extract of rooster testicles first thing in the morning. According to reports, he is capable of sleeping with his four wives on the same night and satisfying each of them without getting bored or tired, even though he is over forty. Who knows? Maybe Zakariyya would prefer Qunbuq's morning regimen now. An idea flashes in his mind: he is going to address Zayni Barakat directly. True, the *Muhtasib* should initiate the contact, since the Chief Spy is his deputy, but Zakariyya is going to take the initiative and test the waters. Flexibility is required now. He is going to tell Shihab al-Halabi to write a letter to him on regular paper and in regular ink tonight. At the same time, the other letters will be on their way to the emirs.

'May God make this land secure.'

To: Zayni Barakat ibn Musa, Markets Inspector

We begin by bearing witness that there is no god but God, One and without partners, a testimony that we uphold in every affair, our swords poised against those who would deny it, rendering them mute. We also bear witness that Muhammad is His Servant and Messenger, and that he is the noblest advocate for justice and charity and the one most justly making it incumbent upon his nation to observe full measures and weights. May God's prayers and peace be upon him, his family and his companions, most of whose toil was for God's Cause.

Now then: know that we have taken the initiative in corresponding with you out of a desire to keep you informed of that which is herein contained, because we seek the security of the people in all quarters and regions, since you will not get to know that which is hidden without the eyes that we send forth among the Muslims. Likewise, you will not hear any of those insignificant whispers with grave repercussions among the emirs or the low-born without depending on us and enlisting our aid. That is how the Sultanate has managed its affairs ever since we began to take note of such matters. It has been customary that these tasks, which shield us all from evils great and small, be undertaken solely by our agency, which is served by thousands without number, who never slumber in the service of the Sultan and his men and who work, sweat and toil for the comfort of the subjects. Therefore we thought we should suggest to you and inform you of what should be done on your part, namely, sending a detailed report to us every night so that we may avail ourselves of the knowledge of what violations you have

uncovered in order that we might know the identity of the perpe-
trators and thus add their names to the lists of wrongdoers and
protect the pious and the righteous. We also hoped that you would
use the heralds working under us so that we might screen what
they announce and convey to the populace. This matter, which
appears to be insignificant and slight, can lead to consequences
that might prove harmful and dangerous – consequences that we
can explain to you at the first meeting between us, because our
goal is peace. And, for your information, that is how it has always
been done, nobody knows for how long. But we have been doing it
for some time and plan to continue to do so if we are granted
sufficient time on this earth. This is no invention of ours; these are
rules set down by our forefathers.

Peace be upon you.

10 Shawwal 912 AH
Chief Spy of the Sultanate
Shihab Zakariyya ibn Radi

Excerpt from Chief Spy Supreme Shihab Zakariyya ibn Radi's communication to the Sultan and the emirs

. . . and were I to elaborate and detail those transgressions, I would take too much space and time. So, for the sake of brevity, I will be brief, and say:

Firstly: for the first time, absolutely without precedent, a notable gathers all the populace of Egypt, low-born as well as noble, and addresses them, agitating and inciting them. Only God knows what firebrand might have wreaked havoc on the entire country had it not been for my men who were deployed to preserve security and lives.

Secondly: his sending forth heralds whom nobody knows. I haven't reviewed the announcements or edited them or given them any particular orientation. I do not need to detail the significance of this grave matter.

Thirdly: his intention, at which he hinted, of creating a special team of spies to work under him, one that he will himself supervise. I have ascertained this after perusing the communications of my deputies, which are never mistaken and which have monitored Zayni's life and everything about him from his youth until now. My purpose in doing so is the common good. I can only point out what things would be like if every official, high or low in rank, were to create his own team of spies, directing it as he pleases without oversight or higher authority. I will never allow that. I shall prevent it. I alone and my men are the Sultan's eyes and ears.

Fourthly: the reports indicate that the populace is beginning to open its eyes, is beginning to look at the emirs. Every man is now saying, 'Why don't they come down and talk to us? Are they greater than the good man Zayni Barakat?'

I am asking nothing of you except to see the way things are, otherwise they would go against our desires and lead to confusion, loss of law and order, security and peace.

God, who uncovers the unknown, is my witness that I am telling the truth.

10 Shawwal 912 AH
Chief Spy of the Sultanate
Shihab Zakariyya ibn Radi

SECOND PAVILION

Zayni Barakat's star is rising; his position con-
solidated, his luck in the ascendant and his
fortune expanding

Announcement

People of Egypt! Our lord the Sultan has commanded that the criminal, son of a criminal, Ali ibn Abi al-Jud, be handed over to the Markets Inspector, Zayni Barakat ibn Musa, to look into his affairs, to extract people's rights from him, and to give him a taste of the treatment he meted out to God's poor, righteous and pious servants. Oh, People of Egypt! People of Egypt! Anyone treated unjustly, anyone robbed of his possessions, anyone whose property was illegally seized by or because of Ali ibn Abi al-Jud should go to the house of Zayni Barakat ibn Musa, Inspector of the Markets of Cairo and of Upper Egypt, and he will give him satisfaction. People of Egypt! People of Egypt!

Said al-Juhayni

HE has long been in love with this house and its inhabitants, its stones, the wood of its *mashrabiyyas*, the decoration of its walls, the light in its rooms, the hall for Quranic recitation during the holy month of Ramadan, with its high ceiling and small windows near the middle of the wall from which the womenfolk could look and listen to the verses of the Quran, safe from the eyes of strangers. Out of one of these windows she looks, watching and examining him. His eyes take in the little coloured marble tiles, which decorate the basin of the fountain in the middle of the small garden of the house. He looks at the comfortable cushions, which protect her tender body against the hard walls. Samah walks these corridors when the visitors are gone. Said has a vague feeling of satisfaction; he is not considered a stranger here. As he listens to Shaykh Rihan he sees her with his heart's eye going and coming in one of the rooms, looking out of a window, leaning her head against a pillow. Seven months ago, on the third day of Eid al-Fitr, she came in. He bowed his head, which was heavy with confusion, shyness and perplexity. He held her exquisitely small hand in his, and it felt like the tremors of hope in the hearts of those awaiting a miracle on the twenty-seventh night of Ramadan or the whispers of a newly born dawn. What a passionate yearning! He doesn't see her as a body, two breasts, a neck or a nape. She is closer to being pure spirit, a vision, an intangible whisper, a lily not for picking. In the street he sees the veiled women without their veils and in his mind he undresses them, taking off one piece of clothing at a time. As the woman sits facing him, leaning her back against a cushion, not covered in silk, he would strip her and then he would dress her again gently, with fingers burning with desire; the flesh of the arm, the roundness of the breast and the flat abdomen would appear. Then his eyes would wander into space and his mind would go to the house of Uns, which his well-off colleagues frequent. It is said that it has a huge room filled with Abyssinian and Turkish and, some even say, Indian women. Last year he made some money copying a book on logic for one of the shaykhs of Upper Egypt and his friends kept trying to persuade him to go to Uns's house, but he shook his head several times and refused. He didn't know why he refused. The students and scholars and the dwellers of the tenements and alleys in Batiniyya know him as a kind, gentle and God-fearing man who rushes to help anyone in a tight spot; he would rescue a woman from the hands of a Mamluk who wanted to abduct her by shouting to call the Azhar students, inciting the men who would then surround the Mamluk. The common people say that if Said had the strength of Qurqmas, the huge Mamluk wrestler, no Mamluk would have dared snatch even the shell of a bean from a basket carried by a little girl. God created him in a small, disease-ridden body. As he lies on his old mattress in the *riwaq*, people of different colours and walks of life come to visit him and inquire about his health. What would they say if they were to learn that he frequented the house of Uns or paid a few dirhams to possess a woman for a few minutes?

'The one does not preclude the other, Said.' He dismisses the thought. Samah appears from a distance in his mind, his most closely guarded secret. In his mind's eye he cannot see her naked or standing in the bath with nothing on except wooden clogs to keep the bath water away from her feet. Samah is the quintessential woman. All other women are mere copies, pale imitations. In the far future he can see her only with himself: looking together from a *mashrabiyya*, walking in a garden or travelling somewhere. It has been cold for days now. When it gets cold, Said sees Samah as a place filled with warmth and peace. Shaykh Rihan said, 'Let's go upstairs.'

He climbed the staircase. It was as if her breath, preserved for ever, had left an indelible mark on the air of the stairs. He was afraid lest Shaykh Rihan should hear his heartbeats or notice his confusion and the changes in the colour of his face. The Shaykh sat cross-legged on a large green cushion, smoking contentedly as the water in the narghile bubbled. He sat up. Said bent towards him.

'This winter hasn't been very cold so far.'

'Not as cold as past years, but at the *riwaq* the cold is unbearable!'

The rooms were glowing with warmth. Something fell in the house, maybe a pot or a box she was holding. The night here is comfortable in the quiet of home and the security of the family.

'Tashtamur's Mamluks were about to run over the people today, had we not come out of al-Azhar and stood between them and the people.'

'Is that so? I didn't hear of that, for I haven't gone out all day. Whose Mamluks did you say?'

'Tashtamur.'

'That's strange; he used to be a peaceful man and his Mamluks were all right. What brought about this change?'

'Nothing really; except that Emir Khayrbak had put in a few words about him to the Sultan. It was rumoured that the Sultan intended to arrest him.'

'Is that so? Well, I've always said that Tashtamur was reckless, very reckless, and didn't listen to anyone.'

At that point Said didn't say anything. It seemed a little funny, but he rationalized it, trying to find something redeeming in it because it came from Samah's father. Whenever the Shaykh heard the name of an emir or a notable, he immediately asserted that a strong bond existed between him and that person. Sometimes Said helped him along by asking a question or requesting an explanation, such as, 'How long have you known Tashtamur, Uncle?', whereupon Shaykh Rihan would sit back and loudly call the servant to fetch more embers for the narghile.

'Oh, well, Tashtamur? I practically raised him myself. He used to come here to me when he was still a weak Mamluk. I knew him before he married Khond Zaynab, his first wife.'

Said didn't know for sure whether Tashtamur's wife's name was really Khond Zaynab or not, but he said, 'I think Tashtamur and Maliktamur al-Saqi of . . .'

The Shaykh didn't let him continue. 'Maliktamur? Maliktamur was the one who sided with me against Musa ibn Ishaq when we had differences over some matters having to do with the treasury. Maliktamur sent for me at midnight. Yes, by God, exactly at midnight. I went up to him in the Citadel. I have gone to the Citadel many, many times and that hasn't happened to anyone else.

Anyway, he kissed my hand. Yes, by God, Maliktamur kissed my hand, as I was older than he was. He said he knew me to be a good and God-fearing man and, for that reason, he was going to abrogate the order given by Musa ibn Ishaq. I remember that he patted me on the shoulder and I held his arm. Yes, Said, my son, I held his arm!'

'When Zayni Barakat himself arrived, Tashtamur's Mamluks dispersed. He even arrested four of them and sent them to the Maqshara Prison.'

'Zayni . . . Barakat? Oh, yes. I was supposed to visit him in two days . . .'

'Zayni Barakat sent for you, Uncle?' Said realized he had asked the question precipitantly. Usually he didn't say a thing. So why now? Why now in particular?

'Zayni is my friend. I was supposed to visit him, had it not been for my health.'

'God give you strength.'

'What is Zayni, my son? The likes of him used to have a hard time trying to come in just to see me or to walk among my retinue. But do tell me: are the people satisfied with him?'

'Yes, very much so.'

'I know him. He is a fair man, but, more important than that, he is wise, very wise. What's his latest news?'

'We no longer see Zakariyya's heralds.'

'Zakariyya ibn Radi? Only God has the power and the might! Lower your voice, my son; he might hear us.'

Said now had a bitter taste in his mouth. No student at al-Azhar dared curse him. Said cursed him, silently. He knew that his shadow extended throughout the *riwaqs* and the rooms to the prayer niche, under the mats of the mosque and in the bedrooms in people's homes. Shaykh Abu al-Su'ud says of him that he is one of the portents of the Day of Judgement. He must stay here on earth as a representative of Iblis, so that the people might receive double doses of torture over and over again. At that time Said got upset at what the Shaykh had said. Perhaps he was saying that because he was unable to catch Zakariyya ibn Radi. The Shaykh could do that; nobody had any doubt about it. But where was Zakariyya? He has to be found before he is caught. Nobody has seen him. It is said that he lives in more than one place. Nobody knows exactly how old he is. People know his original headquarters, far away at the foot of the Muqattam hill where people whisper about hearing the cries of people being flogged or their limbs burned or of people being impaled. But does Zakariyya actually live there? They say that he sleeps in a different place every night, that his face has not been seen by anyone, even Shaykh Abu al-Su'ud.

Said was very upset after the disappearance of three Nubian scholars who had always been together, living together, reading from the same copy of the Quran, eating from the same bowl, sleeping so close to each other that people seeing them thought they were one person. That was their way. From time to time a scholar or a student or somebody from the bazaar would disappear and no one would know anything about that person. His disappearance would leave behind fear and gloom in the hearts. Who knows whose turn it will be tomorrow? Just as the effect of the disappearance begins to wear off, a new person disappears and the hearts tremble anew. Said could not stand it when the Nubians disappeared. He wished he could scream to rouse the earth, the stars, the moon and the planets into some action, to cause feelings to stir in inanimate objects. That day he ran all the way to Kom al-Jarih. The Shaykh listened to him and asked, 'Did they really curse Zakariyya as I'd heard?' Said didn't know; they always spoke their own foreign language, which nobody else understood. How did it reach Zakariyya, then? How? The common people say that Shaykh Abu al-Su'ud has a ring, with the likeness of Solomon on it, which can release the jinn from their talismans and make them do man's bidding. The Shaykh can have Zakariyya ibn Radi transported to the Waq Waq mountains never to return. And if he were to try to come back, it would take him a thousand thousand years. Said didn't tell that to the Shaykh. He knew how angry he got when miracles were attributed to him. In the evening he was ashamed of himself. Did he want the Shaykh to do everything? Said recited, 'Do not throw yourselves headlong into perdition.'

'Stay and have dinner with us,' said Shaykh Rihan.

He craved home-cooked food, some of the soup Samah ate on the same night, perhaps a spoon that has touched her lips. But something bothered him; he couldn't stand being in one place for a long time. Shaykh Rihan didn't insist. Said slipped his feet into his shoes and walked the short walkway in the garden by himself. He almost raised his eyes. If only she were looking now! If he could see her for about an hour, he would spend his life moving from one minaret to another, all over the world, shouting her name to the high heavens, expressing what is in his heart, crossing countries as his master had done, her eyes his only provision. If only she would listen to him! If only the two of them were in a boat on the Nile, their hands in the water making little white splashes in its wake.

He sees her in a city that has known no plagues, where people do not die suddenly in the middle of the street in broad daylight, where a man does not wail over the abduction of his daughter, where the poor are not dragged to the Jubb or Maqshara gaols and where lives are not spent in Arqana Prison, where no hand is severed from its body because it had stolen one cucumber. Samah is looking over a road where nobody has walked before. He has his arms round her. They are laughing. She is chewing on some gum, which has come from some faraway land.

In his nightly vigil, after his companions in the *riwaq* had fallen asleep, Samah would come to him as if she were a whisper of warmth given in a fit of generosity by the mean cold of winter or like a cool breeze in a very hot, stifling summer. He doesn't remember the colour of her hair, but she is the only hope of deliverance in his life. The alleys close in on him as if they were camels laden with hay. But where should he go? What place can contain him? He can go to Hamzawi or Attarin, but he is embarrassed by all the courtesy and attention he gets, since they know him well over there. He cannot stand the idea of staying in the *riwaq* until morning; the feeling of emptiness would be too stifling. Perhaps he should have stayed and had dinner. But he has already eaten there twice in one week; he shouldn't overdo it. Perhaps she and her mother would talk about that. Merely thinking of what might be said fills him with shame. Should he go to Hamza's shop to drink fenugreek with sesame and milk and talk to the people, see what is on their minds? Hamza's shop usually fills up with hashish smokers after the last prayers. The people might say, 'Look how Abu al-Su'ud's disciple is getting stoned to be able to perform the dawn prayers!' Where should he go, then? He must find somewhere. If he kept going to a certain place repeatedly, the spies would take note of him and his name would reach Zakariyya. He is certain that his name will reach him some day; he wants to delay that day until some special event warrants his name's going up there. Who knows? Maybe there are hundreds of pages about him in front of Zakariyya already. Are his men unaware of Said? Anyway, Zakariyya is not taking up all the space as usual. That is what Said feels; nobody has told him, no prominent man has divulged any secrets to him. It is just a matter of intuition.

For the first time, new heralds, who are not working for Zakariyya, are making their rounds on the streets. Only a few people are aware of the fact that all heralds work under the Chief Spy or that even the storytellers in the cafés, the musicians, entertainers, jugglers and mosque preachers, one way or the other, fall under the purview of the Spies' Union. Hence Said understands the significance of the appearance of new heralds wearing blue trousers and green shirts with borders decorated in brocade – a new uniform, which announces that they work under the *Muhtasib* himself. Zayni didn't stop there. He regulated the timing of their announcements: in the morning, after lunch, just before sunset and before the evening prayers. They walked about without guards and with only a short stick, which they used to beat a small drum conveying to the people the innovations that Zayni had introduced. They urged the people to denounce all evil wrongdoers and crooks. When Said heard this particular announcement, he was reluctant to accept it and doubted if a rich merchant, a relative of a wazir, or an emir or even Zayni himself would be subject to the same treatment as others. That has never happened yet and, if it were to happen, it would look very peculiar.

Three days after the announcement, Said heard a noise. Some people had gathered round one of the new heralds. What's the matter? It turned out that a tailor from Megharbilin – not a small-time seamster, mind you, but a tailor who made caftans and coats for the emirs and the notables, a man over forty whom God had afflicted with a pernicious disease – was walking down the Khayyamiyya Market, where tents were made and sold, when he saw a young boy whom he liked.

He asked the boy, 'What's your name, lad?'

And the boy said, 'My name is Kamal.'

And he said, 'Come. I'll take you to your father at the mosque, for he is waiting for you there, and I'll buy you a meat pie.'

The scoundrel, however, took him to a vacant lot behind the

Blue Mosque and raped him. The boy was hurt and injured in three places and went to his father, bleeding. The father went crying to Zayni, who ordered that the tailor be brought forth, and then he asked the boy, 'Is it this man?' And the boy, crying, nodded.

The man shouted, 'The boy is a liar!'

Zayni struck him on the face, saying, 'Children do not lie', and ordered that he be exposed in disgrace on a donkey throughout Cairo and be locked up at Arqana Prison until his case was decided. Some shaykhs went up to Zayni and said that what happened took place every day and they talked a lot, hinting, rather than stating explicitly, that the man knew some emirs and those, well, you know, perhaps . . . It was said that Zayni got up in a rage, yelled at them and ordered them out of his sight, saying, 'No such abomination will ever take place in my administration. I fear only Him!', as he pointed to the sky. It was said among the common people that he had tapped the shaykhs on their shoulders with a stick, the handle of which was made of ivory, with gold ornaments, and shouted at them, 'How are you going to face God on Doomsday?'

Said was afraid for Zayni, especially since no herald had announced the discovery of the hidden assets of Ali ibn Abi al-Jud, whom Zakariyya had taken in custody twenty days earlier. What the Sultan really cared about was the money. Maybe Zakariyya would find it an opportune moment to turn the Sultan against Zayni and he would fire him from his Inspectorship. The current falling out between Tashtamur and Khayrbak may give him some time, but . . . What's this? Is Said concerned for Zayni? Is he wishing torture on Ali ibn Abi al-Jud so that he may divulge the secrets of his hidden fortune? Is he wishing torture on a human being? Even Ali ibn Abi al-Jud? Of course! And how many have suffered at his hands? Besides, God will inflict a much worse punishment on him on Doomsday. Said does not deny that Zayni is close to his heart. When he approached him to convey to him Shaykh Abu al-Su'ud's request, it was at night, and Zayni came out to him with his face covered. His turban was small and his clothes ordinary, such as poor Sufis wore. They walked in silence as Said kept looking furtively at him. The smell of his clothes brought back an old memory of his uncle in the village of Nizzah, the smell of wool mixed with that of a man's sweat. He was overcome by a desire: if some of his friends could see him walking with a man whose name was on everybody's lips all over Cairo! Where does Zayni get this ability to turn down such an important position? All those who were appointed to one of Ali ibn Abi al-Jud's posts were overjoyed and stayed at home to receive congratulations from well-wishers. As for Barakat ibn Musa, when named to the most important post, he turned it down. Such a trait is rare in an age that is very mean with noble deeds. After some silence, Said said, 'My master has commanded me not to come back without you.'

He turned slightly and nodded. Said was embarrassed: maybe he was thinking about matters of great consequence. Suddenly Zayni said, 'I cannot disobey the command of our master.' Zayni's questions followed. Said told him about himself: how he had come from his village, how he had met his master, visited him, kept him company, learned from him and stayed with him all the time. Now he remembers Zayni's questions, then his sudden silence. Said didn't know what took place between the two of them. The Shaykh ordered him to go back to al-Azhar. Since that day Said had not come close to Zayni, except during his procession back from al-Azhar. But he walked alone among the crowds. Zayni was unaware of his being there and paid no attention to what he said.

The last herald had made his rounds two hours ago; Said didn't know what the announcement was about. During the first two weeks, people gathered round the heralds to watch them and listen to what they had to say. As time went by, the crowds thinned out, but the children still gathered round them every time.

Said stopped suddenly; it seems he has come close to Qasr al-Shawq Alley. A man walked by in a hurry. Is that not him? Why did he stop? He stood still, very perplexed. He didn't remember how tall he was. He remembered Zayni stout and thin, upright and slightly bent; the picture in his mind didn't stay the same. But how about that person walking over there? It's he himself! He crossed the Bayt al-Mal Alley. There is one road to Bayt al-Qadi and another to al-Husayn Mosque. He disappeared. But where are the guards? How can he feel safe? If that was Zayni himself, did he see him or recognize him?

Announcement

People of Egypt! We enjoin what is right and forbid what is wrong. Today the Sultan, healthy and vigorous, went to Raydaniyya and began playing polo. May God give him health and strength. People of Egypt!

The falling out between Emir Tashtamur and Emir Khayrbak has not abated; each is lying in wait for the other. So, beware and be warned, people of Egypt! The apothecary Sabir ibn al-Hamzawi has tampered with the weights and sold fenugreek mixed with fine dust; he adulterated *mughat* and he hid Indian *saqanqur*, of which he has a lot, to sell it at a higher price, since he is the only *saqanqur* dealer. Therefore Zayni Barakat ibn Musa, *Muhtasib* of Cairo and Southern Egypt, enforcer of the canon law and preserver of the people's rights and the servant of the Sultan, has fined him 100 dinars and ordered that his stash of *saqanqur* be seized and distributed to all the apothecaries, so that everyone might benefit, and sold at three dirhams a piece.

May God punish all crooks and wrongdoers.

Therefore, people of Egypt, be warned.

Let that be a warning, people of Egypt!

Zakariyya ibn Radi

Tuesday morning, 7 Dhu al-Qa'da 912 AH

HE is all alone. As he looks at a baby or plays with one, he is struck
by how tender the early years are; the feathers of little birds and
the warmth of their soft skin. If only man could remain a baby for
ever, moving his hands at will, laughing as he pleases, crawling
and playing, knowing that when he cries, a kindly soul will rush to
wipe away the tears; delusions and fears would not take up per-
manent residence in the heart; he would see the world with
wondering eyes. It is impossible for Zakariyya to migrate, across
the years, back to his infancy. Sometimes he is quite certain that he
will not have that experience ever again. He doesn't remember
whether any hand has ever caressed him. The most difficult circumstances have never prevented him from seeing his first and, so far,
only son, Yasin, who is usually brought to him in a nappy of black
velvet with golden borders. He would carry him, as the baby's
mother, Zaynab, looked on, talking about Yasin, how many times
she had nursed him, his gentle smile as he slept and as he woke up,
as if his eyes were looking for his dear father, and his disconnected
words. She talked and talked. Yasin was what made her close to
the man. She bragged and looked down on the rest of his harem
and slaves; none of them had given him a child. As for her, she has
given him Yasin. She disregarded Ahmad, who had been born four
years earlier and had died a few months later. His Abyssinian
mother still lived in the house, completely ignored by everybody.

A sharp, searing grief pierces Zakariyya's heart every now and
then; the years have done nothing to blunt its edge or ease the pain.
The most awful circumstances have not kept him from spending
some moments with Yasin; sometimes he even wakes him very late
at night, despite his mother's warnings, to play with him.

A few months ago Zakariyya's men arrested a Turkish merchant in Khan al-Khalili who was said to be secretly corresponding with the Ottomans about matters of the State. Zakariyya watched his torture in person: the wringing of the heels, the burning of the skin of his back over a slow fire. Mabruk was undertaking the torture with great enthusiasm and was in high spirits. Silence descended like a shroud upon the rest of the prisoners as they listened to the cries of the man, which were never heard outside the walls of the compound. Zakariyya knew what terror and pain gripped them as they heard the groans of another human being whose name they didn't even know. It was more painful to them, especially those new to prison life, than if their own teeth were pulled by a pair of red-hot pincers. Who knows? Maybe they will have the same fate as that of the unfortunate Turk. His silence lasted a long time. Zakariyya could only see the convulsions on his face, his protruding eyes, his enlarged nose and his falling jaw. But he didn't say a word. What really bothered Zakariyya was that he was certain that the man had accomplices. After a whole day had passed, Zakariyya grabbed a long skewer as thin as a needle that had been heated for a long time and slowly began to poke it into the abdomen of the Turk, around his navel. Zakariyya choked on the smoke of the burning flesh and as he went out he took deep breaths as if he were gulping water.

He crossed the courtyard to his harem and climbed the staircase leading to Zaynab's room. He asked, 'Is he asleep?' She nodded. He said, 'I want to see him.' She was overcome with disappointment; she had hoped he would spend the night with her, staying until the morning; only then would she be completely distinct from the rest of the harem. Once again he told her that he wanted to see Yasin and she said, 'He's been asleep for some time, Master.' He said in a hollow voice, which made her tremble with fear, 'I didn't say to wake him up.' She led the way. Among the cushions was the tender round face of the child, with his eyes closed, a full moon in the midst of the clouds, his complexion as smooth as an apple clad in diaphanous silk. He brought the candelabra closer; the light flickered and, as he stayed for some time, the Turk's face receded. The woman said, 'Shall I take off the caftan, Master?' He looked up suddenly, didn't look at her and headed for the door. He hadn't reviewed the day's reports. Something had to be sent to the Sultan about the Turk. She hurried after him, not ashamed to let her disappointment show in her voice: 'May safety accompany you, Master.'

Zakariyya descended the tall staircase to the courtyard as the fragrance of sweet basil filled his chest and the palm fronds made a rustling sound. There were all kinds of exotic trees sent to him by the Chief Spies of India, Yemen and Abyssinia. In the right-hand corner of the garden were a few yellow flowers, one of which he didn't forget; it was a whisper of a flower, soft yellow with violet edges and a dark red inside, which had three specks of dark green, which he saw opening up in front of his very eyes. He remembered the moment in wonder. In the garden there were also small cages housing exotic birds that made strange sounds. Now they were silent. In the winter he would see birds flying about freely – birds, he was told by ornithologists, that came from far away, from countries where they had daylight for six months and the other six months were night. They departed with the winter and were no-where to be seen during the summer. Zakariyya noted the day on which he saw the first of the birds in his garden and wondered: is this the same bird that came here last year? How long would it live if no hunter killed it, if it died a natural death? Why do such creatures die? He thought of sending out the heralds to order people to stop hunting the birds, but he didn't go through with the idea. There is no telling what some emirs might think; maybe his orders would be received with derision. Is Zakariyya's world so free of trouble that he is now ordering people to stop hunting birds?

In recent days Zakariyya had spent a long time watching the birds in the cages and playing with Yasin. But worries and stress were weighing heavily on his chest. Had it not been for the birds and Yasin, his going out incognito from time to time, his trips to his fief in Syriaqus, he might have had a stroke. But patience! Such circumstances required flexibility and strength. He hadn't received any response from Zayni. He thought that perhaps the letter had not reached him, but he ascertained that it had actually come into Zayni's own hands. It took a lot of work to make sure of that, since not even a single one of his spies worked in Zayni's house. The Head Spy of Cairo, who had not bothered to place one there before, has promised to get someone inside the house. Even Zayni's servants were unknown, as if he had imported them from another land.

Meanwhile, the Head Spy has kept up the search for that woman who had appeared suddenly in front of Zayni's procession, shouting, 'You bastard . . .' So, she knew him. Perhaps finding her would lead to uncovering the hidden part of Zayni's life. The Head Spy stated in his first report that she was a woman without a family whom the inhabitants of Bayn al-Syarij, Amir al-Juyush Street and Bab al-Shi'riyya had known since their youth and saw from time to time. Nobody knew her to have a house. It was said that she lived in the courtyards of the cemeteries outside al-Nasr Gate and that her name was Umm Suhair. Others said that her name was Miska and that she had no daughter named Suhair. She insulted Zayni in Saliba Street, twice, and also in Mu'iz Street, then disappeared completely, as if the earth had swallowed her up. According to the report of a reliable, veteran spy, an old man, who always sat near the Bashtak drinking-water fountain with a band over his eyes, said that that woman would go to Zayni Barakat ibn Musa and embrace him and the two would cry together as she held his head in her hands and called him the sweetest names; then she told him of future events and everything that was happening to him and about plots against him. The old man said that a number of jinn had fraternal relations with the old woman and served her and supplied her with true prophecies. As for who she was, the old man didn't know; when she got together with Zayni, he had no idea; why she yelled at him in front of the crowd, nobody will ever know. The old man suggested the possibility that secret relations existed between Zayni and the world of jinn.

So, Zayni has ignored the letter as if he had never read or even seen it. Shihab al-Halabi asked a few days ago, 'Did you receive a reply from Zayni?' Zakariyya yelled at him angrily, 'Since when have you asked about the reply to a letter I asked you to write? Is this what I taught you? Do you know the consequences of idle chatter or curiosity? Whatever you write, you must forget.'

Shihab al-Halabi was terrified. His worst fear was Zakariyya's wrath, but even worse than that was Zakariyya thinking there was something behind the question. Perhaps his suspicions would be aroused, in which case Shihab wouldn't know what he might do; his long work record will buy him forgiveness for a slip-up, intended or unintended. Zakariyya always repeated within his hearing the story of the Deputy Chief Ottoman Spy, who had reached the highest positions in spying in the Ottoman State, then years later was found out; it turned out that he was a spy for Shah Ismail al-Sufi, the arch enemy of the Ottomans. Shihab al-Halabi has always been careful what he said or did. That was true not only of him but of everyone who worked in the Spies' Bureau.

Zakariyya was amazed at the fury of his own reaction, but Zayni's being so late in replying bothered him, and Shihab al-Halabi's question needled him. Every day he would say, 'Maybe tonight he will send an answer; perhaps tomorrow.' But Zayni has overdone it. The Emir Jamdar, the wardrobe keeper of the Sultan, shook his head and said, 'The Sultan concurs in everything that Zayni does. Zayni goes up to the Sultan every night and the two spend about an hour together, alone. Nobody knows what they talk about.'

Zakariyya was facing circumstances unknown to any of his predecessors; perhaps even his own name was bandied about in these tête-à-têtes; perhaps a plot was being hatched against him. He was upset anew the night he received a report confirming that Zayni was persisting in creating his own team of spies. Emir Mankali Bugha, who was close to Zakariyya, hinted in a meeting with Zayni that custom dictated that only one team of spies be allowed to operate in the whole Sultanate, and that Zakariyya ibn Radi should work under the *Muhtasib* as usual. But Zayni shook his head, saying, 'I can trust only my men.' What caused Zakariyya real anxiety was this idea of another team of spies. What if one of them penetrated his own household or his private office? He issued strict orders to the head of spies of Cairo, Upper Egypt, Lower Egypt and Nubia to monitor whatever Zayni did and to keep the members of the new team under strict surveillance, to find out who they were, where they came from and how they operated. The reports on this matter were still vague and sparse. Anyway, work on this must be deliberate but speedy. The matter of Zayni must be resolved; the whole future of spying was at stake. He summoned the chief of the singers and storytellers in Egypt, Ibrahim ibn al-Sukkar wa al-Limun. Ibrahim is one of his most loyal underlings. He supervises the storytellers in the cafés, the *rababa* strummers, the chanters on saints' anniversaries and religious gatherings. Everything they told or sang, be it a light song or an epic romance, had to be approved in advance by Ibrahim ibn al-Sukkar wa al-Limun, who would omit whatever he deemed to be against religion or morality or insinuations against notables or emirs. Ibrahim came to Zakariyya every Tuesday to report to him on the singers and storytellers, how they were doing and what was going on among them and what each of them planned to do, be that on a personal or professional level. Zakariyya was secretly full of scorn for Zayni, who suspected none of that. The people listened to the storytellers in the cafés; they heard about Sayf ibn Dhi Yazan, who left no stone unturned all over the world, looking for the *Book of the Nile*. The hearts were aflutter with love for the Princess Dhat al-Himma. They followed the stories of the Barmakids with the Abbasids, Abu Zayd and Diyab and Zanati Khalifa, Solomon and how he controlled the jinn, the martyrdom of the dearly beloved Husayn at Karbala. Nobody knew that one thread ran through what all the professional singers, chanters and the storytellers in Egypt did.

Zakariyya sat alone with Ibrahim ibn al-Sukkar wa al-Limun and asked him to prepare a story to be told to the accompaniment of the *rababa*, about a man of unknown origin, without roots, on whom Fortune suddenly smiled and who claimed that he was going to establish justice on earth. He told him to have four storytellers recite it that night at Lundi's and Bahjuri's in Husayniyya and at Yunis's in Fustat and Abu al-Ghayt's in Bulaq. The first and the second are among the biggest fenugreek, ginger and narghile emporia in Egypt and the patrons are well-off men, who start smoking the real stuff after the evening prayers. As for the third and fourth, they are modest establishments, and the patrons are low-class, mostly labourers. Two days later the story would be told in ten shops in different neighbourhoods in Cairo. In one week it is going to be the talk of the town, and at that point, the spies planted among the different audiences can dot the *i*'s and cross the *t*'s if the idiots have failed to grasp the real meaning.

When Ibrahim ibn al-Sukkar wa al-Limun left Zakariyya's house, Zakariyya got up and went to the garden. He was quite refreshed now, thinking fast as ideas began to race through his head, remembering tens of names and subjects. He hit his palm with his fist, bent over to get a drink of diluted rose-water. He was surprised by thoughts he never dreamt he could have and forgot himself completely. New projects, soon to be realized, were born. He didn't forget the details – nothing, no matter how minute.

Moments after Ibrahim's departure, in his euphoria, he went up to the room of his wife Zaynab, hugged Yasin, lifted him, carried him on his shoulders, crawled before him on all fours, mimicked the sounds of the sheep and the donkey, flung himself into the air with total abandon, in sheer joy and ecstasy when Yasin's laughter grew louder – short laughs like the soft rumbles of an intoxicated narghile emitting aromas of mint, sweet basil and balm. Suddenly he placed him in his mother's arms and went down quickly, leaving his son behind. Zaynab was not surprised; she had grown accustomed to his strange ways.

Zakariyya sent for Master Awad, known among the common people as 'ibn Kayfuh' or 'Son of his Pleasure' because of his addiction to hashish, his sharp tongue and his passion for fornication. He came and stood silently, awaiting what Zakariyya might say. Awad was one of Zakariyya's 'helpers', and Zakariyya was overjoyed at the thought: did Zayni realize that men like these were at his beck and call, that they worked for him? They might appear to him to be insignificant, small fry. But how great their services! Master ibn Kayfuh arrived, huge and broad in the shoulders, with a bellowing voice, and yet he looked shaken with fear. When Zakariyya saw him he rushed to kiss and hug him. The man didn't know what to do: should he return the kiss or stand silently in the presence of the Chief Spy of the Sultanate? He hesitated a few moments, after which he realized that were he to return the greeting it would seem cold. Zakariyya walked him to a marble bench under a tall palm tree, the bottom of which was covered with shining brass plate. Zakariyya inquired about ibn Kayfuh's children and his harem. Did he get reconciled with his second wife whom he had offended four days ago and who had left him for her mother's house or were they still separated? He added quickly that he had heard of the Master's decision to divorce her, then said in a soft voice, his head leaning back, 'Don't you have any other solution besides divorce, Master? You know that divorce is the most hateful permissible thing in God's eyes. But if you insist, there is nothing else I can suggest to you.'

The Master didn't hide his surprise and fear; Zakariyya knew everything about him. He was overcome with shame. Zakariyya turned to him, laughing, and said, 'Between the two of us, Master, it's your fault. You don't give her her due as you should. Your newest, youngest wife has taken up all your time. Come now,

Master: fairness is a must here. It is of the essence. When was the last time you went to her. Let me see ... When? I tell you: two months and a week. You are a very clever man, you know the ways of this world and yet you blame her?'

The man's shame grew more awful, his bellowing voice turned into a hoarse whisper of which only a few words were distinguishable. 'You are right! You are right.'

Suddenly Zakariyya said, 'There's a very simple task that I'd like to see done,' and winked at him. He stretched out his fingers and bent them one by one as he listed a task or a request. The Master narrowed his eyes, listening. Occasionally his eyes strayed here and there. Zakariyya's voice was calm and matter-of-fact, as if he were talking about any ordinary topic. His soul might be agitated for a thousand reasons, but as he began to talk his tone of voice was as normal as if he were saying, 'Good morning', even though he might be discussing the most complex and most serious event. What he wanted now was for a few stories, rumours, turns of phrase to be circulated discreetly among the people.

The Master listened and said: 'That should be easy. I promise you that people will speak of nothing else.'

Zakariyya's eyes narrowed. 'If a single human being were to learn of what we've just said ...'

The Master boldly hastened to interrupt him. 'Insult me, but please don't say that.'

Zakariyya opened his hand. 'I know. I know. Anyway, don't make the stories and rumours sound as if they were intended.'

The Master hit his chest with his palm, saying, 'Ibn Kayfuh knows his job ...'

Zakariyya laughed, saying, 'I like you. You are a prince among men!' After a moment he added, 'And, don't forget to think over that other matter.'

The Master wondered what matter he meant, then he realized what it was when he saw Zakariyya's smile. 'Yes, by God. I'll use my head, Shihab. I know that divorce is the most hateful permissible thing in the eyes of God.'

Zakariyya nods; he knits his brow and narrows his eyes as if that matter had already been settled. 'Take her some fabric or some sweets. Women are like little children when it comes to that.'

The Master concurs and starts to leave, bowing in greeting.

Mabruk follows him out of the garden. His loud voice is heard as he utters a greeting whenever he comes across a door or a crack in the wall or a plant.

The winter days are making themselves more clearly felt; the gravel of the roads has a soft, light sheen; the exotic plants glisten; the birds in their cages are engaged in their uninterrupted, mysterious conversations. At night they are mute, but during the day they tell all. Zakariyya goes into his first-floor room, the one he uses for interviews and meetings. A subtle dampness permeates the soft down cushions. He likes to be alone here. The luscious green plants climb the *mashrabiyya* from the outside. The only sound is made by the plants as they move in the wind. The ceiling is high, inlaid with silver and gold decorations made by Khisrawani, the Persian. Next to him is a brass gong, which he beats once with a short leather mallet. Mabruk comes. If his master but whispered his name he would come right away as if he stood waiting all the time. It is at such moments, when Zakariyya is leaning against the cushion, that the questions begin to assail his mind. How many reports are being written now to be submitted to him in a condensed form on one sheet? Perhaps someone is dying at this very moment. This very moment? It's gone already; another one has taken its place. He is dead; how many people remember his name now? What thoughts might Zayni be thinking now? A woman is giving birth to a baby; what will become of him in thirty years? Where is he going to die? Perhaps a ship's captain right now is uttering a cry of panic, telling of immediate doom in the depths of the sea; the great crack in the total night.

Sometimes, when it is pitch dark, he tries to penetrate the darkness with his mind's eyes. How many men in the city are on top of women now? Undoubtedly innumerable men are. It is at such moments that he realizes that no matter how sharp his insight, certain matters would still elude him. If only the time would come when the spies would know how many men are having intercourse with their women, what babies will be conceived, which of these babies will be born and grow up to be trouble-makers. If he knew that in advance, he would prevent the men from sleeping with the woman who would bear the baby. In this way he could eradicate evil, nip it in the bud, nip it even before it has a bud. If the Pharaoh of Egypt had had a great spy who found out the truth about the baby abandoned by his mother in the river, the world would never have heard of God's Prophet, Moses, and the Pharaoh and his troops would not have drowned. Zakariyya is certain that the time will come when spies will know what is happening in Syria even as they sit on the Muqattam hill. If he looks at the methods he is using at present, are they similar to the methods employed by the spies of the Ayyubid dynasty or even the spy of Ashraf Qait Bey, a mere thirty years ago? Things do change; nothing remains the same. In the past, the minute they caught a transgressor, they would work on him and sometimes he would perish. These days, that doesn't happen: the death of the suspect is the last thing they want. All kinds of pain are inflicted upon him while he is alive and conscious. If he faints, there are ways of making him come to as if he had just awakened, refreshed, from a deep, sound sleep. Of these matters, Zayni is quite ignorant. Otherwise, where are the results of his torture of his predecessor, Ali ibn Abi al-Jud? His heralds had had him in custody for a month and yet no crier has announced the extraction of a single dirham from him or his confessing to any wrongdoing. It was said among the people that Zayni was unfamiliar with the methods of torturing prisoners. Some emirs whispered among themselves about the veracity of the rumours surrounding Ali ibn Abi al-Jud. Emir Yalbugha, the Taster, says, 'If the commoners and the riff-raff speak ill of one of the notables, should we believe what is said? This is not done at all!'

So, Zayni is ignoring him! He hasn't responded to his letter! He is going to suffer the consequences of being so clever! He is under-estimating the thousands of spies who are his limbs, his eyes and ears.

Zakariyya's thoughts wander as he remembers that every human being goes through life with two angels on his shoulders: one on his right shoulder, recording the good deeds, and the other on the left shoulder, keeping track of the bad deeds. That is not enough, though, for in the grave await the two other angels: Nakir and Nakeer, who interrogate, question, cross-examine, beat the truth out of the dead person with angelic clubs that produce unparalleled pain. How many persons are there in the world? Two angels to each human. Do Nakir and Nakeer have agents and assistants? What if two men were buried at the same time? How would they be interrogated simultaneously? Nakir and Nakeer couldn't be in every grave at the same time. Only God Almighty exists everywhere. Zakariyya continues his meditations: what a system! And what splendid organization! That's how it is done; the whole of creation is ordered in such a way that not a single good deed or a single bad deed goes unrecorded. One of these days he is going to sit down and write a detailed treatise, listing his hopes for spies; a wish-list of ways and magical methods that would read someone's thoughts, others that would bring back a whole past era to confront a human being who denied a sin that he had committed.

Zakariyya gets up, paces up and down the room, measuring it with his paces: fourteen, which he walks slowly, with bowed head. Suddenly thoughts assail him and a rough hand grips his heart: Zayni is initiating hostilities, even though Zakariyya has not done anything yet to undermine Zayni or to harm him. Some time has passed; maybe he thinks Zakariyya has given in! He is going to start working. But what if the Sultan persisted in backing Zayni? At that thought Zakariyya's eyes narrow and his pacing grows faster; the room is now only ten paces.

Who backed al-Mu'ayyad Shaykh al-Hamawi when he assumed the throne? Zayni doesn't know. The Sultan doesn't know. Who propelled him to the throne after he was imprisoned for so long at Shama'il Treasury Prison? He swore in gaol that, if released, he would raze the horrible gaol and build a mosque that would be the talk of whole generations to come. He did get out and he did level the Shama'il Prison and in its place built a mosque that became the pride of Cairo. But do the people performing prayers in it or the shaykhs know who it was who backed King al-Mu'ayyad Shaykh? Who was responsible for building the mosque? History books do not mention it, but the matter is well documented in the Spies' Bureau. The Chief Spy was the one who did it. The throne is not out of Zakariyya's reach; he can pry it loose. If only Sha'ban had lived long enough to admit his relationship with al-Ghuri! But killing him was necessary; he was as beautiful as the moon, but even the moon must set and disappear. Today Zakariyya will send for the man in charge of the homing-pigeon houses, a new system that he has introduced and of which he alone can be proud among the spies of the various kingdoms and territories. Each pigeon knows which road to take, avoiding flight over populated areas and cara- vans in the desert; rather it crosses deserted areas, going directly to its destination, no matter how long that takes. Today the flocks will fly so that the officials, fief owners, heads of villages, even commoners, so that all of those who have been deceived by Zayni might know what mistake the Sultan made when he entrusted the affairs of the Islamic nation to a man of unknown origin, a man whom nobody has seen performing the communal Friday prayers, one who pretends to be fair while keeping his thoughts to himself. He is taking his sweet time extracting the monies of Ali ibn Abi al-Jud. Who knows? Maybe they were secret partners in oppressing the people before anyone knew him. The flocks will fly to Emir Tughluq, the Superintendent of Constructions, and Bashtak, known among the people as 'Ful Muqashshar' or 'Shelled Fava Beans'. One fight between Tashtamur and Khayrbak is not enough. Tughluq will learn that Bashtak Ful Muqashshar is casting aspersions on the new mosque, which he had built for the Sultan at Sharabshiyyin. At the same time, Bashtak will learn that Tughluq is making fun of him and mimicking him, hinting at Bashtak's attempts to be like the emirs that are very close to the Sultan and saying that he is *nouveau riche*. Zakariyya is smiling now as his paces get faster. Tughluq will be so angry he will froth at the mouth. Each will turn his Mamluks against the other; confusion will reign; goods will disappear as looting intensifies. A number of tough spies will abduct several virgins and boys. Zakariyya stops pacing. The day is passing quietly, flowing almost inaudibly into space. How he loves the winter! He picks up the leather mallet and strikes the brass gong once. It resounds.

Tuesday evening, 7 Dhu al-Qa'da

Announcement

People of Egypt! We enjoin what is right and forbid what is wrong. We worship, prostrate ourselves and praise God the Almighty who has humbled the wicked and the arrogant! People of Egypt! We bear you good tidings: our lord the Sultan commands the following: having perused the most eloquent report submitted by Zayni Barakat ibn Musa, Markets Inspector for Cairo and Upper Egypt, a report that spells out the truth and explains the hardships facing the poor among his subjects, the tax on salt has been lifted; dealing in it is hereby deregulated, after being a monopoly of the few. People of Egypt! Our lord the Sultan, made cognizant of reality by Zayni Barakat, commands that Emir Tughluq's monopoly over cucumbers and all vegetables be ended and that farmers may sell their produce in the markets with no middleman, so that prices will come down. Any guard or Mamluk, veteran or newly imported, who charges a tax on a load of cucumbers or other vegetables at any of Cairo's gates shall be hanged without further ado.

> *Excerpt from an announcement repeated by the heralds on the same evening, Tuesday, 7 Dhu al-Qa'da*

Our lord the Sultan, having been apprised of the situation by Zayni Barakat ibn Musa, Markets Inspector for Cairo and Upper Egypt, commands that no Mamluk go out on the streets, veiled, after sunset and that no Mamluk enter the alleys bearing arms after the evening prayers.

> *Excerpt from an unusual announcement repeated by Zayni's men on the evening of Tuesday, 7 Dhu al-Qa'da, among the people who went out on the streets and listened happily to what was being announced*

Having consulted the *shari'a* and the learned men and having researched the past, Zayni Barakat ibn Musa, Inspector of Markets for Cairo and Upper Egypt, commands that the custom of mourning the dead by beating tambourines be stopped. Whoever is caught beating those instruments in mourning shall be exposed in disgrace without further ado.

Zayni Barakat ibn Musa, Markets Inspector of Cairo and Upper
Egypt, has designated one of the gates of his house for receiving
complaints and petitions. Anyone suffering an inequity, visited
upon him by anyone, great or small, should go to Zayni Barakat to
receive satisfaction.

*Cover of a letter delivered to Zakariyya ibn Radi by
one of Zayni's messengers*

'By the fig and the olive and the mount of Sinai and this city of
security', as the Glorious Quran says.
   To Egypt's Chief Spy and Deputy Markets Inspector, Shihab
Zakariyya ibn Radi: Peace . . .

*An announcement on Tuesday night, at the same
time as the letter was delivered to Zakariyya*

From now on there shall be hung big lamps, which burn grease,
designed and crafted by Emir Tughluq, Superintendent of Constructions, after listening to the opinion of Zayni Barakat, Markets
Inspector for Cairo and Upper Egypt. These lamps shall be hung
above the gate of every alley, in front of every house, palace or
caravanserai. These new lamps shall be hung and lighted by Zayni's
men every night, so that Cairo might sleep in security. Be fore-
warned that no lamp shall be removed from its place, or else the
owners of the place will be punished and penalized. People of Egypt!
This will not cost you a single dirham. So, co-operate with the
Inspector! People of Egypt! People of Egypt! Our lord the Sultan
commands that Zakariyya ibn Radi remain as he has been, deputy
of the Markets Inspector in all his posts and that the title 'al-
Shihab' be conferred upon him. People of Egypt! People of Egypt!
Take very good care of the new lamps: anyone caught disobeying
the *Muhtasib*'s orders shall be hanged without further ado.

From: Amr ibn al-Adawi
To: Head Spy of Cairo
Re: Events and reactions among the people on Tuesday, 7 Dhu al-Qa'da.

There was consensus among the old men, the scribes of different bureaux, the judges and those truly familiar with events of bygone eras, that what Cairo witnessed on the evening of Tuesday, 7 Dhu al-Qa'da, was unprecedented and unparalleled in any country. I heard that with my own two ears from scholars at al-Azhar, the old men of the Halwaji Chapel, the merchants of Ghuriyya and Batiniyya, the barbers sitting in front of beauticians' shops and the students at the Chapel of the Blind at al-Azhar Mosque. Never before have heralds gone round every half hour, preceded by drums, each time making a new proclamation or announcing a new order. Because the proclamations were so numerous, no single announcement was repeated, even though, according to custom in the past, each proclamation from the Sultan would be repeated five times a day for a whole week, except in times of disaster. The crowds that I saw were tremendous; the whole of Batiniyya, men and women, came out ululating, waving, screaming and shouting. People said various things. To avoid repetition and to cut a long story short, I shall sum up what I heard hereinafter.

Firstly, there were lots of prayers for Zayni Barakat after the first and fourth proclamations. Everybody, especially the women, had nothing but praise for him. The women clamoured, shouted and chanted, 'God save Zayni's days.' They all agreed that Zayni knew the ills that assailed people's bodies and souls, because he was not a stand-offish stranger; rather he knew the conditions well and his whole body shuddered at the mere mention of acts of injustice. He never stooped so low as to condone torture. He performed his prayers at their appointed times. A man (a pastry pedlar; name: Shams al-Ramadani; address: First tenement in al-Rum al-Juwwaniyya Alley; age: over forty; distinguishing marks: grey beard. I know where to get him) said that he saw Zayni go out incognito day and night, checking on people's affairs, feeling their pain. He also said that God had sent him at this time as the friend and helper of the poor. He said that he knew a servant in Zayni Barakat's household who said that his master cried for a long time every night before he slept, because he knew full well that there were sad, oppressed people spending that very night in agony. Zayni suffered a lot on account of that and asked God's forgiveness in this world and the next, because he cannot right all the wrongs. It was rumoured after the fourth proclamation that Zayni Barakat had gone up to the Sultan and stayed with him for a long time, during which he told him, 'You are responsible for these subjects in front of God Almighty on the Day of Judgement. You and I will be held accountable for every sin committed, whether or not we are aware of it. Where, on that day, would we hide from His might?' The Sultan listened to him for a long time. Zayni's talk was filled with verses from the Quran and quotations from the *hadith* and other texts that are known only to the most learned scholars. (The merchants said that Zayni knew the whole Quran by heart and that he had composed an exegesis of it in manuscript form, which nobody had seen.) Zayni spoke about Emir Sharbak and his monopoly over the whole salt trade throughout Egypt, how he was the only one who traded in it and how a poor man caught selling half a dirham's worth of salt would get his right arm cut off; or his left arm if his right arm had already been cut off; or his right leg if the two arms had been cut off; or his left leg if his right leg had already been cut off; or how the Emir would apprehend and similarly punish the son of the violator or his brother or his mother or his father if he had no limbs to be cut off. Sharbak's salt monopoly enabled him to raise its price at will. Sometimes he would be in a good mood and drastically reduce its price. But, when he got angry or ill at ease, he would send the heralds round to proclaim that the price had been raised, causing great hardship for the subjects. Zayni said that when that happened the subjects cursed the Sultan himself and prayed to God to wreak vengeance on him and show His anger with him. Zayni added that when it came to cucumbers it was much, much worse, since Emir Tughluq had prohibited their sale or purchase except through his own agents. The merchants asserted that Zayni caused the Sultan's eyes to flow with tears and that he gave Zayni a free hand, provided the treasury did not suffer a deficit of even one dirham, since the Sultanate was in dire need of all the money it could get, as things were getting tight. Zayni expressed willingness and ability to do that. After the announcements were made, people's curses were heaped on Emir Tughluq and, if people could, they would have torn him to pieces, as some said openly. The rabble cursed Emir Sharbak's grandfathers and prayed to God to punish him. Some poor people tossed tips to the heralds to express their joy and happiness.

Secondly, I heard with my own ears three men talking at Lundi's Café (one of them is known to me; name: Fattouh al-Iskandarani; lives in Bab al-Shi'riyya; owns an oil press; age: fifty-five years). They were singing a different tune; Fattouh al-Iskandarani expressed scepticism about Zayni's announcements. He said things would not go on like that and the Sultan would not allow such things unless they coincided with the Sultan's own interests. He tried to convince those present and waved his hands a lot. I tried to lead him on, to pick his brain, but that was the extent of it. In another café, a man by the name of Abu Ghazala, who works in a dye-house at the Mida Alley, shouted, 'Really? Since when were rulers interested in justice?'

Thirdly, near the Tarbi'a bazaar, where lots of women shop at the stalls owned by the Syrian merchants, the men wondered about the significance of the ban on the beating by women of tambourines in mourning. They were all in agreement that Zayni, as *Muhtasib*, was well within his rights to ban this innovation. The much more serious matter, however, had to do with the lamps. Abd al-Hamid, Head of the Cairo Water-carriers' Guild (he always sits with these merchants) said that it was an innovation that should not be propagated in the nation of Islam. One of the scholars of al-Azhar (name: Jad Allah; Upper Egyptian, lives in the *riwaq* of the Upper Egyptians) said on the same subject that Zayni wanted to introduce another innovation to be named after him. Another said that the innovation might diminish God's blessings among the people. There was a lot of talk about the hanging of the lamps. Others said,

'Maybe this would prevent brigand raids at night.' This was answered with the question, 'Does the light prevent brigand attacks?', meaning that, if the brigands or the Mamluks wanted to raid an alley, would this deter them? They would break the lamps and go ahead with their plans. The Jews said, 'It's all right, since we will not pay a dirham.' Some shaykhs said, 'Nothing but good has come from Zayni. This new order must have some benefit.' After the heralds finished making their rounds, Zayni's men came out and started driving big nails into the walls on which they then hung the lamps and then lit them. As each one was lit, everyone shouted, 'Hey! Long live the lamps!', 'Hey, God save the lamps! The lamps! The lamps!' And Cairo didn't sleep that night on account of that.

Fourthly, as I entered al-Azhar Mosque at dawn, I saw the Azhar student Said al-Juhayni (I have mentioned his name several times already) sitting among some students. He was shaking his fist frequently and showed signs of vexation, discontent and a deep-seated hatred. They were all listening to him. I greeted them and was horrified to find that he was making references to something that absolutely nobody else had touched upon. Said al-Juhayni focused on what occurred in the proclamation relevant to the lamps and pertaining to the confirmation of the Supreme Shihab Zakariyya ibn Radi as Deputy *Muhtasib*. His comments can be summed up as follows:

1) Zayni Barakat ibn Musa was coerced by the Shihab and his assistants to confirm him as Deputy *Muhtasib*;
2) he knew Zayni Barakat well and was sure that he was not satisfied with this decision;
3) all the proclamations announced in such quick succession were meant to divert people's attention away from the most important matter, namely, confirming the Supreme Shihab and giving legitimacy to his posts;
4) he said, verbatim, the following: 'Things are beginning to get messy. This is a bad omen. God help us and protect us.'

As of the time of this writing, he hasn't ceased moving round among the students, making public his intention to go to his Shaykh Abu al-Su'ud to explain things to him and ask him to intervene. He has continued to curse and insult the Supreme Shihab, using most loathsome profanity.

Fifthly, some preachers preached from the pulpits of mosques against the lamps. Storytellers in the cafés made fun of the new order and composed verses, among which was this one: 'A numbskull will end up with a lamp on his head.'

Friday, 10 Dhu al-Hijja 912 AH

Announcement

People of Egypt! We enjoin what is right and forbid what is wrong. Today the Sultan received the Envoy of the King of Abyssinia and the Envoy of the King of Venice and conferred on each a velvet Kamili overcoat with sable trim. People of Egypt! A sudden rift has developed between Emir Bashtak Ful Muqashshar and Emir Tughluq, Superintendent of Constructions, because Bashtak reviled the new minaret in the Sultan's mosque. He said it leaned a little and looked ugly! People of Egypt! Beware the two, and beware Emir Khayrbak and Emir Tashtamur, for the rift between those two still goes on. People of Egypt! Matters of great importance will be announced soon about the monies and treasures sucked from the blood of the poor and hidden by the criminal Ali ibn Abi al-Jud. People of Egypt! Selim Loz, maker of Kunafa dough, was caught selling his fare at prices higher than those set by the *Muhtasib*. Zayni Barakat has punished him: he ordered him to sit on the hot tray on which he baked the dough and ordered further that he be tied, naked, to the tray. People of Egypt! People of Egypt! Whoever sees injustice and pretends not to see it is an infidel and his life shall be forfeit.

Said al-Juhayni

THIS is the age of perplexity, when doubt is master and certainty extinct. Details vanish. A desire overpowers him. If only he were to wander in an endless desert of unknown dimensions, where his hair would wear off and his body dissolve! Maybe then he would know what has eluded him, that which is cloaked in clouds and veiled in mist. His life and his passion are consumed by a love that is hopeless. His only sustenance comes from his awareness that she lives in a house that he visits only twice a week. All he hopes for is to see her. The sun rises from the East and sets in the West. How far is the first heaven from the second and the third? Is the distance measured in space or time? How distant are the stars from the earth and what huge chains bind them, keeping them from falling? And those stars that do fall: are they evil souls that have been expelled from paradise? They appear only for a few moments in the dark and then they get lost, neither reaching the earth nor staying up in heaven. Even the trails of fire that follow them vanish completely, as if they were an unwelcome dream. How come the seas do not run over and inundate the land? How come the Nile fills up, reaches inundation and then recedes anew? When Zayni Barakat was born, did he know what was written on the sacred tablet foretelling his fate? Did he know that one day he would become *Muhtasib* and that a man named Zakariyya would be waiting for him? How? How does he accept Zakariyya ibn Radi continuing as his deputy, surrounding the Inspectorship with the toughest, most frightening spies, who inspire terror wherever they reach: the stones of buildings, the holes in the walls, the corners, on pillows, on mosque minarets, in the prayer niches? Did he make a mistake when he went to Zayni's house to accompany him to Kom al-Jarih? But he is still announcing that whoever had a complaint should go to him. Indeed, those with complaints daily go to him and to nobody else. They forsook the emirs and the judges. It got to the point that there were rumours that he intended to combine the Markets Inspectorship with a judgeship. To counter that, Zayni rode his mule and went to al-Azhar Mosque to perform the Friday prayers and then addressed the people denying all those allegations, saying that the Inspectorship required him to be sharp and vigilant and that he couldn't bear the combined load. The people hailed him and shouted, 'God is greater!' and they tried to kiss his cloak, but he snapped at them and expressed anger and annoyance. At that point Said was overcome with worries. He saw the Supreme Shihab Zakariyya ibn Radi, Zayni's first deputy, walking behind him, clad in a yellow embroidered cloak and an ordinary turban that was unmarked, except for a ruby in the middle of the white cloth wound round it. He complained to Mansur, his friend and colleague at the *riwaq*, but Mansur was worried; the *riwaqs* were once again crawling with Zakariyya's men and lackeys. One must be careful what one says. Said is not unaware of them; he hears their stealthy steps behind him and senses the way they vanish. The glances of Amr ibn Al-Adawi get to him; Amr has bought a new cloak and a pair of shoes. It is rumoured that he goes to a woman in the house of Uns and that he buys meat and vegetables and meat pies for her. Said wishes to sit and talk to him, open his heart to him and ask him what impels him to report every sigh and whisper to Zakariyya. But how can he think like that? His friend Mansur is not annoyed about Zakariyya, saying, 'Zayni doesn't run the whole show. He is new to the post. A man like Zakariyya should not be underestimated, and it is impossible to ignore him. Besides, who knows? Perhaps this is a deliberate move on the part of Zayni. Even if he were to fire Zakariyya, he would be a potential threat, like a camouflaged pit, since he is in possession of the secrets of the State and the emirs. So, should Zayni clash with him or contain him?'

Said didn't say a word. Which is the right path? He sees everyone in this world following an unalterable course, unalterable but crooked, enveloped in fog and thick smoke. Mansur is sitting in a corner at Lundi's café. He reaches out his hand to arrange the tobacco on the narghile and is completely enveloped in the smoke, the quintessential refuge from grief. His faraway beloved draws near; he opens his arms and embraces her. She cleaves to him and sits at his feet. He migrates to the Waq Waq lands at the end of the earth. He invades the islands of women and he sees Zayni as a messenger sent by Providence and Zakariyya as his loyal disciple, providing security, staving off calamities and guarding against strife. Before his migration to the world of oblivion, Mansur says, 'Nothing concerns me, so why should I care? I have been allotted a certain number of years to live on this earth, and this world is transitory. So, let me drink at the fountain of pleasure and take the path of safety and not be light in the head, convulsing and twitching and worrying myself sick.'

He invites Said to accompany him, as he feels lonely the moment he steps into the world of blue mist, where the houris and boys are. Said is irritated; he leaves Lundi's café. The roads are lit by lamps. So far, the matter of the lamps has not been resolved. Strife is about to break out over these lamps. Is he for the lamps or against them? He doesn't know. He hasn't been to see his master for four days. If only he could just pick up and leave for Upper Egypt, throw off his shoulders the loads they have been carrying ever since he came to al-Azhar. If only he could go to the Mosque of al-Husayn and attach himself the rest of his life to the Green Portal, never leaving the side of the beloved Husayn, reciting invocations of the memory of the Martyr. If only he could go to Samah, tear away her veil and embrace her as a cherished treasure, a talisman, unparalleled poetry and a lost paradise. But she is a mirage that offers nothing but thirst. He doesn't know what to do. Samah made other women look like monstrosities. Only she is left; all else is a wasteland. His safety lies in being away from her. Desire has been tormenting him for several nights. His bedding in the *riwaq* is always burning with a slow, undying fire. He tries to learn about what happens in the house of Uns, how a man would enter and pick the woman he wants. A man doesn't know the name of the woman with whom he sleeps. Mansur told him, 'The first time, I asked the girl her name, and she laughed and said, "Rawya"' and he knew it was not her name. If only he could go to the house of Uns! Couldn't he? In his mind's eye, Samah never disrobes. He doesn't remember the colour of her eyes, the taste of her glances, the features of her face, which make her Samah and not somebody else. Years ago, Said was a blank page with no writing on it whatsoever. Now his world is filled with letters, exclamation marks, question marks, a thousand perplexed questions seeing no way to an answer. The whole world is a question that has no beginning and no end, eternally preserved in an old, torn, worn-out manuscript, the words of which have been scraped off.

Special section containing excerpts of what was said about the lamps

1) Part of the Friday sermon delivered from the pulpits of mosques on the last day of Dhu al-Qa'da 912 AH. This section was delivered by all preachers, regardless of their rites.

People of Egypt! The Messenger of God, prayers and peace be upon him, says that a learned man, if asked about something he knows nothing about, should not be too embarrassed to say, 'I do not know.' We say that to those who have decided that it is permitted to hang lamps in front of homes and shops, pretending knowledge of history and past events. All they've stopped short of is claiming knowledge of what will be. If they hadn't, we would have included them among the infidels. They say that in many a nation in the past, rulers have hung lamps in the streets. Would they mention one specific example? Did our Messenger walk in the light of lamps? On the two journeys of the summer and the winter to Syria and Yemen, was his path lighted by lamps made by human hands? We say it without embarrassment and are ready to die for it; we say it to those who claim knowledge of the wisdom of history, the *hadith* of the Prophet, the hidden texts and custom and tradition, when in reality they are ignoramuses trying to disguise their ignorance. We say it without fear or timidity. People of Egypt! It never happened before that lamps were hung. The Noble Messenger has enjoined us to lower our eyes so that we may not see the nakedness of people. But the lamps reveal our nakedness. God has created night and day: dark night and lit day; God has created the night as a cover and a shield; do we remove the cover? Do we do away with the shield that God has given us? Do we give in to our arrogance and dispel the darkness of the night from every span of the hand in the city? This is heresy, which we do not accept. It is deviation from the law and we reject it. Had it not been that all of us were convinced that Zayni Barakat meant well, we would have said that he had ulterior motives. But ever since he assumed the Inspectorship, he has done nothing but good. The lamps are not going to shake our confidence in him or make us suspicious of him. People of Egypt! Go to the house of Zayni Barakat ibn Musa, individually and in groups, by yourselves or with others! Go to him! Go to his house! Demand that he ban the lamps, which pierce the veil of modesty, which encourage women to go out after the evening prayers. Go to him in supplication and with resolve, begging firmly! Let not his slick talk dissuade you from that which you have decided. Do not stray from your goal. The lamps are a sign of the end of time. They are indications of a world deviating from God's design. Demand that our Sultan cut in two halves whomever has suggested this idea to Zayni, burn him, stone him. Those ignoramuses who pretend to be learned. Woe the day when the lamps rule! God protect us against this evil abomination! God keep it away. Oh, God, do not extend our lives long enough to see such a day. (At that point people in the mosques cried loudly and some of them shouted, 'May God destroy the lamps! May God pulverize the lamps!')

> *Judicial decision handed down by the Chief Justice of*
> *Egypt*

Lamps take away God's blessing from the people.

> *1 Muharram 913 AH. The Judge of the Hanafi rite*
> *has a dissenting opinion*

The lamps drive away devils, light the roads for strangers at night and deter the Mamluks of the emirs and the brigands from attacking innocent people at night.

One of the distinguished jurists has strayed from the path, contravened the foundations and disregarded the specifics of jurisprudence by siding with the lamps.

The leading emirs go up to the Citadel

Our lord the Sultan, the hanging of lamps has encouraged common women to go out after the evening prayers, to roam the streets and sit up late in front of the tenements and bazaars. This is against all modesty and decorum. (Khayrbak)

The children no longer go home early. Rather they stay in the streets for hours, singing and chanting, sometimes making fun of our Mamluks and throwing stones at them and bandying obscenities. (Qusun)

Such a matter could have been devised only by someone who wished to sow seeds of sedition, strife and profligacy. (Tughluq)

Illuminating the city and people staying up in lamplight is injurious to the establishment and insulting to the Sultanate. (Qunbuq)

Zayni sends his men in the evening. They climb the wooden ladders to light the lamps and clean them. That is what he says. But, my lord, fellow emirs: they spy on the people and on us. They invade people's privacy. (Tashtamur)

Exactly. Absolutely right. (All emirs)

Chief Justice Abd al-Barr

The Judge of the Hanafi rite has instituted a grave, unprecedented precedent; he disagreed with us. He said no. This is a horrifying development.

Some of the scholars expressed approval of the opinion of the Chief Justice Abd al-Barr ibn al-Shahnah. They said a man of such calibre wouldn't bother about the lamps unless it was a very serious matter, not as some would imagine.

Said said, 'You exaggerate!' He pointed to the main thoroughfares in the city of Cairo and how their shops were lit all night.

At that point one of the scholars said, 'Not true. The shops close after the evening prayers, and by midnight everybody is asleep at home.'

Said shouted, 'Does anyone here hate to see the alleys and the homes well lit so that people might feel safe? What the emirs want is for the dark to prevail so that their Mamluks might engage in as much mischief as they wish.'

Amr ibn al-Adawi's voice rang out, 'Exactly! What Said is saying is true.'

A Syrian scholar said, 'Oh, Said, you always disagree.'

Said said, excited, 'I only disagree with what I consider wrong.'

A Nubian scholar wondered, 'Can the Chief Justice be wrong?'

Mansur turns to Said; he disagrees with him. 'What reason is there for introducing this innovation of the lamps? Aren't people's affairs more important and more worthy of Zayni's attention and his concern? Besides, honestly, Said, this innovation only makes matters worse.'

Said bowed his head: who knows? Perhaps this innovation of the lamps had purposes that eluded him.

The Syrian scholar wondered, 'Everybody has raged and foamed at the mouth and threatened to move heaven and earth, but has anybody, great or small, dared to remove the lamp in front of his house?'

A scholar from Manfalut shouted, 'They fear Zayni.'

Amr said, 'Exactly.'

Mansur jeered, 'Does the Commander in Chief of the Armies himself fear him?'

Said bit his upper lip: if only he could tell them, 'Instead of wasting your breath and your time, watch what Zakariyya is doing, how he has imposed himself on Zayni.' But is it true? Did he really impose himself? Who knows? Perhaps he got the post with Zayni's blessings.

Amr ibn al-Adawi said, 'It is not a question of lamps at all.'

The people in the mosques and the streets shouted, 'God damn the lamps! A curse on the lamps!'

Said al-Juhayni

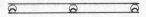

SAID had visited him before, one day after dawn, to accompany him to Shaykh Abu al-Su'ud. There's the house. The gate is open. Zayni had added nothing to it. As Markets Inspector he is entitled to move to a larger house, but he has stayed here. In front of the door stands a Nubian wearing a green shirt with a collar and yellow sleeves – something new introduced by Zayni – a uniform for his deputies, agents and men. On the opposite side many are standing in a line extending to the other side of the house overlooking the back road. The Nubian asked, 'Do you wish to see Zayni himself?' Said said, 'Yes, definitely.' The man left him. The voices of the people with complaints are soft, even though there is a large number of them. When he meets Zayni, he will speak to him with an open heart. He will say to him, 'God help you with what you have to contend with!' When he walked next to him that night a long time ago, Zayni didn't talk much, didn't get into any details. If he saw him now, talk between the two of them wouldn't stop. Said will tell him about what caused him to start doubting. Zayni will mention all the things that bother him, what the post of Inspector requires and what the people say about him in return.

The Nubian came back. 'Zayni left the house in the morning. He may be back in the late afternoon.'

It was as if Said had stopped suddenly after running. He asked, 'Don't you know where he is?'

The Nubian said, 'Zayni has his own tours, about which nobody knows a thing, to reassure himself about the people's welfare. But I know about one of his errands today. As you know, there is that rift between the Mamluks of Tashtamur and those of Khayrbak, and there is a disturbance around the Juwwaniyya Alley. They seized the opportunity presented by the quarrel and looted several shops in the area. Zayni has gone to the alley to make an estimate of the looted property and the damage and to submit the matter to the Sultan.'

Said wondered, 'When did that happen?'

The Nubian, amazed, said, 'All night long.'

How did that happen without Said being aware of it? Was it perhaps because he had stayed in his classes until noon? 'But wasn't a reconciliation between Tashtamur and Khayrbak supposed to be imminent?'

The Nubian shook his head. 'Not at all. After they both had agreed that it was necessary to get rid of the lamps as the rest of the emirs had done, Khayrbak said, "I'll never agree with Tashtamur." When Tashtamur heard that, he shouted, "Is he disparaging me? I swear by God to bring it tumbling down on his head."'

Suddenly there was a big clamour: peasants with dusty faces and wandering eyes. Said saw little children in his faraway village, with big heads, necks as thin as sticks, chewing the dust of the road, their eyes providing havens for the flies. He found himself praising God for not creating him a peasant toiling in the fields, raising water from the irrigation canal, paying protection money, being flogged by the tax collector, going to the city to complain and never going back to his children. He didn't interrupt his thoughts but kept on. What if he had been born a peasant?

After a few moments of silence, the Nubian gatekeeper said to him, 'But you didn't tell me about the purpose of your meeting with Zayni,' and assured him that Zayni's deputy, who was available, could listen to what he had to say.

Said said, 'Zayni knows me. I must see *him*.'

Said was not turning anybody in, but he had strong evidence that Burhan al-Din ibn Sayyid al-Nas, the fava-bean merchant who owned several boats on the Nile and storage facilities at Minyat ibn Khasib, had been buying up fava beans from the peasants and storing them; that he had built innumerable silos at the Athar al-Nabi harbour in Misr al-Qadima; that he had been bribing a number of emirs in order, ultimately, to obtain an official decree from the Sultan, giving him monopoly over fava beans. That would bring back to life an old plague, which Zayni was trying to stamp out, namely monopolies by certain individuals or groups in certain commodities such as vegetables, or legumes or other merchandise. Think how much worse it would be when it is such a staple food.

What if Burhan al-Din ibn Sayyid al-Nas decided to hold fava beans back from the markets until they became scarce? That would be an unheard-of event; no merchant has ever tried to have a monopoly over fava beans in Egypt before. Zayni will not accept that. Said wondered if he was really upset over that or if he was trying to test Zayni's sense of justice. The truth is that he doesn't know at this time.

He crosses the Amir al-Juyush road; hammers are pounding copper, shaping it into pots and pitchers. A donkey driver has tied his donkey to a pole on the street and sat down next to it, chewing on a radish and a piece of bread. There it is, Hamza ibn al-Eid al-Saghir's shop. He feels comfortable sitting here, since nobody knows him. He is totally by himself; even his friend Mansur is away.

'Welcome! Welcome. Such a beautiful day!' A warm greeting from Hamza, which he returns by raising his hand and laying his palm on his chest. He ordered a narghile. The first drags produce a nice light dizziness, even though it doesn't contain any hashish. He likes it. He needs very much to reflect on what has happened and what was happening, to go over what he would tell Zayni Barakat if he met him in the evening. As for seeing Samah in his mind's eye, it has a different flavour as he sits here.

Sultan's Decree

Shaykh Said ibn al-Sakkit is hereby removed from his post as Judge of the Hanafi rite.

From the Chief Justice of Egypt to the Sultan

You have protected justice and truth and strengthened Islam by removing the dissenters. God save you as a protector of this land.

Sultan's Decree

The custom of lamps shall be discontinued. Those lamps that have been hung shall be removed as if they never were.

From the emirs and notables of the land of Egypt

What you have done is right and just. God damn the lamps! A curse on the lamps!

Said al-Juhayni

'TELL me about your world.'

He is at a loss to know where to begin.

'Shaykh al-Balqini, the *hadith* scholar at al-Azhar, has died. He was ninety-three years old.'

The Shaykh does not show any sense of mourning. 'God have mercy on him and on us.'

'Zakariyya and Zayni are in agreement.'

'I know that.'

Said is surprised.

'Zayni came to see me yesterday. After I heard the news, I thought of sending for him to get to the truth, but he came in and explained the situation.'

His master has taught him not to ask too many questions or to inquire insistently, but rather to listen to what is said, to draw conclusions and try to understand.

'Master, everything puzzles me.'

A smile that is the essence of serenity: 'Everything?'

'Master, I accompanied Zayni to your house; I walked in front of him in the procession as if I were one of his aides. I enthusiastically supported him and defended him. Right now, I have my doubts, my misgivings, about him. A month ago I said to myself I should go to see him and inform him of what I had learned for a fact about a man named Burhan al-Din ibn Sayyid al-Nas.'

'Burhan al-Din?'

'Yes, Master. This Burhan had started a scheme to have a monopoly over fava beans. I found out his methods and his storage facilities. I knew that the price of fava beans would go sky-high. When I finally sat down with Zayni, after several futile attempts to see him, he complained to me about the controversy over the lamps. He said that the emirs had so misled the people and deceived them that they turned against the lamps – a fact that made the Sultan ban them. He spoke for a long time about the lamps, saying that he had pinned great hopes on the lamps. He spoke of his intentions to end many unfair practices and eliminate injustice. He spoke about being frustrated in his post as *Muhtasib* and the loss he was incurring. Imagine, Master! He complained that he had little money, because, before the Inspectorship, he used to go to certain towns and trade in certain commodities and oversee a small farm in Damietta. But now he has neglected the land and the business. His fifty-dinar salary from the Bureau is hardly enough to keep the appearances required by the post of *Muhtasib*. Even if he were to discontinue these appearances, he still has to wear certain types of clothing whenever he goes up to the Sultan, and this costs him plenty. He didn't hide anything from me. He told me the most intimate details. I swear by God, Master, that I felt so close to him that I almost told him what was disturbing me: why did he accept Zakariyya as his deputy? I wished I could tell him what Zakariyya was doing to the people. They haven't changed; they are still all over al-Azhar. Does he accept that? I was about to tell him, but I didn't say a single word. I told him what I had actually gone there to tell him. He shook his head and said, 'I'll ask my deputy to put him under surveillance, and, if his wrongdoing is confirmed, he will be punished.' Imagine, Master! Who will administer justice? Who will stop Burhan al-Din ibn Sayyid al-Nas? Zakariyya ibn Radi. But I told myself that perhaps Zayni was trying to employ Zakariyya for the good of the people. I continued to watch what Burhan al-Din was doing and found out that he had kept doing what he had been doing. I went up to Zayni again and he said, 'These things take time', and he mentioned the story of the tailor whom he had punished despite the intercession by the emirs most influential with the Sultan. I do not know, Master, what Zayni is planning to do. So far he has done absolutely nothing to Burhan al-Din. Should I regret that I once walked in front of him? On the other hand, acts of injustice fill me with pain. Why are the peasants flogged? Why does a great Azhar scholar deny his mother who had come from the countryside to visit him? Why? Just because she is a peasant woman? How can I believe that people were created equal? How, when what happened, what is happening and what will happen belie that and contradict it? How? I wish I could go before all humanity and proceed to uproot all oppression and corruption, not only in the land of Egypt but all over the world. But our lives will pass and will be wasted without being able to do that. Imagine, Master, I am filled with fear whenever I see Amr ibn al-Adawi. I wonder what he will write in his reports about me, things that will make them lock me up in al-Maqshara, al-Arqana or the Jubb. What would they do to me? They may cut short my study at al-Azhar, cut off my stipend and my livelihood, bar me from employment. Let them. What is the value of all that? If I saved one human life from oppression, what is the value of all of it? But then I find myself fearing deprivation, gaol, chains and torture. I tremble whenever I hear the name Zakariyya. Imagine, Master, that I, who feel great pain when I see flies on the eyes of the children in our village, I praise God. Imagine that, Master! I praise Him because he didn't create me a peasant suffering the hardships of life and the oppression of the tax collector. Forgive me, Master, for laying all my burdens in front of you, but what can I do when time is holding me down, breaking my jaw and entombing my thoughts in my chest?'

The night passes in silence. At the beginning its colours are deceptive and the day recedes; they turn dark and deep, until everything is drowned in blackness. Voices are stilled. The Shaykh's fingers chase each other. Said fears the night and never faces it in the *riwaq*. He sees the dying lights in the streets. After a pause with his head bowed down, his eyes look round the small courtyard, the solid trunk of the palm tree, which the years have watered, a little mound in the middle of the courtyard, which he had not noticed before. The Shaykh is silent. Said points to the mound of earth: 'I didn't see it before.' He seeks a question to break the silence.

'From time to time I need to be by myself. For that purpose, I have dug this cellar. I dug it so that I could rest my body in it whenever the soul is perplexed and let down by time.'

This narrow opening leads to the cellar. All alone, he has snatched for himself a place in the earth. In it he lays down his burdens, and then the soul can soar where it can reach primeval truths, where he can bang on the gates of the universe, speak his innermost thoughts and secrets, so that the heart might see.

Announcement

People of Egypt! We enjoin what is right and forbid what is wrong. That which was hidden is now known! That which was buried has been unearthed! Ali ibn Abi al-Jud's shameful wrongdoing has been exposed. This evening, before sunset, the preachers in the mosques will read a document from which you will find out and see how the oppressor had sucked the blood of the Muslims, hence deserving severe punishment!

THIRD PAVILION

Beginning with details of the imprisonment of
Ali ibn Abi al-Jud

In the Name of God, Most Gracious, Most Merciful.

Praise God who has uncovered all secrets, laid the earth flat and raised the heavens. We address the Muslim nation, uncovering a matter that has been long awaited, so that it might be a lesson for those who would learn, those who are alive and those who are gone. The details of that matter are as follows.

About a year ago our lord the Sultan ordered the detention of Ali ibn Abi al-Jud and his remanding to the custody of the Markets Inspector to punish him and to find what he had hidden. From the beginning we had planned to be patient until the very end, because we were opposed to torturing the body. We do not permit any human being, no matter who, to be burned anywhere on his body or to be shod like a horse. This explains the lapse between our receiving Ali ibn Abi al-Jud and the uncovering of the affair. We have discovered such monies that nobody could believe, all sucked from the blood of the Muslims.

Following is what we have seized: his daily revenue from his properties, lands, warranties and protection operation has reached 1,000 dinars. His estate is appraised at 150,000 dinars in gold. We found rubies, each of which weighed 1½ pounds; 6 chests filled with jewels; diamonds and cat's-eye: 100 pieces; gold: 1 *kantar*, approximately; silver bowls and pitchers: about 6 *kantars*; 100 caftans with the fur of grey squirrels and 400 caftans without fur; golden saddles: 20. We found also 50 horses, 100 mules and 100 camels. Of sheep, slave girls and Mamluks, we found a great many. In the latrine we found something that looked like a fountain. When opened, it turned out to have been filled with gold. Of wheat, fava beans and barley, we found 100,000 *ardebs*. We found out that he had 70 ships plying the Nile.

The accursed criminal hid his wealth and exerted a great effort so that no one might suspect anything. But our patience and perseverance paid off, and we were able to uncover that which he had hidden. Tomorrow we will bring out all that he had, loaded on mules, and these monies will be added to the treasury of our lord the Sultan, at a time when we are in most dire need of money, as our enemies are moving against us. Whoever among you wishes to watch the spectacle may wait at exactly the fourth hour, Arabic time, at mid-morning. Besides, Ali ibn Abi al-Jud will also be shown to you and you will see that he is safe and in good health, that he has not been tortured or hurt.

We have impounded thirty slave girls, one hundred and twenty male slaves and forty eunuchs, whom the accursed one had castrated with his own hands.

Nation of Islam! People of Egypt!

I have an appeal for you. Please let us know immediately of anyone who hoards money at the expense of the suffering Muslims. We can never allow the majority of the people to go hungry while a few are enjoying themselves. Please let us know. No matter how high the status of those hoarders of gold, silver, mules, slaves and slave girls, we will exact your rights from them.

In the Name of God, Most Gracious, Most Merciful.

'May God make this land secure.'

Details of the torture of Ali ibn Abi al-Jud, submitted to Shihab Zakariyya ibn Radi, Chief Spy of Egypt and Deputy *Muhtasib*, by the Head Spy of Cairo.

As per your instructions, a team of our most trusted spies conducted a very intensive search and investigation of what happened to Ali ibn Abi al-Jud. We penetrated very well-fortified walls and overcame enormous obstacles to unmask the secrets of the case. After tremendous effort, we were able to recruit one of those working with Zayni. But we didn't rely on him alone, he being the only one among Zayni's men to join us. We double-checked with other sources, some of whom are well known to you, the others we would hold on to until we've had a chance to communicate with you orally.

Now then: it turns out that there is no gaol in Zayni's house at Birkat al-Ratli, as it is a small house that cannot contain a gaol. Besides, any screaming inside would be heard near by. Ali has been moved to a faraway house, close to Helwan. The building is surrounded by trees and plants. We do not know when it came into Zayni's possession or who built it, but we are investigating. Under the house lies a gaol made up of fourteen cells. These are not cells in the usual sense: each is a rectangular room, three paces long (measured by an adult male); height: only one and a half handspans taller than a man of average height; its width is hardly enough for a man to extend his arms. In the middle of the ceiling is a small opening to the outside, from which the sky can be seen as a piece of silver, but the opening doesn't show at all from the outside. On top of the door on the inside is a lantern, which is lit in the same way as those famous lamps. That lantern faces one wherever one turns, and there is no escaping it, even if one were to sleep directly under the door. If one turns one's back on it, one would inevitably see it facing him. The lantern makes a hissing noise day and night that one doesn't perceive right away but which turns into a roaring sound in the ears after a while. A short wooden board drops from the wall for the prisoner to place his food tray on while eating.

The gaoler here is a handsome young man, who has a pleasant face and is soft-spoken – a departure from usual procedure. He smiled as he talked politely to Ali, telling him, 'If you need anything, just knock once with your fist on this door. When I say "Who?", you don't have to say your name, just say, "One". From now on, you are "One".' The smile never left his face as he spoke. On the face of it, his words sound like a polite request, but in essence they are an order. The cleanliness of the place didn't reassure Ali, who was overcome with a mysterious unspecific fear that was not acute but quiet, almost like the strange place. The door gives you the impression that it could be opened suddenly and the walls make you wonder if they could move in on you. The smile never changed. When the food was brought in, he was quite amazed: in front of him was placed rice pilaff, a bowl of *mulukhiyya* soup, a piece of meat and an orange. This is unprecedented in the history of gaols. However, something has to be explained here: Ali ibn Abi al-Jud and the other prisoners whom luck had sent to this gaol never felt full or satisfied but lived in constant, mysterious hunger. The food, on the surface of it, is more than enough and it does produce an immediate sensation of fullness, but it doesn't end that secret, mysterious hunger, which gnaws at the innermost marrow.

Ali ibn Abi al-Jud stayed for ninety-three days, during which he saw nobody but Uthman. If he knocked on the door at any time, Uthman would come right away, smiling, as if he never slept and never left the place. It was as if he anticipated when Ali intended to knock and waited. As time went by, Ali ibn Abi al-Jud began to fear the smile and the two calm eyes and tried to avoid them. He would sometimes have a desperate need to pass water and be about to explode, yet he wouldn't knock.

He recalled his life moment by moment. Night and day got mixed up. Time appeared to him like a disfigured body without any features. He knew that there were others next to him. He always heard Uthman asking, 'Who?', then his footsteps until he stopped at a nearby door. He completely failed to hear the voices of the other prisoners. He began to think about how to think. He hoped they would just burn him so that the world might go away from his head. The sharp point of the lantern tore his flesh and dried his blood. At a moment when he was feeling extreme distress, Zayni Barakat himself entered.

He said in a voice that was devoid of any pretence of friendliness, 'I am Zayni Barakat.'

Ali ibn Abi al-Jud looked at him in amazement. He had never seen him before. The following is an approximation of what Zayni said: 'As you see, Ali, we haven't done you any harm; we haven't hurt you. I know that you have a lot of money. You are a genius at hiding it. Tell me about it, and, as you know, I will not pocket one dirham of it; it is all going into the Sultan's treasury. As for your harem and your children, I guarantee their livelihood. Where is the money?'

Ali ibn Abi al-Jud shook his head.

'You deny?'

He persisted in denying. Zayni stood up.

'I wash my hands of any responsibility for you.'

After an indeterminate period of time, Uthman came in. He blindfolded Ali ibn Abi al-Jud with a wet cloth: a long-awaited moment. He doesn't know what they will do to him, but he will leave this strange place. That in itself is enough. He went down some stairs and passed through some doors, and Uthman left him in an empty hall. His joints trembled; he was afraid to sit down. Time passed with the heavy tread of a dying horse. His limbs trembled. Numbness crept up his back. His whole body shook. Suddenly a strong hand gave him a blow on the neck, producing sparks and blue stars in the dark emptiness surrounding him. Three blows created a hot belt round his neck. And here begin the actual details of the torture of Ali ibn Abi al-Jud.

The first day: they brushed the underside of his feet with water and salt. They brought a small black goat with a white spot in its head, and it began to lick the salt water slowly. His lips twitched, his ribs trembled. He started to scream. His screams turned into laughter until he fainted. They poured cold water on his face.

'Where is the money of the Muslims?'

He didn't answer.

The second day: it has been established beyond any doubt that Zayni Barakat never left the room adjacent to the room where the truth was being extracted. Early in the day he was annoyed by Ali ibn Abi al-Jud's steadfastness. He came into the room himself and kept pressing his middle finger into Ali's chest; at the same time one of his men raised a pitcher of water and caused it to drip, one drop at a time, at regular intervals. Before long, his neck shuddered and then his whole body shook as if it were about to split into two halves. He uttered a horrendous scream that came from his guts. At that point Zayni shouted, 'The Muslims' money, Ali.'

He didn't answer.

Mid-afternoon of the following day: they brought one of the forgotten peasant prisoners and took off all his clothes. They looked at Ali ibn Abi al-Jud and Zayni said, 'Look, I am going to do to you what I will do to this man.' They produced two red-hot horseshoes, which they began to nail to the heels of the terrified peasant. The screams of the peasant got to Ali's ribs, and, whenever he tried to close his eyes, Uthman slapped him on the back of the neck with a piece of leather.

The fourth and fifth days: three of the forgotten peasants were slaughtered and their necks were propped up against Ali ibn Abi al-Jud's chest. Zayni kept going in and out, feverish with vexation. 'Hasn't he talked yet?' Nobody answered. He hit the stone wall with his hands.

The seventh day: when they brought in Khalil, Ali ibn Abi al-Jud's youngest son, Ali appeared to be distracted and in a daze, but when Khalil screamed, his father's eyes grew wider and he didn't hear the screams of his son.

Comment: this is some of what we have received concerning the details of the torture of Ali ibn Abi al-Jud. But what is certain – and this is puzzling – is the fact that he didn't disclose where the money was. Where then had Zayni found out the amounts and places that he announced? What is amazing also is that, after a certain period of time and after the variety of new torture methods, which Zayni calls 'uncovering the truth', Ali ibn Abi al-Jud is healthy again. The only change is what has happened to his eyes: now he looks only straight ahead, as if he were blind, except that he is sighted. When somebody calls his name, he does not answer; rather he bends down and lets his tongue drop like a dog. We have no explanation yet of what happened.

Head Spy of Cairo

Announcement

People of Egypt! We enjoin what is right and forbid what is wrong. Our lord the Sultan has ordered that Ali ibn Abi al-Jud be executed by slaps of the hands: he will dance, like a woman, throughout the procession. Slap him! Slap him! Whenever he stops, slap him. Whoever wishes to watch the spectacle and to exact retribution against God's enemy should come out after the mid-afternoon prayers. People of Egypt!

Excerpt B, containing some of the observations of the Venetian traveller Visconti Gianti, who was passing through Cairo for the first time, coming from the Sudan and the lands of the Negroes, heading for the sea for a passage to his country after a long journey

Rajab 914 AH

I left the inn. I found the crowds to be oppressive; women mixed with men; little children tried to pass through the legs to watch. On the two sides of the road stood tough, armour-clad men, wearing blue uniforms with yellow collars. I learned from my interpreter, Ali, that the procession had already started from the house of Zayni Barakat, the *Muhtasib* of Cairo, that it stopped at the ibn al-Zaman school, turned at the Nile Island, came to Shubra, continued until Abu al-Manja Barrage, went from al-Hajib Bridge and entered Bab al-Shi'riyya. I was standing at Bayn al-Surayn (a big bazaar) in front of a shop that sold dyes. Anticipation spread among the people, who started shoving each other; a child screamed; a woman let out a long sound, which they call here a 'Zaghruda', which means an 'ululation'. The procession gradually began to come into sight: several saddled horses, all white, then four horses, the riders of which beat drums. They stopped so that a short man, who had the strongest voice I have ever heard, might make an announcement. Ali, my interpreter, informed me that he was asking the people to hit Ali ibn Abi al-Jud whenever he stopped dancing, until he dropped dead. The spot where he drops dead will receive a baksheesh (a tip) from Zayni. The truth of the matter is, this is the strangest manner of dying I have ever seen or heard of. Ali also told me that he was giving the people the good tidings that the Sultan had ordered that Zayni Barakat be appointed Governor of Cairo, in addition to his present post, and that Zayni had accepted the new position out of a desire to serve the people; whoever had any objection to his assuming the post of Governor should express his views after the Friday prayers in the biggest mosque in the capital (al-Azhar). The post of Governor is like that of our Province Governor. As for the Inspectorship, it has no parallel in our country, since it is a post that combines religious and temporal authority. Its functions consist of upholding what is right and forbidding what is wrong. In truth, I didn't believe what Ali told me about his urging the subjects to go to al-Azhar to make their opinions known. This is a custom that I have never seen or heard of prior to this time, in spite of my extensive travels. I heard the name of Zayni repeated many times. It seems he is an extraordinary person, and I will do my very best to meet him. When the herald finished, the noise of the bank of drummers sounded as if it were coming from one person. Shouting and hand-waving increased. I pushed past the people until I came close to a flat cart with small wheels pulled by two mules. On it was a man of medium height, who stood precariously, his eyebrows and beard shaven, his eyes lined with kohl, like women; his cheeks were scattered with red spots and on his head was a triangular multicoloured cap with a long tassle, which swayed whenever the man bent or gyrated. He is twisting his waist wildly in a non-rhythmic manner. As the drumbeats continue, he bends his torso backwards and shakes his chest frantically, then he stands straight and suddenly pushes his buttocks backwards. All the time the people are stretching out their hands, slapping and beating him. A man pushed a stick between his buttocks. On his forehead, sweat poured profusely; his tongue was sticking out. The people are displaying excessive zeal in slapping him and beating him, since if he drops dead, the people round him will get the reward. Zayni's men try in vain to prevent the hands that carry sticks or shoes from reaching him. The cart moved away, vanishing in the huge crowd. I swallowed my saliva; the face of the terrified and disfigured man blocked all else from my sight. In truth, I was afraid.

Announcement

Our lord the Sultan has ordered that Emir Kurt Bey, former Governor of Cairo, be remanded to the custody of the *Muhtasib* and Governor of Cairo, Zayni Barakat ibn Musa, to punish him and to recover what the accursed criminal has stolen from the Muslims.

Zakariyya ibn Radi

ZAKARIYYA ibn Radi thinks that his meeting with Zayni had taken place on the same night. Usually nobody disturbs him during the last hours of the night, except for something very serious. That night he listened to Wasila telling him about her country. He likes to listen to descriptions of people's customs, habits and different kinds of food. He asked her why the slave merchant hadn't deflowered her after her abduction. She has got used to the strange questions and no longer feels ashamed. She said that he coveted her as everyone who saw her did. 'It happened near Aleppo that . . .'

Zakariyya reached out and placed the tips of his fingers on her lips. 'Tell me about Aleppo.'

She was not perturbed; she has got used to his changing the subject suddenly. She began to recall the city, the roads leading into it, the postmen in the small buildings that stood by themselves in the middle of nowhere, the eyes of the Syrian women as they watched the caravan and how they hurried to lock their doors. She remembered how the guards greeted the caravan. Mansur, the merchant, knew them all and paid them a certain amount of gold regularly, and they not only never bothered him but guarded him as well. Zakariyya is holding a polygonal glass. He never drinks wine. He doesn't like his consciousness to be affected for one moment. It happened two hundred years ago that wine was responsible for the downfall of one of the best spies that Egypt had known, during the reign of al-Zahir Baybars. Ibn al-Kazaroni became an alcoholic and started to babble in private and in public about all he knew of the affairs of the State and people. This resulted in his disgrace and later the loss of his life. He had perfected a new wine concoction, which, it was said, got a person very drunk if he as much as smelt it. The new wine was later named after him: the

'Kazaroni wine'. The Sultan Nasir ibn Qalawun was later to ban it and dump what had already been made. Zakariyya loved fruit juices and had imported a device from Tlemsen to squeeze the toughest kind of fruit and remove the seeds.

Zakariyya was sipping grape juice, passing his hand very softly over Wasila's neck as she kept on talking. Her words suddenly trembled as his hand went up and down and as his fingers got close to her ear. His hot breath at the back of her neck made her whole body tremble; he felt that as he followed the tremor on her lips. Suddenly he took her little ear into his mouth, sucking it. She gasped, her limbs convulsing and her hands reaching to cup her breasts. She closed her eyes and felt transported far away. Suddenly, with one stroke, he tore up her dress; he didn't unbutton it; he just ripped it and listened to the sound of the cloth being torn. The beginnings of the soft world appeared to him. A movement of her eye betrayed how young she was, opening up from a bud into a flower, a girl at the threshold of her feminine life, surprised as she was brought to the edge of the world. Did such pleasure really exist?

At that moment, at exactly that very moment, Shihab al-Halabi struck the brass shield that hung in the lower courtyard. Zakariyya went down to him. Zayni Barakat had sent a messenger requesting that Zakariyya come right away for a matter of great gravity. Zakariyya made a gesture with his head, went up to the wardrobe and selected an Azhar shaykh's garb. Since his confirmation as Deputy *Muhtasib*, Zayni has not sent for him; the only contact between them has been in the form of a daily report sent by Zakariyya to Zayni. Naturally it is a specially prepared report. Only a few times did Zayni send inquiries about matters of 'general interest', as he said. Zakariyya responded, amazed at how petty the requests sometimes were: for instance, the names of the slave girls that Emir Bashtak had purchased in 907 A H; how much wine Emir Qusun drank every night; the name of the mother of a pickle vendor in Husayniyya; favourite dishes of Chief Justice Abd al-Barr; the number of metres of fabric needed to make an embroidered cloak for Khond Zaynab, Tashtamur's wife; how many Mamluks had six fingers on each hand and how many of those were in each garrison.

Zakariyya received these requests in disbelief at first, but he quickly changed his attitude; there should be no room for derision here. A man like Zayni wouldn't make these requests unless they were really important. When he met him the first time at Birkat al-Ratli, he realized what a rare kind of man he was. Each of us was born to meet the other, he thought. He went downstairs quickly. When he gets close to Zayni's house, he will not show his surprise but will talk calmly to him. Nothing comes as a surprise to Zakariyya. He will suggest to him that he had anticipated Zayni's intention to summon him. He went out to the big courtyard; the leaves on the trees rustled audibly. How wonderful it would be to go back to Wasila; he hasn't had his fill of her yet. His eyes wandered, looked for Mabruk. Mabruk is the only one who would always spot him, even if he were disguised as a jinnee. To strangers he is a mute, but he does speak a little. Sometimes he takes Zakariyya to task and upbraids him. Zakariyya accepts that and listens to it and does what Mabruk tells him to do. Zakariyya asked, 'Where is Zayni's messenger?' Mabruk led the way. Zakariyya whispered, 'If I am not back by tomorrow noon, tell the Head Spy of Cairo to take his orders from Shihab al-Din, the Private Secretary. Understood?'

Zakariyya entered the sitting-room in the hall. A veiled bedouin got up. 'Welcome to the Supreme Shihab Zakariyya.' Zakariyya looked at the veiled face, the wide leather belt studded with metal spikes. He examined his outfit. These little details helped him get rid of his surprise when he saw that the messenger was none other than Zayni himself. Zayni got to the point right away, with no beating about the bush. 'Very briefly, I want to know exactly where Ali ibn Abi al-Jud has hidden his money.'

Zakariyya leaned his forehead on two fingers of his right hand. Briefly, as if in an official document, he said, 'Don't know.' A strange bird made a strange sound in the sky; the night was getting old.

Zayni got up in one movement and slowly came close to Zakariyya. 'You, Zakariyya, know exactly where Ali ibn Abi al-Jud's belongings are. Nothing is hidden from you. If anything were, I wouldn't have risked my reputation and confirmed you as Deputy *Muhtasib*. You know, not because you were Ali ibn Abi al-Jud's deputy, but because you are Zakariyya. Do you understand me? Because you are Zakariyya ibn Radi, the ablest man to assume the post of Chief Spy of Egypt.'

Zakariyya didn't answer. Let Zayni say what he will. A secret was about to be divulged; the light is faint and trembling, about to glow, but something was holding it back, about to snuff it out.

Zayni Barakat ibn Musa said, 'My friend, you know where his money is, just as I know where Sha'ban's grave lies.'

Now, some time after Zayni's visit at the end of the night, the heat of what Zakariyya had decided after Zayni's departure has not cooled off. It may take many years, but what he has decided must be carried out; he must see it accomplished, a real fact. What force has ever been able at any time to prevent a chief spy from achieving a goal he is bent on? Neither man nor demon nor a thousand talismans will prevent him. He will never forget the days of his self-imposed seclusion following the visit. He ordered that no reports be sent to him. He told Mabruk not to let him see anybody's face. He chewed his food with great reluctance when he had to eat. When he ended his seclusion, his men came to congratulate him, but they turned back in disappointment. He met them in a despondent mood. He was secretly pleased when Shihab al-Halabi told him that the Sultan's Chief Physician was willing to come and see him throughout his seclusion. One week after Zayni's visit, Mabruk came in and said, 'Zayni Barakat is here.'

Zayni stood in the courtyard, feeling with his cane the huge trunk of a palm tree covered with brass plate. He said, 'I prefer to sit in the sun. My house at Birkat al-Ratli doesn't see the sun.'

Zayni poked the earth with his cane. Zakariyya leaned his forehead on his right hand.

'Please listen to me and bear with me.'

Zakariyya nodded. Zayni had come in his regular clothes, not in a bedouin outfit.

'Many thoughts are running through my mind, but they will come to nothing until I go over them with you. Please correct me, if you think it is warranted. You are more knowledgeable and more experienced about the matters that I will touch upon than I am.'

His words betray a clear tentativeness. Zakariyya is secretly reassured.

'I wanted to share with you what I envision for the system of spies. Can anyone imagine enjoining what is right and forbidding what is wrong without strong, loyal eyes that can see what I can see, everywhere?'

Zakariyya said quickly, 'You have your men.'

Zayni shook his head quickly; there was pleasure in his voice, perhaps because of Zakariyya's responsive participation in the conversation.

'I knew you'd say that. But you, Zakariyya, overestimate my men. Isn't it better to see the world with two eyes, instead of one? True, you will say, and you are absolutely right, we have thousands of eyes. True. I have no quarrel with that. But if there were another group, with a different system, a different method; wouldn't that be useful? First of all, you've got to forgive me, because we don't see enough of each other. I am very, very busy, Zakariyya. Imagine a man administering justice in this day and age! You know what the Ottomans are planning and, no matter how long it will take, war is inevitable. There is no doubt about it. I've told our lord and I am telling you now – my confidence in you impels me to tell you even more – the East is not big enough for both the Ottoman State and the Mamluk State in Egypt. It is either us or them. Don't be surprised, Zakariyya. Or, in other words, don't feign surprise, for you know that better than I do. If someone sneezes in Constantinople, you hear him here. You are aware of every movement there. And, God willing, we will beat them thanks to the blessings of the house, which our lord is protecting. As you see, then, things are hard. We've got to meet often and to co-ordinate. Whatever my men report, I will submit to you in summary form. You have tremendous experience, the most precise system in the world for utilizing the mails and the homing pigeons. You and I are brandishing the sword of justice. You and I are keeping the scales absolutely even, going neither this way nor that way. What I want, Zakariyya, is for our men to be the instrument of justice among the people. Everybody has to know that.'

Zayni suddenly stopped talking. Zakariyya kept looking at the floor. Moments later he said, 'And then what?'

As if Zayni had not stopped talking at all, he said quickly, 'To save your time I have brought you a few pages in which I've written what I envision. Please look them over and tell me what you think.'

At the door he shook Zakariyya's hand. 'I invite you to dinner at my house. What time would be good for you?'

Zakariyya said, 'I hardly ever leave the house.'

Zayni's smile grew broader. 'I will have quite a spread for you!' Zakariyya said, 'I'll send word and we'll meet soon.'

He went back to the garden to postpone thinking about what he had said until the evening, after he had read those pages. Every letter must be scrutinized. This was no joke. He was getting more and more convinced of what he had decided that night, but the truth was, Zayni was a man the likes of whom he had not known. Sometimes Zakariyya thought that he should have come years later than this age; how many years he didn't know, but it would be more fitting to live in a far-off time, where he could find those devices he dreamt about but couldn't quite define because of his inability and his age's inability to realize. This Zayni has also come from that mysterious, far-off era, in which he wanted to live. A man like Zayni should not be underestimated.

With nightfall, Zakariyya is beset by an annoying thought that has been recurring since Zayni's secret visit. He goes back to doing something that he hasn't done for a long time, roughly since assuming the post of Head Spy of Cairo, before being promoted to the post of Chief Spy. Tonight he goes way back in time, to the time when he used to trail people himself. He used to disguise himself as a craftsman of one kind or another. At that time he started a new method of shadowing somebody: trailing a person by walking in front of him, and that is something that only a very able spy can do. Zakariyya started as a spy from the very bottom of the ladder; in that he was unprecedented. Tonight he is tuning those senses that had served him very well when he began as a spy. But where? Here in the house? How did Zayni learn of the Mamluk Sha'ban? As was his custom when he wanted to think through something puzzling, he got hold of a pen and began to draw figures and lines and circles, which appeared to have no meaning but which helped him to focus his thinking. Who accompanied him when the prisoners were slaughtered and Sha'ban buried?

*Mabruk

He is not going to make any exceptions to the suspect list. Nobody is above suspicion. Mabruk will be placed at the top of the list until the opposite of what he thinks is proved true. Then, who can be presumed to have followed them or watched them during the burial? On that night the house was completely empty. But he is going to make a list of those who frequent the house.

*Shihab al-Din al-Halabi
*The Head Spy of Cairo
*All the men of the Bureau, all of whom are known to him

Perhaps one of them was able to penetrate, was able to see them in a manner that couldn't yet be determined and conveyed what he saw to Zayni. This is a real disaster. How can a stranger look through the walls? He has to review what has been written about his men, one by one: where they came from, their circumstances, likes and dislikes and thoughts. Then he would narrow down the list, extend the lines, draw the circles until the noose is tightened round one particular neck. Then he would move on to his acquaintances and relatives outside the Bureau.

*The Harem
  (a) His four wives
  (b) The slave girls

As of tonight he is going to see each of them. He will start with the oldest, Hekmat, the first of his women. He has deserted her and hasn't visited her for some time. Tonight he will start with her, and, when he smells the musk, sips the grape juice and eats the chicken smothered in ghee and rose-water, the questions will come from him at random. The rest will have their time later on. The slaves: Wasila – but she is only a child who came to him weeks before Zayni had taken office. Who knows? Nobody will be above suspicion. Then there remains the possibility that Zayni may have used a new trick that is unknown to Zakariyya. That is what he must find out. He must go to Birkat al-Ratli. So, Zayni is proposing to him an investigation of the ways and secrets; he wants to learn his methods. Zakariyya is not unaware of the annoyance that came over him. Admittedly he is careful with everybody, including those closest to him, but he has never gone so far as to investigate each and every one of them. And where? Those closest to him; those who work in his house; his harem! Let those who criticize and curse him come and see his worries and his suffering. He drew several circles. From now on, each one in his household shall be a spy against the others, each woman and each man will watch the other. He remembers some history of spies: the Mongol king, one of the grandsons of Genghis Khan, was able to penetrate the operations of the Baghdad spies. One man, by himself, assumed the post of Deputy Chief Spy of the whole Abbasid Empire and thus was able to learn all the secrets of the Abbasid Caliphate, which he conveyed to the Mongols for a long time, until they sacked Baghdad, fully familiar with the terrain. The rest is history.

Zakariyya got up with a great longing to take a stroll in the city wrapped in darkness. But he is not going out. When he finds out who had informed Zayni of what happened! He imagines it now as anger mounts in his heart. He sees in his mind's eye the new varied methods of torture that he will devise for the perpetrator of that deed. What novel method that can occur to neither man nor demon is he going to invent to end his life? What technique? As for what he has decided in the case of Zayni Barakat ibn Musa, he will never go back on that, even if it takes all the rest of his life.

In the Name of God, Most Gracious, Most Merciful.

'Call unto the path of thy Lord with wisdom and fair exhortation and reason with them in ways that are best. Your Lord is best aware of those who have strayed from His path and those who have gone aright', as the Glorious Quran tells us.

What I offer you here is nothing more than a few ideas and thoughts that have occurred to me. If you think they are valid, I hope we can work together to implement them so that justice might be established and strengthened. In this endeavour, we shall care about nothing except pleasing God, for, as you know, the noblest of God's creatures, peace and prayer be upon him, has said, 'He who pleases God by displeasing people shall be protected by Him from their evil; and he who pleases people by displeasing God shall be placed in their charge by God. He who does good in his relationship with God, God will make good his relationship with people. He who does good in his private life, God will make good his public life. He who works for his afterlife, God will spare him the evils of this life.'

Now then: the corner-stone of our work (yours and mine) is the establishment of security and justice throughout the Sultanate. I shall confine myself, for the moment, to my own jurisdiction (Cairo and Lower Egypt, which the Sultan has recently added to my Markets Inspectorship). As for Syria, that is a region on which *you* are the expert and over which I have no say. In order for justice to be established, strong and solid foundations have to be laid. As we both know quite well, this post is hated by the people, since those who have preceded you have only shown its brutal aspect. This has been done so successfully that the people have forgotten how necessary it was and how the world couldn't go on without it.

Hence the goal for which we should work is to have every spy enjoy the love and respect of all men, religious or secular. This shall be accomplished by several means, which we will discuss together. My most immediate concern at the moment is to break down the groups and classes among which we will work and to determine the relative importance of each and the different degrees of emphasis to be placed on them.

Egypt is divided into classes ('We have placed some of you above the others in rank'), as the Glorious Book says:

(1) The Sultan and leading emirs;

(2) lesser emirs and Mamluks;

(3) sons of Mamluks, men of the turban (shaykhs), members of the guilds; artisans and merchants;

(4) common people.

As far as the first group is concerned, it could only be penetrated by specialized spies who are very sophisticated, learned and presentable, have debating skills and are knowledgeable of this group's traditions and arts. Our aim here is to protect our lord the Sultan and the key emirs. I think the spies to be assigned to penetrate this group have to come from within the group (a departure from current practice).

The lesser emirs and Mamluks are covered by a team that works for you and is doing a good job.

The third group requires emphasis and great attention, as it exerts great influence on the groups closest to it, the upper (key emirs) and the lower (common people and the rabble).

Common people are always the trouble-makers and might occasionally sway men of the turban under certain circumstances. I find I must break down this group further:

(a) Azhar students and students of lower grades in Quranic schools: these have to be trailed constantly. From time to time, trouble should be stirred up to find out those who stray and are prone to support dissension and sedition and instigate the rabble against their masters. These should not be brutalized in public, for that might create resentment among the common people; rather they should be treated in different ways, using different methods, which the two of us will agree on.

(b) As far as the common people are concerned, they are just a herd that moves whichever way you move it. They are a sea at the mercy of the winds, a beast with no mind, which, once you tame it, will obey you. Lives in this group are worthless, for the harder life gets, the less value it has and the less the effort to hang on to it. Hence it wouldn't hurt if some of them were to disappear from time to time, by means unknown to anybody. This terrifies the rest of them.

I need your help in preparing lists that contain the names of all craftsmen, artisans, manufacturers and merchants; one list for the butchers, another for the masons, marble-workers, dyers, painters, thread and tassel makers, mother-of-pearl workers, weavers, pastry and beverage vendors and others.

We must make an inventory of the new-born babies as they come into the world. Each father who sires a child and does not report it to my deputy in his region shall be flogged, and, God willing, I plan to hang a number of them at the beginning so that the rest might be deterred. In this way we will be able to keep track of the numbers of those coming, those who will succeed us. We will then record their names in special registers so that we may follow them as they grow up and receive an education, religious or temporal, in a guild or military body (that would be for the sons of emirs and the Mamluks). Reports about them would be filed periodically, so that we may learn of their leanings, predilections and of points of potential danger about them so that if we leave this world when our time – which only God knows – comes, we would leave for those who come after us a useful record, containing what we have experienced and seen in our time. Regarding this point, I have decided to make a public announcement of it and to start implementing it, now that the Sultan has concurred with me on it.

Now that we are approaching an era beset by crises and troubles and in view of the numerous factions and races now living in the land of Egypt, I think that little tags made of leather should be prepared and carried by all, young and old, sighted and blind. Each of these tags will bear a number corresponding to the person's number in the register. It will also show the person's occupation and his address. The tag must bear two stamps, one of which is that of my deputy in the quarter where the person lives and the other that of the head spy of the same place. Whoever is caught without the tag shall be severely punished. Upon the demise of a person, his family shall hand over his tag to the head spy, who would then forward it to the Bureau so that the person's name may be struck off the register and entered into the registers of the dead. Women shall not be excepted.

Since I assumed the post of *Muhtasib*, I have noticed that from time to time certain stories have begun to circulate among the people, aimed at slandering some key figures in the Sultanate and at defaming me personally. This is a matter, you will agree with me, that must be stopped once and for all in order to preserve the dignity of the emirs and key figures. To give you a simple example: when I wanted to illuminate Cairo using those lamps, there was a lot of talk about the subject, and it was considered a great event, which was recorded in the history books, a fact that forced me to go back on something that I had decided and begun to execute. That didn't make me angry; maybe my timing was wrong. What really bothered me and hurt me were those stories that were bandied about among the common people, even though they loved me. This has led me to thinking that those stories and anecdotes have been deliberately fabricated. As Deputy *Muhtasib* and as my deputy in all my posts (I have just decided that), you are likely to suffer tomorrow from what I suffer from today and be beset by the same problems. For that reason, I think you are the only person capable of stopping and nipping these stories in the bud. I shall accept no excuse. No insurmountable obstacle stands between you and whatever you want.

Accept my greetings. I pray God to make this a secure country.

Muhtasib of the Land of Egypt
Governor of Cairo
Zayni Barakat ibn Musa

Amr ibn al-Adawi

HE doesn't let him out of his sight, and, when he goes anywhere, he learns about his comings and goings from his colleagues. He would sit quietly among them, then would ask casually in a tone that he now knows how to manipulate completely, 'Has anyone seen Said al-Juhayni?'

One of them would say, 'He has been out since this morning.'

Another might say, 'Said is a regular at a coffee-house near Qalawun Mosque.'

And Amr would say, 'Said is a good man,' and fall silent.

A few days ago Amr went out on the street. He recalled faraway days in which he held on to his mother's *galabiyya* as they went out to the fields to dig up some sweet potatoes. His nose hasn't forgotten the smell of the mist nor the smell of baking bread at noon. He remembered the reeds, the glowing fire of the oven, running with the boys when the *Muhtasib*'s agent came and the heart-gripping fear in the eyes of the women behind the small windows. At the Nahhasin market he smelt the smoke of the ovens adjacent to the Qalawun bath where the fava-bean pots were cooking.

'Good morning.'

Hamza ibn al-Eid al-Saghir raises his hand. 'Welcome! Welcome!'

For the last three weeks he has been stopping at Hamza's place every day, drinking a cinnamon milk drink and paying a whole dirham instead of a half-dirham. One day he didn't show up. The following day Hamza expressed concern and hoped that nothing bad had happened to him, then prayed God to give him a long, protected life. Amr comes here at specific times. By keeping tabs on Said, he has found out when he usually goes to the coffee-house.

The Head Spy of Cairo had said, 'Said's frequenting Hamza's coffee-house is a new development, which only you have reported.

Also his spending time smoking tobacco cured in molasses is a new sign. What made him choose this café in particular? These are matters that have to be cleared up. In the beginning there were suspicions that he might be using the shop as a place for suspicious meetings, but close surveillance has proved that he spent the whole time alone, speaking to nobody but Hamza ibn al-Eid al-Saghir. The words exchanged between the two of them were also thought to be suspicious, but it turned out that they never went beyond ordering fenugreek or greetings and words of welcome – all words that a customer and café owner might ordinarily exchange and nothing more, even though they were a little too friendly. Also, the way he ordered fenugreek was not suspicious; he never accompanied his order with any surreptitious gestures or secret codes. Maybe his words contained very profound meanings that eluded even a sharp and smart observer. What is puzzling is what he thinks about during the hour or two that he spends at the café.'

On another occasion the Head Spy said, 'You must stay close to Said al-Juhayni.' Amr knows him; he sleeps in the same *riwaq* not far from him and is familiar with his temperament, his moments of joy, dejection and the accompanying signs and the grimaces of his face. Hence, it would be possible for Amr, if he had a chance to observe him closely, to follow the twitches of his face, the tremors in his eyes and the movements of his hands. Maybe they will find out something. They had to be careful, though. Amr had to sit in a place where Said couldn't see him. Amr wondered how that could be done when the café was so small. At that point the Head Spy spread out a wide sheet of paper on which was a sketch of the café, its utensils and built-in benches. He pointed to a gap in the wall close to the charcoal-burner and the fenugreek and salep.

'Here you will sit. Said doesn't come in but stays outside. You can monitor his movements without his seeing you. But your sitting here should not come about all of a sudden. As of today, go to Hamza ibn al-Eid al-Saghir; treat him in a friendly way, be liberal with him. The fenugreek there is half a dirham, pay him a whole dirham. Do you like fenugreek? Oh, I forgot that you loved cinnamon milk. It is the same price, anyway. You will get all your expense money at the beginning of every week. As of today, you will go to the café for fifteen days after the sunset prayers or any time after the evening prayers. You may sit anywhere you like;

Said doesn't go at those times. On the sixteenth day, go early to the café and ask Hamza ibn al-Eid al-Saghir to let you sit here at this gap. Stay put and don't move. Pretend to be sad with no desire to speak. Said will come and will sit here. See? From where you are sitting, you will see him quite well, whereas he will not be able to see you. Do you understand?'

Amr marvelled at the precise details and at how the shop had been reduced to such a size as fitted on the paper. The Head Spy said, 'Go, with God's blessings. Listen, do you need money?'

Amr shook his head. 'Your kindness has been too much already!' His hand remained in the hand of the Head Spy.

'How's your mother?'

It was as if a bitter pill dissolved in his mouth. He has had no news of her. When the Shaykh of the Chapel of the Blind came back, he rushed to him, because he knew that she would send him something from the village: some bread or some aged cheese to resume that which time and distance had interrupted. Amr will never forget the man's voice as he said, 'I couldn't find a trace of her. They said in the village that she hadn't died.' For some time she had been talking about a voice coming to her in her sleep, warning her that she did not have long to live and that she had to see Amr, her son. And in order not to interrupt his studies, she told her friend Sikina al-Duda, who made clay pots, the very woman whose hands had received Amr at his birth on a clover-stack and cut his umbilical cord, 'Duda, I am going to Cairo to see the love of my heart.'

Duda said, 'Cairo is far, and you've never been to it.'

But she insisted and told every man and every woman in the village. She even stopped the children on the street and told them about her son, Amr, how she had to go to him and how she wished they'd grow up to be like him. Duda gave her some provisions and one day Duda got up and Amr's mother was nowhere to be found. They looked all over, in the sweet-potato and water-melon patches, but they couldn't find a trace of her. After a little while, no one remembered her any longer. Nobody had needed her; it was she who always needed people. The Shaykh of the Chapel of the Blind was amazed and said, 'I thought she had come here to you.'

Amr's eyes were blurred; he saw his mother on a deserted dusty road, connecting two villages. He saw her crossing many irrigation canals and ditches and going through palm-tree groves. Night fell and she had not eaten anything to warm her stomach; she asked people who were coming and those who were going how to get to Cairo. Sometimes Amr is certain that she is close, that perhaps he will meet her suddenly. Will he know her? Perhaps time and the trip have changed her. Perhaps her eyesight is so poor now she wouldn't be able to see him. For three years, he hasn't heard her voice, hasn't seen her twitching eyelids. He himself has changed. At times he harshly blames himself for being away from her for three years. How could he do that? It is no use. A wound has firmly planted itself into his guts, his heart. But what would happen if she passed in front of him in the street while he was watching Said? Would he rush out, blowing his cover, to embrace her? Said would then figure out what is happening; the Head Spy would know that the whole plan had been undermined. Amr is not alone in the café. He knows that full well. There is another eye watching him, perhaps Hamza ibn al-Eid al-Saghir. Maybe someone else. There is only one person who is not a suspect: Said al-Juhayni himself. Who knows? Maybe he was being put through a harrowing test as a prelude to promoting him up the spies' ladder. The Head was very visibly touched. He said that that was a condition worse than death and that he would tell the deputies throughout the land to look for her: she must be found. At his meeting with the Head Spy he saw an unmistakable, noticeable change in the way he talked to him and treated him. His tone now is more gentle; he is showing excessive interest in his personal affairs and is not threatening him as usual. That's better. Amr feels closer to him after the meeting.

Amr was now sitting, cramped, in the gap. He learned from the Head not to get bored or tired with the passage of time; he may be forced by circumstances to peek through the lattice-work of a *mashrabiyya* for a whole day, awaiting the arrival of a specific person who may never come. He shouldn't allow boredom to find its way to him. There is a dampness in the gap, and in the heart there is a yearning for an old woman whose whereabouts are unknown to him. He doesn't know what land she is in or in what land she is going to die. But that yearning has to make way; he is working now, earning his living. Hamza left him alone as he had requested.

Three Quranic schoolteachers came. One of them was making a

loud noise drinking his salep, which annoyed Amr. The oldest of the teachers mourned the passing of the good old days when the boys themselves sought to memorize and recite the Quran. But times have changed; a ten-year-old sits in front of you as if he were sitting on burning coals. No sooner is class over than he bolts away.

One of them said, 'Mischief is rampant! God help us!'

A third man said, 'These are the signs of the Hour of Resurrection.'

Amr wondered to himself what he meant by the 'signs of the Hour'. He should prick up his ears. It is true he is here for Said, but he should listen to what is happening; maybe he will get a valuable conversation. Maybe he can get by accident that which he cannot by design and planning.

The oldest man said, 'Yes, by God. I wouldn't be surprised if someone told me about a mule giving birth.'

The third man, the shortest of them, said, 'I take refuge in God, Master. If a mule got pregnant and gave birth, that would be a sign that the world has come to the end of time!'

The one with the gruff voice said, 'And how do you know it is not coming to the end?'

Amr listened. Nice conversation, but there must be a point to it. What code are these old men using? He should prick up his ears to the full. When he met the Head Spy for the first time, he had told him, 'An able spy is two ears and two eyes; he hears and he sees; he memorizes and conveys what he sees and hears even while asleep.'

'Well, we thought we had seen everything! But now, look at these wondrous innovations! Now a man cannot go from his house to the mosque without this piece of leather. Isn't it amazing?'

The short one said, 'This is unheard of!'

If only Amr knew which Quranic school they ran! He is going to ask Hamza about them in the evening or tomorrow so as not to arouse his suspicions and so that he may prove that he is following correct spying procedures, if it turns out that Hamza is the one watching him. Amr noticed that two merchants had arrived.

The first one, with grey hair, asked, 'I wonder whether the Sultan has taken off his light turban and put on his big one?'

'If that were true, it would mean that he has recovered from his illness, but there has been no drum beating the good news.'

Amr wondered what quarter they were from.

On the other side, the eldest shaykh was saying, 'One of the signs of the Hour is the appearance of the Antichrist.'

The grey-haired merchant said, 'I am sure he put on the big turban and met Emir Tuman Bey.'

The second shaykh said, 'By God, I feel as if the Antichrist is among us already.'

Amr's heart is beating faster; this is serious stuff!

The young merchant said, 'I don't believe for a moment that the Sultan has put on the big turban. Otherwise, where are the good tidings? Where is the good news?'

The grey-haired shaykh remarked, 'The only thing missing is for the sun to rise from the West!'

The young merchant said, 'Anyway, that's not impossible . . . maybe.'

A thin dark man with a small blue turban, a Christian, entered. Hamza ibn al-Eid al-Saghir had told Amr a lot about him. He doesn't speak much. Waiting for him to speak is like waiting for rain in Ba'una. He comes here four times: once after sunrise as soon as the shop opens; before noon; in the mid-afternoon and just before closing time. Oh . . . the shaykhs are laughing. Did he miss anything?

The grey-beard says, 'God will make me live long enough to take pleasure in the calamities of my era!'

They laugh. He must remember this sentence well.

The young merchant says, 'We bought the *ardeb* for a dinar and a half and now we have to . . .'

They had changed the subject. The Christian, each time he went to Hamza's place, drank a cup of anise without sugar and smoked two narghiles. He didn't use the tobacco provided by the café. He carried a cracked leather pouch filled with good, golden tobacco, which had a unique aroma. Hamza didn't know where he got it. He used exactly the same amount every time. He would ask Hamza to set up the narghile, arrange the charcoals and followed him closely with his eyes; then he would begin to smoke, exhaling the smoke from his nose as if he were in pain, moving his head right and left, complaining in silence to the narghile, telling it about a terrible injustice visited upon him. Towards the end of the narghile he would look at it, arrange the coals, press them, place his hand round them, bend over to blow on them, with a mute supplication that the tobacco might not die out.

The short shaykh says, 'Yes, by God! Yes, by God!'

The grey-beard says, 'But I didn't believe him. He swore by all that is sacred, but I didn't believe him.'

Hamza told Amr what he knew about him. He lives in the poultry quarter, near Khan al-Khalili, no wife or children. Once Hamza saw him crying, shedding tears that flowed freely from his eyes, without sobbing. Amr wondered where he got the tobacco and what made him so depressed? It was as if he were talking to men who were invisible to all eyes except his own. Oh! Said is sitting in front of the café; a sudden arrival that he hadn't noticed. He is not going to mention that he saw him all of a sudden. That would be to his disadvantage. He sat on the bench. Amr is trying to be calm and to slow down his heartbeats. It is a long way indeed before he attains perfection: to be able to see whatever there is to be seen, yet with his feelings unchanged, unmoved. That is a very sophisticated level, which only very able spies can reach. If only there were a way by which a person could get to what was going on in another person's mind! Then spies would know the significance of a tremor of the eye, what thoughts produced a quick twitch of the nose. Amr sat back, so that his back was pressed against the walls of the café.

Announcement

People of Egypt! We enjoin what is right and forbid what is wrong. That which was hidden is no more: six months ago Zayni Barakat ibn Musa, Markets Inspector and Governor of Cairo, took Emir Mamai al-Saghir in custody. After he made him talk, he seized his property. It turned out that he had 90,000 dinars. That is 20,000 more than the Sultan had assessed. All the monies were handed over to the public treasury.

People of Egypt! Zayni Barakat ibn Musa, Markets Inspector and Governor of Cairo, has levied an impost on the houses of sin and ordered that admittance to said houses be denied to those under twenty, to preserve morality and the *shari'a* law. People of Egypt! After two days Zayni will travel to Damietta and Daqahliyya to inspect conditions, keep the bedouins out and establish law and order there. In his absence Abd al-Azim al-Sayrafi, Treasurer and Financial Officer of the Inspectorate, shall be the acting *Muhtasib*. Everything will remain the same: violators shall be punished.

People of Egypt: Zayni Barakat ibn Musa, Markets Inspector and Governor of Cairo, has pledged to our lord the Sultan to hold Emir Baktamur al-Saqi, Prince of Ten, and to extract the monies of the Muslims from him. Zayni estimates these monies to be 50,000 dinars, net, not counting hidden assets.

Urgent

To: Head Spy of Cairo

On Monday morning when the people went out to celebrate Shamm al-Nasim and mark the advent of spring with fun and merry-making, I saw Said al-Juhayni. I immediately took cover. He was not alone; rather he was accompanied by two women, one of whom was advanced in years. I followed them closely from Bab al-Khalq to the Bulaq gardens. There they were joined by a shaykh wearing a turban; name: Rihan al-Bayruni. I know that Said visits his house frequently.

Said seemed, I am absolutely certain and have no doubts whatsoever, to be madly, deliriously, head over heels in love with Shaykh Bayruni's daughter. I have learned from my colleagues at al-Azhar that he frequently repeated the name 'Samah' during his sleep. Samah is the Shaykh's daughter. They spent the whole day at the Bulaq gardens. Said was alone with her twice and they spoke to each other. I shall follow up developments.

Amr

Announcement

People of Egypt! Abd al-Azim al-Sayrafi, Treasurer of the Markets Inspectorate, announces that everything stays the same, that prices are the same as set by Zayni. Any merchant meddling with the prices shall be proscribed until Zayni comes back.

Announcement

People of Cairo! Abd al-Azim al-Sayrafi has ordered that an egg merchant be hanged on the door of his shop because he raised the price of eggs.

Announcement

People of Cairo! Abd al-Azim al-Sayrafi has ordered that the tongues of three young men be cut off. They were caught making a disturbance.

Announcement

People of Cairo! Abd al-Azim al-Sayrafi has ordered that three Moroccans be handed over to the Supreme Shihab Zakariyya, First Deputy of the Inspectorate and of the Governor of Cairo. It was proved that the three were in touch with the Ottomans.

Announcement

People of Cairo! Abd al-Azim al-Sayrafi orders everyone to prick up their ears and inform against whomever they suspect has any connection with the Ottomans. There is a reward.

People of Cairo! Tomorrow, Supreme Shihab Zakariyya will go to Shaykhun Mosque to lead the prayers and deliver the sermon: the mosque will be open to all who wish to go.

In the Name of God, Most Gracious, Most Merciful.

'May God make this land secure.'

Secretariat of the Bureau of Shihab Zakariyya ibn Radi.

Memo sent by homing pigeons to Zayni Barakat ibn Musa, Markets Inspector of Cairo and the Land of Egypt and the Governor of Cairo, in Damietta.

1) Who is Shaykh Rihan al-Bayruni? He is Shaykh Rihan ibn Zayd Muhammad al-Asyuti ibn Amir al-Fadil Ahmad ibn Ibrahim. As for 'Bayruni', it is an agnomen, which has stuck to him ever since he studied logic under a blind shaykh who came to the old mosque at the end of 805 AH from the lands of Shah Ismail al-Safawi. His name was Shaykh Bayruni; he was neither a Shiite nor a member of any of the Rafidite factions. Rather he was a very learned Sunni. He lived in Egypt, never married, died in 883 AH and was buried in the Eastern Cemetery with the pious scholars.

Shaykh Rihan worked as a junior clerk in the secretariat of the Chief Justice. During that period he composed the judgements and judicial decisions handed down by the Chief Justice. He was good at his work, which gave him a chance to see at close quarters the emirs and key figures of the State whom he had only seen in processions previously. When he saw them, he used to wonder and his thoughts ranged far and wide. Do these notables laugh like the rest of the people? Do they tell jokes or engage in repartee with each other? Are they on intimate and affectionate terms with each other? He frequently wondered how they ate and how food was offered to them. He would close his eyes and see himself as a protégé of one of the leading emirs and close to the very circle of the Sultan but who didn't know what to say to them. It has even been established, and there is evidence to support this, that he wondered aloud with one of his friends sometime between 863 AH and 875 AH about whether a person like Emir Tamurbugha, the Commander in Chief at the time, urinated and did what everybody did, i.e. defecated? He even said to his friend, 'How does the Sultan take off his pants and bare his huge posterior when he mounts one of the women in his harem? Does his saliva run? Does he close his eyes? Do the corners of his mouth tremble in lust and desire?' Bayruni considered these to be very important questions, which deserved a huge tome. He wished he could get close to the great notables, sit with them, talk to them about the times and about their dreams and hopes. He saw himself sitting with the Commander in Chief, smoking together after a delicious supper, the Commander in Chief turning to him and telling him a secret that only he knew, or Emir Jukandar al-Muhammadi, the Polo-stick Bearer, telling him a very private matter concerning the Sultan and asking him not to tell anybody, because if the Sultan were to learn that it was disclosed, he would cut off the heads of the one telling it and the one listening to it. His happiness and bliss are unimaginably great when secrets that nobody else knows are confided to him, when he would walk on Saliba Street or through the lime market under Bab al-Futuh Gate, surrounded by the crowds of people buying and selling, their heads filled with the petty and trivial matters of life. As for his own head, it is filled with secrets. When he sits in a shop drinking fenugreek or salep and milk, he sees himself as having spent the whole night at the palace of a great emir, without sleeping or rest, and yet he has to go to the Bureau to compose the judicial decisions and judgements. At that point, he would actually feel that his eyes are really tired; he even would yawn several times and look around him. People sitting around would notice his lassitude. If they ask him, he will explain the situation to them immediately; he has been sitting up all night with the emirs, being the boon companion of the high and mighty. They would understand his excuse and would seize the opportunity of his time of rest to beg him to take their petitions or pleas to his acquaintances in authority and to intercede for them, for he is a good-hearted man who never turns away a person in need.

The judicial decisions that he has to compose keep piling up, and he gets upset with Abd al-Barr's urging him to hurry up. He sees himself going in to see Shaykh Abd al-Barr, the Chief Justice, and standing before him. Abd al-Barr is taken aback: what has so changed his employee? His glances are fixed, his turban big, smelling of perfume. Calmly Shaykh Rihan turns to him and asks him simply not to hurry him up. His voice is soft. No, loud. No, it would be better if it were soft and confident. His words are eloquent. He will tell Abd al-Barr that he stays up late with the emirs, that he is part of the inner circle of Emir Baktamur, the boon companion of Mintash and the confidant of Emir Tuman Bey himself. As for Emir Tamurbugha, he leans on nobody else's shoulder but his. Abd al-Barr will be frightened and stricken with awe. He orders Shaykh Rihan to take his time and never to hurry up, to dispose matters however he sees fit. It is not improbable that the Sultan would dismiss Justice Abd al-Barr and he would run to Shaykh Rihan, begging him to intercede for him with the Sultan to restore his judgeship.

It happened around the year 876 AH when Shaykh Rihan was twenty-five years old, that he found the way, with one of his friends, to the house of Saniyya ibnat al-Khubbaiza near Fustat. There he was introduced to a peasant girl, whom the woman had picked up from the street and taught to fornicate. It has been established that that was the first time in his life that the Shaykh had slept with a woman. During the first encounter, he told her that he had a very important position, one that was very close to Emir Aqbugha. The wench asked him who Aqbugha was and he said, 'The closest man to the Sultan.' The girl beat her firm, erect breast and gasped, 'God Almighty!' He pursed his lips and warned her not to tell that secret to the madam or else her head would be cut off. His secret post made it impossible for him to appear in public with women or to go to them. The women of any of the emirs or notables are at his beck and call. He was actually convinced that many of them in fact desired him. But he couldn't do anything about it; his secret post stood in the way, and even before the post, there was his conscience. As he talked, he paused several times and shook his right-hand finger, warning her never to divulge what he was telling her, even to herself. The wench was frightened; she believed what he had said, especially since he had given her something that she rarely got, a sizeable tip.

Every Monday and Thursday, Shaykh Rihan went to Fustat. One time he didn't find the wench and refused to sleep with another woman, despite Madam Saniyya ibnat al-Khubbaiza's entreaties. When he went back, he found his wench all made up and waiting for him. When he disrobed and laid down next to her, he struck his forehead with his hand saying, 'Oh!'

The girl was afraid. 'What's wrong?'

He answered, 'Something terrible! I forgot a very important matter that Emir Mintash had asked me to look into.' He fell silent for a few moments. Merely hearing those names and the simplicity with which he utters them make her very frightened. He apologizes, saying, 'By God, I have done him wrong! Mintash is very generous with me and gives me every consideration, but I pay no attention to him. Yet he should forgive me: I am too busy. Yes, by God, too busy!' He blows and hits his knee with his fist.

The girl doesn't know what to say and, when she is overcome with confusion, she creeps towards him and presses herself against him, saying, 'Don't worry, my love; don't think of it, darling.'

Another time he would lie down next to her, laughing in content-ment. 'That Tuman Bey! What a man!' Her eyes grow wide as he talks about the Sultan's executive secretary as if he were his closest friend, without titles or formalities.

She asks him, 'What about him?'

He says, 'He stayed up with me all night. What a man! And what strange, very strange stories!' Then he would say, 'But I don't know how that happened. How?'

Once he had the nipple of her left breast in his mouth and as he was passing his lips over its edges – his favourite practice – the wench said, as her body trembled, 'Saniyya ibnat al-Khubbaiza is having a difficulty with the *Muhtasib* – it was during Ali ibn Abi al-Jud's administration. He raised the tax on her operation.' She was hoping that Shaykh Rihan might talk to one of his high and mighty close friends.

At that point the Shaykh's naked body shook and his veins almost burst with anger. 'You are mad! We are dead. Did you, mad woman, tell ibnat al-Khubbaiza anything of what I told you?'

She trembled all over, swearing by his life, by the Prophet's family, by her late father whom she had never seen but of whom she thought – and that is true – that he was the only high and mighty man she knew. She cried in his arms until his anger subsided and he regained his composure.

He said, 'I wouldn't object if it was a reasonable request in which I had no stake. But what would I tell any of my friends the emirs? Do I tell them that I want justice for ibnat al-Khubbaiza? They will ask, "How do you know ibnat al-Khubbaiza?" Yes, when the matter has to do with my high and mighty friends, one must weigh things, not take them at face value.' Shaykh Rihan remained perturbed for some time. Whenever he met ibnat al-Khubbaiza he would look at her and try to detect any indication that she knew what he was saying. He feared that she might surprise him with a request for intercession with the authorities or that her tongue might slip when talking with the patrons of her establishment, revealing anything about his numerous stories to the wench. He learned from her the identities of some of those patrons: employees in the bureaux of emirs, in the Inspectorate of Markets, and some shaykhs. Some lesser emirs went secretly.

It happened at that time that Justice Abd al-Barr summoned him. As he went to him he kept thinking that maybe his stories had come to Abd al-Barr's attention. The Justice will punish him twice: once for going to a house of sin and the second for the nonsense he has been saying. He kept preparing what he was going to say; he was going to ask the Justice to forgive him for going to that house, as people's tongues showed no mercy. But what would he say about the stories that he had been fabricating about the emirs? Abd al-Barr received him warmly, smiled to his face and made him feel at ease. That was unprecedented; Abd al-Barr was usually very stern, unkind and spoke harshly. He told him that he had been visited by Emir Salamish, the Jamdar in charge of helping the Sultan get dressed; the Sultan would stand up, turn his back and stretch his arms, whereupon Salamish would place them in the sleeves, then make sure that everything is on right. This is a post that only the most trustworthy person ever got: the Sultan had to trust him to the point of turning his back to him, making himself so vulnerable. Justice Abd al-Barr said that Emir Salamish had asked for a trustworthy man to write his letters. The Justice searched for a long time and could find no one more faithful than Shaykh

Rihan. But, in order for the matter to be concluded, he had to find a good bride to marry, since Emir Salamish never accepted bachelors in his palace. Then Justice Abd al-Barr said, 'Besides, you are not young, Shaykh Rihan.'

Shaykh Rihan got up and kissed Justice Abd al-Barr. He walked in the street, dancing with joy: finally he is going to see the emirs and the guests, write the letters, be privy to the secrets of the State. He wished he could tell that to the wench, but she would only wonder. Hasn't he always told her how intimately close he was to the high and mighty?

He put on his best clothes and went to the palace of Emir Salamish, showing excessive politeness and decorousness, to suggest that all his life he has been serving in the houses of the high and mighty. He waited to meet the Emir, but he didn't meet him. He said to himself that perhaps the Emir was too busy. When the Deputy of the Emir asked him about his marriage, he told him, 'I married two weeks ago.' And indeed he had gone to one of his relatives, Master Mahmud ibn Salamah by name and a lentil merchant at Athar al-Nabi by trade. He owned three freight boats on the Nile, which transported the crops, in addition to earthenware jars and clothing, from Upper Egypt. (He died in 909 A.H.) Anyway, Master Mahmud lauded Shaykh Rihan, who had memorized God's Book and was safeguarding *al-Bukhari*, where the Prophet's *hadith* was preserved. A week later his marriage to the Master's daughter was consummated in his house at Fustat, until he could find a house of his own to settle in. The Master used to say, 'My daughter's husband is a chief with the Emir Jamdar.'

In the palace of Emir Salamish, Shaykh Rihan was given a small room in a building unattached to the palace. It was a dark room illuminated by a lantern, day and night. The second and third day, the Shaykh was not received by the Emir, nor was he the first and second week or the first month. It has actually been established that he never met the Emir.

Whenever Master Mahmud ibn Salamah met him, he would ask him about the health of the Emir Jamdar and he would make a gesture with his hand saying, 'Yesterday he was not his usual self. When he got up he discovered that his right eye was twitching, and that was not a good omen. So he spent the whole day depressed.' The Master would express alarm and would shout so that his fellow merchants might hear him talking about a great emir, and he would wonder, 'Has the physician seen him?' Shaykh Rihan would say, 'Yes, he came and bled him.' At that point Master Mahmud, in a loud voice, would ask his son-in-law to convey his greetings to the Emir and tell him about his sincere prayers for his recovery. Shaykh Rihan would nod and answer him also loudly, for he knew the Master's purpose, 'I will tell him. He has sent you special greetings with me. Yes, by God!'

Frequently he would come to the Master and, while approaching from a distance, would shout, 'Emir Salamish sends you Islam's greetings', whereupon the Master's face would light up; he would twist his moustache and run his fingers through his beard, saying, 'When you see the Emir, please convey my greetings.'

This kind of talk began to hurt Shaykh Rihan and cause him sorrow. He hasn't seen Salamish in person once. Even his deputy he met only once when he took the job. All correspondence was sent to him with one of the eunuchs. It has been established that he never saw the Emir, even when his first daughter Samah was born. (She was born in 902 AH, three years after his marriage; no other children. This happens only to a few men.) Rather Emir Salamish sent some dinars and some garments with his deputy. To be exact: ten Ashrafi dinars, some fabric and an embroidered shirt for a little girl.

Two years after Samah was born (904 AH) our lord got furious with Emir Salamish – and that is a well-known fact – when he did not wind the white cloth around the turban carefully, which led to its coming undone the moment our lord the Sultan sat down to receive the Abyssinian envoys. This caused the Sultan some perplexity and almost embarrassed him. He summoned Salamish, interrogated him and then threw him to the floor and beat him up until he almost perished, because he thought that that improper winding of the turban was a deliberate act. He ordered him to be gaoled at Maqshara Prison. Salamish is still there in gaol, almost twenty-two years after the incident.

As Shaykh Rihan's luck would have it, before that incident Emir Salamish had sent him to Emir Tughluq to compose letters going to Yemen. While Shaykh Rihan was at Emir Tughluq's, the turban incident took place, and Tughluq invited him to stay on. Shaykh Rihan accepted and his happiness was greater, since he was in direct contact with Tughluq and went out with him more than once. He told Master Mahmud and some of his close friends that some of his friends among the high and mighty had secretly told him of what was going to happen to Salamish, advised him to stay away from him and put in a good word for him with Tughluq, who was no stranger anyway and took him in. Whenever he rode with Tughluq, he would try to get closer to him and would keep looking round, hoping that somebody who knew him would see him riding a mule with a high saddle in Tughluq's procession – a status that very few attained.

Years ago a Southern Egyptian boy, a distant relative of Shaykh Rihan's, came from the village of Juhayna. He stayed at his house for some time until he moved to the Southern Egyptian *riwaq* at al-Azhar. In truth, we couldn't be certain whether he spent any time alone with Samah, Shaykh Rihan's daughter, especially since she was no more than ten years old when he arrived.

According to what we can verify with our own eyes and ears now, we cannot pin-point the date on which his heart began to conceive love for her. But after analysing the patterns of his walking and talking with her on Shamm al-Nasim in the Bulaq gardens, his love for her has been established as fact. The passage of time makes his passionate love even stronger, although he sees her only rarely (of that we are certain).

It has also been established that the Shaykh is unaware of Said's feelings for his daughter. Currently we are in the process of gathering more precise details in order to arrive at the quintessential truth and its secret essence.

Secretariat Bureau of the Chief Spy,
Deputy *Muhtasib* and Deputy Governor of Cairo
Seal: Zakariyya ibn Radi

Announcement

People of Cairo! Abd al-Azim al-Sayrafi announces that Zayni Barakat ibn Musa, *Muhtasib* of the Land of Egypt and Governor of Cairo, will soon arrive back from his trip to Southern Egypt. Shop owners, singers, *rababa* players and dancers are hereby instructed to go out to welcome him as he comes in from Giza at noon on Tuesday, the day after tomorrow. Whoever fails to come will be severely punished.

Kom al-Jarih

DISTANCES without beginning and without end in the eyes of the seeker, travelling on foot, his only sustenance love of the Higher Essence, a yearning that draws him to the ends of the earth. He travels, reflecting on the lessons of the beginning and the end. How painful the sorrows of the heart in ruined homes and in populated cities where the people had forgotten the first and the last! How beautiful the mariner's stand at the helm of a ship under sail! The whole universe is a sea; the ship tilts to turn upright and turns upright to tilt. The mariner shouts a cry from the heart of the throat, the deepest voice, the essence of hope and the end of pain, the cry of a mariner in the face of an infinite void with no land to be seen. The Shaykh doesn't remember where he fought off the vertigo: he placed his hands around his mouth and from the arteries of the heart, the pupils of the eyes, the deepest recess of the liver, the passion yearning to the last horizon, the years of life, the secret well of the heart, the pain of an old passion, the remnants of an orphaned love, he shouted a single scream that nullified the inside, lightened the burden of the body; the innermost secret loomed; the primeval truth was on the point of revealing itself; the stars whispered and the reluctant sky shed a few tears: Oh, One! One! Where are you? Save me! Save me!

He doesn't remember the name of the sea. When he travels all over the world he doesn't care to know the names of the countries. The house is big, with no visible width or length. Giving oneself hope of arriving is a great sin. Neither this year nor the one following it bears good tidings. In his scream he posed the question, crossed the seven seas and the seven lands, went beyond the Qaf mountain, the Waq Waq lands, the Islands of Women and went through the belly of the whale. In his passion's eye he sees the lote-tree of the utmost boundary, the ultimate hope. His feeble, saddened voice was heard there. Oh, if only the sea were all around him now! If he were standing at the top of the big mast shouting in anguish into the wind, his scream turning into a long rope of passion and yearning. Now, however, it is no more than a whisper, distilled perplexity, a cry for help whispered by a bird with feeble wings, which migrated alone and was now lying down, companionless. He has witnessed many moments at which he thought deliverance was at hand and that only a few short steps separated him from the primeval truth. Events, however, would intervene, cloud the vision and bring shame on the soul. But in an age like this, it would be in vain for divine light to appear; it is impossible for the body to grow so delicate and light that it becomes translucent. He was now seeing his faraway days, when he saw the world, rested his cheek on the Black Stone, played with the wild tigers, sucked pebbles, seeking a little moisture that would tame the scales of thirst encrusted on his throat, and talked to cannibals. If only he would bid farewell to stillness and emerge into motion, depart from stagnation to ceaseless everlasting! Never before in his life have events forced him to seek a long seclusion, but after only a few years in his homeland he is forced to dig a cellar with his bare hands, in which he can close his eyes to the prison and his ears to human voices. At the beginning of one's life, one discovers that the world is crooked and one tries to straighten it out, but at the end of one's life, when everything appears as it really is, there is no hope in any change. Even his children are unknown to him. When he tries to comfort Said as he cries, he sees him as one of his own children. He hasn't seen any of them as a youth. Early in his quest for the truth, he married in Khwarazm, but before the end of the first year he left for the mountain, leaving a vestige; he didn't know whether it came into this world in a city in eastern China, in a village on top of a very high mountain in India or on a small island in the big eastern ocean, with a total population of forty males and females. He never embraced any of his children. He doesn't know how many they are, but his heart is filled with love for them. Wherever he went, he was certain that he knew how they were doing and that they knew where he was, for the whole world is one. Maybe he saw one of them in the crowded bazaars of Persia, in the port city of Basra, in one of the regions of Kazakhstan, not knowing them and knowing them. Had it not been that the tears had dried up and permanently deserted his eyes, he would have cried with Said. It was the first time he saw him cry, a hurt child. Evil deeds are like Siamese twins. Now the spies no longer bother to hide when they follow him. Some of them would loudly exclaim when they are near him, 'A man like that marry this beauty!' He would hear someone calling her name, 'Samah', and would turn around in fear. The whole universe is listening. The Head Spy has sent for him four times; no one could disobey his orders. As for Zakariyya ibn Radi, he was now leading the prayers at the Shaykhun Mosque, loudly reciting the Opening Chapter of the Quran, the people kissing his hand, seeking benediction from him. From the Citadel, the head of the State, its very nerve centre, letters were being sent freely to the land of the Ottomans; everything, every secret whisper was being sent by Khayrbak, Janbirdi al-Ghazali and Yunus al-Qadi to the Ottomans.

On the night of Samah's wedding, Said, like a bird whose slaughter was not completed, wandered about. All those high and mighty men came to the wedding. The bridegroom was the son of a great emir who had left the service and died two years earlier: a young man with a future. They surrounded Shaykh Rihan, whose joy overflowed all bounds. They made small talk and joked with him. Zayni Barakat had a sumptuous banquet for the wedding party. As for Burhan al-Din ibn Sayyid al-Nas, he had total monopoly over fava beans in Egypt. If someone were to ask about that, he would be told, 'Has this affected the price of fava beans? It hasn't increased one fraction of a dirham.' Zayni had a ready, convincing answer to every question, no matter how tough. Everything appeared to make sense: a man was nothing but the product of his time. It sometimes happened that the product of the time is concentrated in one single, specific person, who epitomizes all the good with all the bad. The Shaykh could see the epitome of all turbidity. When he shared his sorrows with the pious, ascetic Shaykh Baha al-Haqq Ulwan (he hasn't stopped yet; he is still a great traveller; every night he invokes God's name in a different place; stillness will come at his death), Shaykh Baha al-Haqq said that whenever he thought he had got rid of the loads and burdens, he saw the illusion. Many a time has he thought of retiring from the universe, spending the rest of his life in the cellar. But he has been blaming himself. How come harm was hovering over the land where he had come into the world, where he had chosen to spend the time remaining before the final deliverance? To see the country tranquil is an impossibility; what he considers is as simple as the letters of the alphabet, as legitimate as breathing, is in reality an impossibility.

Shaykh Baha al-Haqq shook his head. 'We are all burning: you in your stillness and I in my travels. But if the soul shied away from what time has allotted it, we'd all be lost.'

FOURTH PAVILION

Zakariyya ibn Radi

THE letters and cards of invitation were dispatched to the Maghrib, to the kings of Fez, Abyssinia, Venice, India and China. None was sent to the Ottoman State. The present situation does not permit the Chief Spy there to come to Cairo to attend a big convention where all the top-notch chief spies from these countries will meet to discuss matters of the profession, the state of the art and exchange stories and anecdotes about what it is like to be in the field. History books will mention this convention, perhaps in one line. What takes place in it will remain classified and confidential, but its effects will be felt everywhere.

Only two men in Egypt know of the convention: Zakariyya ibn Radi and Zayni Barakat ibn Musa, whose idea it was. This will be the first time that something like that takes place. Zakariyya didn't hide his pleasure. Zayni hinted that when he sits with them he will be able to figure out their methods and techniques. Of course, none of them is going to disclose what techniques they use. It is up to Zakariyya to find out their secrets, using whatever methods he likes, so that, should hostilities break out between Egypt and any of the kingdoms represented, Zakariyya would find that he is in possession of the most vital secrets of the country in question. He would become so familiar with the methods of its spies that he would be able to figure out the most complex developments while sitting here in Cairo. When Zakariyya heard Zayni's ideas he wondered where he got them from. But, after a short silence, he told him, 'You know, two years ago I intended to do exactly that, to gather the chief spies of the world, but I got distracted by other things.' Zayni tapped Zakariyya's knee, saying, 'Of course, a matter like that couldn't have escaped you.'

Zayni was now touring Southern Egypt, visiting every village, accompanied by a group of his tough men and agents carrying scales and weights. Zayni is now the *Muhtasib* of all the land of Egypt, over which he administers justice. Reports of his tour reached him day by day. He has managed to recruit two of Zayni's men, but could not find a single Inspectorate spy. After Zayni's tour in Southern Egypt, he will go to Damietta. A few months ago he pledged to the Sultan to pay a certain amount of money for Damietta and Mansura. Zakariyya doesn't remember now how much, but it must have been about thirty thousand dinars. After the pledge a number of emirs went to Zayni. They said among themselves: 'If Zayni succeeds in collecting 30,000 dinars, the Sultan would be very angry at us and would say, "Look at the integrity of Muslims: that is how it should be!"' They met Zayni and expressed fear for him. Damietta and Mansura yield no more than 10,000 dinars a year. What would happen if the year ended and Zayni couldn't pay the Sultan's money? Besides, how much money would he make? Is he going to overtax himself? Will he let the peasants chase him away whenever he goes there? He would spend his own money and hang some people. In return for what? Zayni answered them, saying, 'I am not going to kill or hang anyone because they are late in paying. I will find an excuse for whomever is suffering a hardship.' He was silent for a few moments, then he added, 'May God help me collect the Sultan's money; if Damietta has never yielded more than 10,000 dinars a year throughout the ages, I will improve its conditions and will get out of it amounts that no one can imagine.'

The emirs left him, extremely vexed. Zakariyya sent secretly to each of them; he would never forget what he had decided one day. He hinted to them that Zayni had evil intentions towards them. They got angry and excited and went to the Sultan and spoke to him harshly and showed solidarity against Zayni, but the Sultan answered them vehemently, telling them: 'This is just like you; the minute a man who wants justice appears on the scene, you fight against him!' And when they exceeded the bounds of decorum, Ghuri flew into a rage; he threw down his turban: 'I swear by God I shall depose myself and you may take it over, a bankrupt wasteland. The coffers are empty; the Ottomans are trying to pick a fight with us; the populace is restless, the Frankish merchants no longer cross from Alexandria to Damietta, and we have lost the revenue. When a man appears who has a genius for collecting money, we oppose him and thwart him. This is a state of affairs that pleases neither Muslims nor infidels.'

Zakariyya himself was at a loss to understand. How is Zayni ever going to gather the 30,000 dinars from Damietta and Mansura? On the same night he decided to send to the Head Spy of Damietta some experienced men who would monitor Zayni's methods and his innovations. During the last few months, Zakariyya has not denied his secret admiration of Zayni's planning and execution. Zakariyya holds certain men in esteem, no matter how much he hates some of them. Take the Chief Spy in the Ottoman State, his enemy number one now. He has never seen him, but he has a full profile of him: how much he likes boys and women, his ability to make decisions concerning destinies. The Bureau has compiled a whole book on him. It was as if Zakariyya had been his companion for a long time, even though he has never seen him. Zakariyya thinks he is one of the greatest spies. Two years ago he created a special unit, some members of which spoke the language of the Ottomans as if they were born in Constantinople itself. He divided the men into several groups, one of which specialized in the history of the Uthman family members, their likes and dislikes and their conditions. Another specialized in the affairs of the Ottoman army and its new weapons. Zakariyya holds the Ottoman Chief Spy in perfect esteem, especially after a certain fact had been established beyond a shadow of a doubt, namely that a number of Mamluk emirs were in touch with the Ottoman State. When Zakariyya found out, he was very alarmed, not because some Mamluks were in contact with the Ottomans – that was natural and easy to uncover, and, if the Ottoman Chief Spy couldn't do that, he wouldn't deserve to be in that post. What really alarmed Zakariyya was their ranks. They included, for instance, Khayrbak, one of the emirs closest to the Sultan. Zakariyya didn't inform the Sultan; more evidence had to be obtained. He decided to monitor Emir Khayrbak's correspondence, but he found nothing. There must, then, be a secret method of contacting the Ottomans, which has eluded his men thus far. All the evidence is hearsay. And even after definitive evidence became available, he would keep it under wraps; there may come a moment when he could use it like a sword over Khayrbak's neck if he started something against him. Without concrete evidence, the Sultan won't believe it. Khayrbak has got so close to the Sultan that he gave him the governorship of Aleppo, so close to the Ottomans. However, hints must be made to Khayrbak that Zakariyya is closing in on them. True, they would become more cautious, but they must know that Zakariyya knows and is not doing anything about it. There is an idea deep in the recesses of his mind: who knows how things will turn out? Maybe one of them will take over. Zakariyya hates it when the idea comes to the surface in his mind. He hates to think how low they have sunk, betraying their master and the country that nurtured them until they grew up to be strong men. Now they offer it all, fully cooked and ready to eat, to the Ottomans. That is a crime of which Zakariyya is well aware and about which he has a definite feeling, unlike many other things. Zakariyya has often wished he could recruit one of the Ottoman emirs; he would make him welcome and pay him handsomely, but he would also secretly despise him. But, so far, the Ottoman Chief Spy has beaten him by recruiting more than one emir, whereas Zakariyya has not managed to recruit even one comparable to Khayrbak or the others.

When Zakariyya learned of the meeting of the emirs who hated Zayni, he wondered what they wanted: would they go along with what he has been planning so carefully, for such a long time? But getting rid of Zayni will not come about by a dagger thrust or a potion placed in his food or horsemen ambushing him in Southern Egypt or on a rural dirt road in Damietta. That won't do. Zayni is the challenge of a lifetime. How easy it would be for Zayni to get rid of him the same way, despite Zakariyya's precautions. When he decided to finish Zayni off, he didn't mean to kill him but rather to finish him while he went on living, eating his meals, sleeping with his women; killing him and keeping him alive at the same time. That is much more difficult and might take a lifetime to accomplish. But not everybody is treated in the same manner; a man like Zayni is very rare! Zakariyya gives him his full due of esteem; he studies his techniques and adopts those that help him, even if these techniques had been used against him personally. Zakariyya kept the emirs under surveillance and sent spies after each of them. How are they going to get rid of Zayni? The ears conveyed to him the conversations in the closed halls; the old women brought him fresh news. The emirs were even more upset when Zayni had Emir Ozdamur al-Saghir turned over to him and pledged to extract one hundred thousand gold dinars from him. Among themselves they said, 'If we let him do what he likes, he will get us one after the other. We will lose the respect of the populace, and the Mamluks in Egypt will have no dignity left.'

Zakariyya realized that the situation was quite serious. The following night he went out in disguise to Birkat al-Ratli. At that time Zayni was getting ready to start his second trip to Southern Egypt. At Bab al-Futuh Gate he slowed down. How did he decide to do that? Is he really going to Zayni to warn him that his life is in danger, to suggest that he change his place of sleeping every night in a house picked by Zakariyya and surrounded by guards and monitors? At the same time, he would monitor every movement the emirs make. He hasn't forgotten the annoyance that Zayni caused him. Is he weakening before him? Isn't that his chance? No, that is a quick way to get rid of him. If the emirs slay him, the populace would mourn him and cry over him. His stature among them dead would grow more than it did when he lived. When Emir Taibugha, during the reign of al-Nasir Qalawun, began to call for justice and helped the poor against the rich, the emirs were very incensed and they killed him slowly with poison. The populace figured that out and they wept over him and lamented and mourned for a long time; whenever anything happened they would say: 'If only Taibugha were among us!' Even when the Chief Spy at the time commissioned the scholars to write a booklet and several treatises casting aspersions on him, the populace grew even more fond of him. They made a sugar doll and named it after him: the Taibugha *balaliq* are still displayed in pastry shops on the anniversary of al-Husayn or Sidi Ismail al-Imbabi or Sidi al-Layth or any other saint. But the emirs are stupid and don't understand these things. Has Zayni offended or harmed any of them as he has Zakariyya?

Zakariyya will never forget the night he had incontrovertible evidence about a matter, which he was reluctant to accept or be convinced of for a long time. That night he went into the room, unable to breathe and unkempt in appearance. When he faced her in the light of the new day stealing through the lattice-work of the *mashrabiyya*, he was certain that what he had been reluctant to accept was true. He knew he had been duped, and that was a feeling he had never had before, even when he started as a junior spy, relaying all kinds of information. All the evidence had not succeeded in convincing him, but the look in her eyes at that moment ended his reluctance, slew all doubt. He remembered Egypt's greatest spy, Kazaroni, when he caught one of the emirs of al-Zahir Baybars and dismembered him, beginning with his male organ, keeping him alive in pain until the emir finally died after forty-five days. He began by shaving off her hair, which flowed like the hate in his veins. He disfigured the face so that the heart might not relent before the young features. He inserted the red-hot tip of his dagger into her and twisted it slowly. She couldn't bear it and expired after only one night. An overpowering grief gripped his heart, and, when grief knows its way to the heart of a man like him, it is a bad sign of weakness. He blamed himself for being so hasty in killing her. But she couldn't bear it at all; he had tortured her too much. He had to know from her where and when Zayni had got to her and was able to recruit her and introduce her into Zakariyya's household weeks before he became *Muhtasib*. He had to learn from her whatever he could about the team of spies working with Zayni. The Head Spy of Cairo said, 'This team of Zayni's is either so well knit that it is impenetrable or it doesn't exist at all.' Zakariyya was certain that it existed; otherwise, who did Wasila belong to? Indeed, he was over-hasty in killing her: were there others in the house facilitating her contact with Zayni? He has to monitor the household, check times when Wasila went out, find out which fabric and perfume shops she went to, the merchants she talked to. All these matters will be taken up by Zakariyya personally. The story of Wasila should not get out; it is a blot on his record that would make him the laughing stock of the spies of the future. Oh, she must have told Zayni how he slept with her. A shiver ran down his back. It was as if Zayni was with them every time they were alone, his gleaming eyes scrutinizing his bare posterior. Who knows? Maybe one of his women now is in touch with Zayni. Whenever he thought of that, he backed away and didn't touch any of them. Has Zayni harmed anyone as he has him? And yet he is knocking on his door to tell him what took place among the emirs, to protect him. When he undertakes to protect him, he is sharpening a secret, unbending blade ready for Zayni's heart.

Zayni met him with open arms. The conversation started with talk about what was happening in al-Azhar. Many scholars were publicly saying bad things about the Sultan. They were even attempting to tarnish the reputations of Zakariyya and Zayni himself.

Zayni said, 'I'll send you the names of those trouble-makers at al-Azhar. And by the way what's the latest on that boy . . . what's his name . . .?'

Zakariyya said, 'Said al-Juhayni.'

Zayni shouted, 'Right!'

Zakariyya smiled. 'None of his movements escapes us. We know him better than he knows himself. After his beloved's marriage, he was very sad. We thought he was going to jump into the Nile or swallow some poison pill. Then he began to sit by himself very frequently at Hamza's café. Sometimes a friend of his named Mansur sat with him.'

Zayni asked, 'Mansur?'

Zakariyya said, 'Mansur al-Rakaybi. I have enough information on him. He is more rational than his friend and more promising.'

Zayni made a gesture with his hand. 'Anyway, let's go back to that boy Said.'

Zakariyya said, 'Addiction to tobacco and the new drink that we got from Yemen: coffee. Months after his beloved got married, he began to frequent the house of Saniyya ibnat al-Khubbaiza. He goes there every Tuesday. We do not know the reason for that.'

Zayni bent forwards and rested his chin on his hand. 'Send a lot of men after him, not so much to monitor his movements, but to make him feel that somebody is monitoring them.'

Zakariyya said, 'We did even more than that. I ordered my men to follow him, then loudly call out Samah's name. He almost went mad.'

Zayni laughed, 'Good! Good! And the prayers?'

Zakariyya smiled. 'Everybody is kissing my hands now.'

Zayni's laughter grew louder. 'Listen, Zakariyya, you've got to win their hearts even more. Tomorrow, ride your horse, have one of your men dress as a peasant and another as a Mamluk. Get the second to give the first a sound beating. Naturally, your procession will happen to be passing there at the time. Get off your horse to come to the aid of the peasant and justice and arrest the Mamluk. Once you've done that several times, the people will love you. And when the spies of the future arrive, they will find, for the first time in human history, a great spy who is not only good at his work but one who is loved and respected by the people. This will help us administer justice.'

Zakariyya fell silent; he liked the idea so much he almost forgot what he had come for. Did Zayni know why he had come and decided to distract him? Should he postpone talking about the emirs? If Zayni didn't know why he had come, he would be perturbed and would be trying to work out the reason behind Zakariyya's visit. However, after a few moments of silence, rendered more oppressive by a faint light from a solitary candelabra, Zakariyya suddenly said, 'You, Zayni, are going to be killed.' Zayni listened. Two days later, as Zakariyya was going on a stroll in his garden he recalled Zayni's face as he rose suddenly and embraced Zakariyya. He actually saw tears well up in his eyes as he said, 'A man like me cannot live without you, Zakariyya.' At home Zakariyya noted that he had developed a secret liking for Zayni, especially after Zayni had agreed to go to the places that Zakariyya had selected and to sleep under his protection. But, will his heart ever forgive Zayni? Never. To succumb or back away from the old decision would be suicide for Zakariyya. In order to reassure himself that he hadn't changed his mind, he began to revive an old project buried deep in his mind. He sent for Abu al-Khayr al-Murafi', an old spy who had worked for a time deep in the South. A few days ago he arrived in Cairo. He bragged, 'In my life, I've wrecked tens of homes, destroyed families that no one ever thought could be destroyed.' If Abu al-Khayr hovered around any man, he would bring him down, especially if it came to his knowledge that that man was enjoying a peaceful life or was happy with his wife and children. He loved to turn joy into grief, happiness into misery and wealth into poverty. He was dedicated to closing down homes and ruining people's happiness and joy. He danced and rejoiced when a woman was divorced. Zakariyya looks at his elongated face, his hunched back, his eyes, which look upwards all the time. From time to time, Abu al-Khayr breathes in hard through his nose as if having difficulty. He wonders what will happen in the following moments.

Announcement

People of Cairo! We enjoin what is right and forbid what is wrong. Zayni Barakat ibn Musa, Markets Inspector of the Land of Egypt, Governor of Cairo and Controller of all Lower Egypt, announces that he will deliver a speech on Friday and will inform the people everywhere of the truth of the matter and the secret behind what was and is being said.

If you want to find out the truth, go to al-Azhar Mosque on Friday, after prayers.

Excerpt C from the observations of the Venetian traveller, Visconti Gianti, who arrived in Cairo for the second time in 917 AH, stayed there for some time, travelled to Syria and Hejaz, then returned to Cairo and stayed there.

By this time he had learned the language of the country and no longer needed an Arabic interpreter.

Dhu al-Qa'da 920 AH

I didn't put on the garb of a Turkish merchant, especially since the people and the police have been seeking out every Ottoman they could catch. At best they would hand him over to the Chief Spy of the State to punish him severely and make him confess what information he was assigned to gather and send to the Ottomans. I went out holding a short stick to fend off the dogs. I saw the city seething. It is rare to see people, especially women, out after supper in oriental cities, especially Cairo, which is kept in order by a strong man, very religious and greatly respected by the people, who is the object of this seething. I mean Zayni Barakat. No one has had more longevity in his post than him, even though conditions here are very volatile; a man may assume a post in the evening and lose that very post the following morning. I saw torches here hanging only in front of the shops. I saw an old man sitting next to an old wall. I see him in the daytime and at night, absolutely motionless, as if he were a stone protrusion in the shape of a man. I remember having seen him on my previous visit: he doesn't change. I wish I could watch him to see when he eats, when he loosens his grip on the stick. A fat woman is sitting in front of a big crate, on which parsley and watercress are displayed. A man is selling a delicious pastry made of flour, butter and sugar, which the orientals love and which they call 'basbusa'. A number of people in Cairo are famous for being good at making it. Of these, I remember a man who is short and has one bad eye. Before sunset he goes out of his house to an alley inhabited only by herb and spice merchants. He would stand there, expressionless, as men, women and children thronged around him. None of them speaks loudly; if a person were to raise his voice, urging him to hurry up with his order, he would never sell him any, even if he came to him several times. He uses a short knife, which has a wide, triangular blade, to cut the *basbusa*. The movements of his hand are deliberate and precise, as if he were shaping gold or sculpting alabaster. The tray would become empty, except for some sweet crumbs that glisten on top of a thin layer of butter like golden rays. He would gather the crumbs with the knife in the corner of the tray. The moment he has finished gathering them, a tall thin man with a band around his eyes, walking noiselessly and carrying a little child who does not cry, comes. The vendor gives him the crumbs wrapped in a piece of paper. Then he places the wooden triangular stand under his arm and leaves. I like standing near him, watching his hands and his expressionless face. I haven't gone to him yet. All the food shops are open. As you walk in front of them, you hear the clatter of plates and pots and pans and smell the aroma of the different dishes: fried fish, chicken stuffed with onions, meat pies that are made of dough shaped like triangles, filled with meat, then fried in clarified butter until they turn brown.

From a distance a clamour arose, approached, then turned; a group of carpenters is riding in carts drawn by animals. They were cheering and shouting rhythmically, 'Ibn Musa! Ibn Musa!' I couldn't make out the rest of what they were saying. From time to time, thundering shouts made by a group would rise to a roar, then their words would be scattered and lost in confusion and then stop. I hear someone saying, 'Ibn Musa doesn't come twice in the same era.' Another said, 'If someone came to do good by them, they must find fault with him.' Strangely enough, yesterday I heard an old man at an old apothecary's shop in Hamzawi saying, 'The fact that ibn Musa has appeared is a sign of the imminent destruction of the world . . . I know things about him that would make your hair stand on end!' But those present looked at him, fell silent for a moment, then tried to outdo each other in praising ibn Musa, as if fending off some hidden evil, as if negating having listened to the old man. What a perplexing affair!

I haven't seen anything like it in any country. The people love a specific person, everybody says good things about him, praises him, but at the same time there is a secret undercurrent, an imperceptible feeling permeating people and even inanimate objects, a fear of Zayni, which does not show on anyone's face but which can be felt. This has really puzzled and confused me.

I heard the drumbeat of the herald. So, ibn Musa will address the people tomorrow! The city is staying up. I didn't see a single Mamluk on horseback. I learned from my servant that their mischief had increased to an unbearable degree a year ago. It got to the point that going out after supper was a very risky business. The alley dwellers closed the gates of their alleys and assigned some men to sit behind them as guards. When the mischief became too much, ibn Musa went up to the Sultan and interceded for the people, saying, 'If things go on as they have been going, with women being abducted and innocent men slain, everything will come to ruin!' The Sultan responded favourably to Zayni's plea and decreed that no Mamluk should leave his barracks and go to the city after supper without a special pass. He also decreed that no Mamluk should wear a veil covering his face. I didn't live through that period in Egypt, but my servant told me that prayers for Zayni Barakat on the pulpits of the mosques continued for three days – and that was unprecedented – until ibn Musa ordered them to stop doing that. My servant told me that three young men were slain at that time because of disparaging remarks they made about ibn Musa. The populace slew them when they said that what Zayni did was suspect and that it was he who instigated the Mamluks so that he could go up to the Sultan and intercede for the people, whereupon the Sultan would curb his Mamluks and ibn Musa would call for prayers for him to stop. I went back to my house, dizzy. Undoubtedly, people were living in security and peace. I couldn't get over the people's noise and their merry-making.

On the following day I got up early. Entering the mosque would be a difficult undertaking. What if they caught me? I would ask Zayni for help. Any foreigner, especially a Frank, who entered the country must register his name and where he came from. This is a new system that was not in effect on my first visit. If he asked me what I was doing in the mosque, I'd tell him about my travels, my desire to see the world. Ibn Musa would understand me. I must meet him this time. I saw him only in procession the day his predecessor was executed in the strangest manner of killing I've ever seen: dancing until death. I thought to myself that I wasn't going to miss hearing him and so I entered the mosque. I saw men wearing blue uniforms with yellow collars, standing among the people performing the prayers, watching them. They grew in number the closer one got to the front rows. For the sake of safety, I sat next to one of them. I didn't make any mistakes rising and kneeling down. I know the prayers here – much easier than in the villages of India, with their rituals and movements without end. A murmur went through the people, like the circles growing wider after a stone is thrown into calm waters. The eyes were fixed on the wooden pulpit and the wooden ladder, which the Governor of Cairo and the Markets Inspector of the Land of Egypt, Zayni Barakat ibn Musa, was climbing. I listened carefully: he was using the colloquial dialect, which, to my knowledge, was a departure from the usual practice. I had to cup my ear for a time in order to hear what he said.

Ibn Musa began speaking softly, then got louder. I heard about Zayni's assuming his post, making sure that justice was served and how establishing justice in this world was a matter that some people liked and others hated. He had the chance to loot money and hoard rubies and pearls, as predecessors had done and as successors would do. But he refrained out of fear of Him alone (meaning God). And here he was today, barely subsisting. He said he had pledged to collect money from certain regions and was able to extract several times the amounts those regions usually yielded, and not a single human being complained. He didn't detain a poor peasant who worked there or caused any of them to flee their villages. He put a stop to the raids of bedouins on houses of peasants. That was as far as the countryside was concerned. As for taxes here: has anyone complained about them? He has eliminated many imposts. At that point Zayni slowed down, and the people were treated to a State secret that no man alive would dare divulge. The Sultan had intended to levy a new tax. (Here the people shouted, 'God protect you! God save you!') The Sultan's mercy and his fairness chose to respond favourably to ibn Musa's intercession and to abrogate that which he had intended (God save you! God protect you!). For what is the value of intercession if it isn't met by a merciful heart like that of the Sultan? After that, Zayni went down from the Citadel on a Saturday and left for Southern Egypt to make sure that things there were all right ... (Here he stopped talking and sounded overcome with emotion.) An agitation spread among the people. I noticed certain sounds, coming from a faraway place in the mosque. As for the men in the blue uniforms, they began to get closer to each other, then dispersed to stand in places other than the places they stood in earlier.

As ibn Musa continued he said that at noon on that Saturday, this man, God forgive him, Abu al-Khayr al-Murafi', Abu al-Khayr, who in one year destroyed thirty-three families, went up to the Citadel. Ibn Musa is not disparaging Abu al-Khayr; he is just stating facts supported by incontrovertible evidence. Those whose homes were wrecked were still alive; as for the orphans, they could testify for fathers who had departed this world prematurely. Who was it gave him these details? Who revealed to him the truth about Abu al-Khayr al-Murafi'? It was his faithful, loyal deputy, his deputy who zealously guarded justice the same way he guarded the honour of his own family (he pointed to the front rows), Zakariyya ibn Radi. The people strained their necks trying to see Zakariyya, but they couldn't, so they shouted, 'God preserve Zakariyya! God preserve Zakariyya!' The men in the blue uniforms gathered at one of the corners of the mosque. It seems there was some kind of disturbance going on there. Ibn Musa's voice rang out. I saw him beating his chest with his hands. Abu al-Khayr al-Murafi, accused him wrongfully; he pledged to the Sultan to extract sixty thousand dinars from Zayni Barakat after he took him in custody and tortured him. (The people shouted, 'God damn Abu al-Khayr! God damn Abu al-Khayr.') But the Sultan, with his insight, acuity and sagacity ... Do the people know what the Sultan said? First, he ordered that Abu al-Khayr al-Murafi' be put in irons. Then he said, 'Do you think that I do not know what ibn Musa has? I will tell you a little story. When we had our evening gathering, Emir Mamai Tabardar, the halberdier, apologized to me, saying: "Until today I had thought ibn Musa was a rich man; I thought he had so much money he didn't even have to reach for it. But he came to me, perplexed and with wandering eyes, and asked me for a loan of . . ."' The Sultan asked how much the loan was. He apologized to the Sultan once more and said, 'Five dinars. Yes, by God, five dinars!' The Sultan said, 'Do you think you can extract thousands of dinars from a man who seeks to borrow such a sum of money? Ibn Musa has brought into my coffers thousands upon thousands of dinars, of which he didn't keep one dirham for himself. I have my own men who tell me of everything that goes on in his house.' (Here, some murmurs from the corner of the mosque got loud and whispering spread among the people.)

Ibn Musa stood silently on the pulpit, his head bowed and his hands holding the sides of his black cloak. People shouted, asking each other to be quiet. I saw men on the roof of the mosque, which overlooked the inner courtyard, coming and going, then three of the men wearing blue uniforms appeared and they pushed away the men who were watching from above. I was certain that I would get a beautiful sight if I could climb the new minaret built here by the present Sultan, which resembled the four-headed minaret rising above his new mosque at the entrance of the Sharabshiyyin market. I have become addicted to looking at that minaret. I love to pass underneath it; the glow of its coloured marble bathes my soul. I see in it bygone eras in the morning and when I come to it as the afternoon dust envelops it, I see a different sight. I sit in a beverage shop near al-Azhar, watching its peak sink its four heads into the night until it blends in its darkness. I fear to lose it and I go back to it.

Ibn Musa didn't speak until the hubbub had subsided. 'Please excuse me if I have told you some of my most private affairs. You are my brothers. Did I steal anything from any of you?'

The throats, in unison, block out everything. 'God forbid!'

'Did I commit an abomination?'

'No!'

'Did I oppress any of you?'

The voices got mixed up and grew louder. I saw ibn Musa making a gesture with his hands. When the people were quiet again, a short man wearing a leather shirt stepped forwards. I tried in vain to hear what he was saying. Ibn Musa raised his hand, saying, 'This man is complaining about an injustice that he has suffered. One of my men beat him up because he was walking, carrying a water-skin – for he is a water-carrier – in the middle of the road. This causes the clothes of passers-by to get wet; the water dripping on the street causes it to be covered with mud, and this is in violation of the regulations laid down by the *Muhtasib* for water-carriers. However, the water-carrier must have his satisfaction. It is unacceptable that one of ibn Musa's men beat up any human being without due process. It is totally unacceptable to the *Muhtasib*.

'After the prayers, come to my house, tell me where you were walking and I will bring before you all my men who work there and you will get your satisfaction.'

At a specific moment, before the people cheered, a shout rang out from the far end of the mosque during a silent lull in the middle of Zayni's speech.

'Liar!'

Ibn Musa was incredulous. A dissonant voice? I didn't hide my amazement. The truth of the matter is that I haven't seen a man like this one in all the years I have spent travelling in different countries. My admiration of ibn Musa increased when once again he bowed his head. He did not talk until silence returned. I noticed that he was slightly irritated. Of course, he must be irritated at this impudence. Perhaps his enemies had come to spoil his address to the people. Once again he pointed to the first row: his faithful, loyal deputy, Shihab Zakariyya ibn Radi ('Long live Zakariyya! Long live Zakariyya!'), was the one who arrested Abu al-Khayr al-Murafi' and imprisoned him, not because he went up and spoke against Zayni. No. Actually, ibn Musa thought of forgiving him. It was enough that the Sultan knew who the righteous ones were! The Supreme Shihab was going to give him a taste of what he himself had inflicted on others. Ibn Musa was not going to turn back; he was not going to back away from what he believed to be justice. The Sultan was on his side; the people's hearts protected him! Let his enemies do their worst. All he hoped was for the person with the complaint to come to him. If it turned out that he had done anyone an injustice, he would accept retribution just like everybody else. (A noise arose from the same place where the shout had come from.) Ibn Musa began to descend the steps of the wooden pulpit. Some people shouted, 'God is greater! God is greater! Zayni! Zakariyya! God give you strength! God protect you!' Some dervishes beat brass cymbals, and the voices that had sought to interfere with Zayni's speech were drowned out. I didn't hide my delight. I became more determined to meet him before my departure.

Announcement

People of Cairo! We enjoin what is right and forbid what is wrong. Today we have the good news that the Sultan has taken off the black wool and has put on white, with the coming of the hot season.

People of Cairo! The Supreme Zakariyya ibn Radi, Deputy *Muhtasib* of the Land of Egypt and Deputy Governor of Cairo, has ordered that Abu al-Khayr al-Murafi' be hanged. His body shall remain up for three days, as a reminder and a lesson for the present and the future.

People of Cairo! It is forbidden for beverage and pastry shops to remain open after the evening prayers. Anyone caught in violation shall be flogged with fifty lashes.

People of Egypt! News has come that a battle has taken place between our valiant cavalry and the Ottomans. The cavalry of our Sultan killed forty Ottoman horsemen.

This is the first blood.

Look out!

People of Egypt!

Look out!

Announcement

People of Egypt! We enjoin what is right and forbid what is wrong. Our master, the Sultan, has ordered the appointment of Zayni Barakat ibn Musa as Controller of the Armoury and deputy of the Chief Executive Secretary, Emir Tuman Bey.

You have been informed.

People of Egypt! If any of you should hear any heretic or enemy of religion say anything against the Sultan or any of the high and mighty, he should inform the Deputy *Muhtasib* Shihab Zakariyya ibn Radi and he will be rewarded. He who hears and does nothing shall be eradicated without further ado.

You have been told!

You have been warned!

Said al-Juhayni

IN the heart are wounds that do not heal. The soul is a forest of
sharp spears and blades that are deeply imbedded and cannot be
pulled out. No dam stops the flowing sorrow engulfing the first and
the last, the beginning and the end, the dual and the singular. The
death of hope is born of two lovers separating. The wishes recede.
As your life is just about to begin, a secret voice coming from deep
inside you whispers that your forehead is as yet unwrinkled. You
are surrounded by a terror, regulating the orbits of the planets,
monitoring the whispers of the stars, connecting earth and heaven.
The people's hearts are labouring under the bitterness of trial and
oppression. And yet, be patient. In a few years, the happy days will
come; things will not remain the same. Early in life he closes his
eyes and he sees bright days ahead and a youthful spring; he sees
people going out on the streets, safe from the harassment of the
Mamluks, unafraid of the attacks of brigands or sudden raids by
spies who keep following a person. Man doesn't love twice; hers
were the first beats of the heart, beats as yet unbanished, not yet
smothered. The heart had not yet been snatched out of the chest
and given to a bird of prey to amuse its little chicks. He is hoping
for a time when little children's vocabulary will not contain the
words 'impale', 'cut the throat', or 'plague'. The faces will have a
serenity that he is used to seeing in the face of his master, Shaykh
Abu al-Su'ud. This will not be long in coming. He says to himself,
five years. Only five years. The days keep passing and moving far
away. He asks in sorrow, 'Haven't the five years passed yet?'
Perhaps after another five years. No, never. Even his sweet,
harmless desire to have his own lodging, which he can close behind
him, and a bathroom that he doesn't have to share with anyone,
even that is difficult, impossible. Mansur, his friend, says, 'We came
into the world and we will go out of it. We are not immortal, nor do

· 175 ·

we have longevity. We will leave behind others who will hope that the happy days will come. Why do we deceive ourselves, Said? What we are doing has been predetermined.'

After five years, then another five; the fingers cannot keep up with the passing of time. Twenty-seven years have passed. The rottenness of the world is eternal. There is no end to the mischievous tricks that the demons play on humans. Injustice, like the fires of the Magi, never goes out.

He doesn't go to Shaykh Rihan's house any more. In the days of his loss, it was locked and the bolt was planted into his heart. Mansur said, 'Time has a great medicine called forgetting.' Sometimes the pain would not be so sharp for a few days at a time, and his exhausted mind would say that the medicine was beginning to work. But at a specific moment, any time of day or night, while sitting in the morning as usual at the shop of Hamza ibn al-Eid al-Saghir, while taking a sip of fenugreek, or in the courtyard of the mosque while attending his class, suddenly, at that moment, a heavy load descends upon him. The veins of his heart fill with dark blood, which darkens the spirit. He would remember a certain moment and all his pains would jump back into life. He would rise to his feet. Life is nothing but links in a red-hot brass chain, which burns the soul. Life is a long, painful memory, which covers him, envelops him. On what planet is his saviour? Which of the stars can mitigate that catastrophe or warn him about its coming before it comes from far away? What enchanted bottle can he hide in to escape his age and his world, one that would be opened only when the future, happy days had come? The bottle would be opened by a simple fisherman, and out of it he would come as a ray of light, a serene spirit that would offer him life and restore the lost love. He would be offered shelter by the fisherman. Eternal life would embrace them both. He wasn't going to lose his way to his love. As for this time of his, it does not accept what the sad heart offers. It doesn't heal open wounds. No, it doesn't. It never does. Said says, 'The happy days will come.'

Mansur shouts, 'When? Why do we keep hitting our heads against the obstinate rocks? Said, no intercession for people is to be hoped for; even if our beloved Prophet were to come back and try to fill the earth with justice and peace instead of the injustice and oppression with which it is now filled. Oh, Said, I have given up hope for the long-awaited Mahdi; if he were to rise and come from the Kaaba, brandishing his golden sword, Zakariyya will confront him, ban him from entering the country, arrest him and throw him in the Maqshara Prison, the only reality in the world. The first and the last reality is Maqshara; all else is vanity. No, all else except Shihab, Zayni and Saniyya ibnat al-Khubbaiza.'

Said listens a lot to Mansur, mulls over his words, turns them around, changes the order of their letters. A few days ago he climbed the new minaret. He saw the city enveloped in the dark. There was no sound at such a tremendous height, and the emptiness was like a bottomless sea without shells or oysters. He saw himself completely alone, the first man in the world. He saw himself removing one of his ribs and in its place was Samah. His throat was hardly able to keep up with his breathing: he glowed from the pain. His spirit became transparent and light. It was liberated from the prison of the flesh and soared over wings of pure tears. The stars on high were mute, communicating in a secret, unspoken, inaudible language. Isn't he right? Then why doesn't his prayer turn into a thunderbolt sent down to shake the earth to its very foundations, to expose hell's devils cloaked in angelic caftans, promising good and delivering evil, their warp evil and their weft harm. They lead the prayers and climb pulpits! He shed tears that were as true as the rise of day. In his mind's eye he saw tender Samah, of whom he wondered one day whether she actually chewed and ate and did what human beings did when they went to the bathroom; he saw her stark naked, and on top of her was a moaning faggot with bare buttocks, swaggering to and fro in a land that had been a no man's land. He was burning its grass, ravaging the figs and the olives, harvesting its crops, putting out its fire. He remembered Samah's hand, her little hand, gentle as a whisper, exquisite like a well-wrought verse. He held it on that orphaned day of his ascetic existence when he went out with them to take the air on Shamm al-Nasim. That tender hand must be feeling the rough back bending over the generous spring. As for Shaykh Rihan, he can speak of nothing except the visit of the high and mighty. On the wedding night, Emir Sudun whispered something to him. Shaykh Rihan laughed. Zayni Barakat later came to ask him what Emir Sudun had said. Shaykh Rihan laughed in modesty, spread his hand on his chest and said, 'Please forgive me for not repeating what he said. I don't divulge what was said in confidence.' Zayni laughed and said, 'Do you know that this is the first time that Emir Sudun has bent over and whispered a secret to anybody?' Shaykh Rihan went out of his mind. The joy was too much: his daughter was the wife of an old emir's son in whose veins flowed the blood of the very high and mighty emirs. Oh, what use is it to try to capture these poisonous thoughts? What a rotten, barren soul he was! Is this a soul that has lived only twenty-seven years?

They do not take pains to hide themselves. They appear openly before him. They cross the street in front of Hamza's shop, so many, coming and going. Their disguises do not fool anybody: a poor, old peasant walking slowly. One glance of his eyes, however, gives him away, revealing who he is and why he is passing through this place in particular. Sometimes it is a young woman, at others a very old one, or even children. Innumerable children are working for Shihab, who is turning son against father. The only testimony he truly believes is that coming from children under five, and this is a new thing. Said doesn't walk with his friend Mansur; they will follow him and do their best to get to him. Said knows well that all his movements are monitored, his breaths counted. He talks a lot at the *riwaq* and in the mosque. They might twist his words, add to them things he didn't say. Strangely enough, he has heard some scholars publicly disparaging Emir Tashtamur and he said to himself that they could be spies. But he heard a Syrian scholar from Aleppo, swearing on the *Bukhari* that Emir Khayrbak was secretly corresponding with the Ottoman Sultan about the people's affairs in Syria and Egypt, conveying everything to him. The fingers went through the beards, perplexity danced in the eyes. What disaster was coming next? What catastrophes were looming? What surprised Said was not that Khayrbak was in contact with the Ottomans, for perhaps thinking about such matters was not unthinkable for someone without family and without roots. What really frightened him was the tone of voice in which it was said. What are they thinking? He saw himself for a long time as someone labouring under a heavy load with nobody helping him with it. Even Mansur, his friend, if asked about his friends and colleagues would say, 'They are hopeless. The Mamluks came to them suddenly and did to them what turned them into eunuchs the likes of whom never existed throughout history: they are eunuchs who can sire babies, castrated men who impregnate women but they have no tongues; their master is a spy and their nursemaid Saniyya ibnat al-Khubbaiza.'

Now he is hearing them saying things that he is reluctant to say himself. What happened? Has he grown old? Has the razor blade reached his heart, his mind and his tongue? He comes and goes to their circles, listening to the news. The Sultan's envoys came back from the Ottoman State after they were humiliated and insulted by its head: he shaved the head of their chief, Emir Mughulbai, put him in irons and would almost have killed him, had it not been for the intercession of some wise Ottomans. War is inevitable. The ambassadors of the King of Abyssinia are going up to the Citadel. The people go out to watch them because they look weird. Janbirdi al-Ghazali goes to the Sharqiyya province, using his sword on the peasants. He kills thousands: irrigation canals are ruined by the corpses. An old man who had a unique talent for making *basbusa* has died. With his death, an irreplaceable pastry recipe disappeared. He had given the secret to no one. Zayni Barakat intended to address the people. Did you know that maybe some emirs were behind Abu al-Khayr al-Murafi's going up to the Sultan and accusing Zayni?

The mosque is overflowing with worshippers. The fragrance of ablutions and old mats permeates the air. Zayni climbs the pulpit. A certain moment comes and changes everything around. On the wooden pulpit, Said sees himself going out with Samah on Shamm al-Nasim, attaining the pinnacle of his joy. He spoke to her for a whole day on which the sun never set. He sees it now devoid of any hope; the words resound in his ears. He listens to the sounds of the wedding, the night he was slaughtered and not ransomed by the Angel Gabriel, peace be upon him. His heart didn't cry over him. He wandered about like a leper who saw the world as a little hole. A drink of water is offered to him. When they prevented him from running, his blood was shed in a desert, eradicating the confession of love in his chest. Zayni is talking from the pulpit. Ibn Sayyid al-Nas is trading in fava beans as he likes. The lips are competing to kiss Zakariyya's hand and touch the hem of his cloak. The men in front of the shops are nodding their heads, narrowing their eyes. 'My God! Has Cairo ever seen a man like him? Look at his piety! See how he fears God!' Time will not bring forth a spy like this one. Zayni is addressing the people softly and with humility. Did he arrange Samah's marriage? Why did he attend the wedding? For what purpose? Where is the old woman who appears in the midst of people and shouts two words only to his face? Nobody has seen or heard her for a long time. Maybe he killed her or banished her from this world. They said she went to him in the evening, that he cried before her in front of the door of his house and that she told him what happened and what would happen, what time would bring, but that she was the only one who shouted at him. Said himself had heard her at the first procession a few years ago when he danced with joy. People were shouting their prayers, 'God save you! Long live Zakariyya! Zakariyya!' Let Said say what she had said. His shoulders are weighed down by a heavy burden and stones are heavy on his chest, but he is not lying down in the heat of Mecca, scorched by the fire of the sands. He is not shouting as Bilal and Ammar ibn Yasir and other early Muslims persecuted by the heathen Meccans did, 'One! God is One!', unyielding and un-wavering in the face of iron chains and harsh shackles. 'One! God is One!' Say it and utter the profession of faith in preparation for death. 'Long live Zakariyya! May you live long, Zayni!' What is there left for him to care about? This is an age whose imam is Zayni, whose shaykh is Zakariyya, whose custodians are the spies and whose confidential secretary is Amr ibn al-Adawi. Let him end this premature old age, recover the youth of his life, remove the sharp blade from the tongue.

'Liar!'

A slight echo rang out in his ears. The blue uniforms with yellow collars, blue, yellow. The arrow has been shot and the hand froze in mid-air on the pulpit.

'Liar!'

He is not afraid of the heat. Let him be covered by glances of resentment from water-carriers, blacksmiths, marble-workers, masons, coal dealers, carpenters, bakers or spies. Let them converge on him. They don't know. Let the rocks and stones of the mountain come tumbling down. It doesn't matter. If they were to slaughter his son right in front of his very eyes, if they withheld water from him, if they took the severed head and toyed with the lips, it wouldn't matter. Al-Husayn has prior claim to the honour of bearing torture.

'You are lying!'

Was it an echo? No. Maybe. This is wonderful and puzzling. Other voices scarred by fear and yet they shout with him in a unified, martyred voice, 'You are lying! You are lying!'

Head Spy of Cairo

HE doesn't see what his men are doing now. But he knows what is happening. He hasn't seen Said's face, but he knows him thoroughly from what he has read about him. He knows things about him that Said himself doesn't know. He wishes time could hurry up so that he may see his face sooner; the face about which he read much and how silent it was. Now he was going to know every tremor that passed through it. What is it that makes his face always silent, not given to much talking? His old hobby was to watch the first moments on the face of a man whose life has been put in chains. At the outer door he is going to offer him half a glass of water, which he would drink, blindfolded. What effect would that produce? The Supreme Shihab says, 'The step by which a man crosses our threshold should be a clear line of demarcation separating two eras. That moment should divide a man's life into two parts in such a way that the man comes out of here, bearing the same name, but, in reality, a different person.'

Kom al-Jarih

THE trunk of an ancient doum tree is encircled by an iron fence. A heathen city stones a hermit. Muslim Baghdad gathers around a high platform on which is Mansur, al-Husayn ibn Mansur al-Hallaj; men and women are slinging mud at him. The martyred tongue does not stop. 'I am the Truth! I am the Truth!' The harsh hand rises, its arm covered with leather studded with iron spikes. The whip comes crashing down on the thin body whose owner has mastered true knowledge. The executioner's hand gets tired of whipping. Al-Husayn's arms and legs are cut off. The smile on the lips of the pious hermit tells all that is apparent and that which is hidden. His face is spattered with the flowing blood of his arms, which doesn't stop gushing in conspicuous profusion. The sharp blade removes the tongue. During the night the ashes of the burnt body are strewn over the Tigris. The head is banished to Khurasan. Baghdad gathers; it drowns al-Husayn ibn Mansur.

Time here is nothing but the continuation of those oppressive long-bygone days, a viscous shadow that never leaves. Good is spilled, evil is master and prostitution rules. Where does one take refuge? What path does one take? An unexpected dilemma, one that one doesn't wish to have at the end. Said has been shaken to his very foundation. They wasted him. The noises of the city recede. How he needs to be away from it all, to surround the soul with the wells of silence, to recall the faraway days in order to unlock the secret of the frozen smile while the arms and legs are gone. He would try to gather the ashes and ask the soul about that secret. Mansur is gone, chased by the ghosts of the treacherous age. Mansur is shaking, trembling. Perhaps he came seeking security. But what security? At the back of his neck are two eyes, which nobody can see, which constrain his vision, decide his path. Mansur reports what the people are saying: 'Our master has chosen Zayni and supported him. What intercession can he hope for?' If only he would shout the cry of deliverance and go! But where would he go? Undoubtedly he would meet the Antichrist. Where? To the cellar that he has dug with his own hands. Is this the end of the road? Oh! He has fallen in a well-planned ambush, carefully prepared by an evil oppressor.

Excerpt D from the diary of the Italian traveller Visconti Gianti
(922 AH/AD 1516)

It seems that I have been destined during this, my third, trip to the land of Egypt to witness great events. Three days after I arrived from the Sudan I went into the city. I heard that the Sultan had gone to Syria to fight the Sultan of the Ottoman lands. I heard the muezzins praying that the Sultan be victorious. I was told that Cairo had been shaken greatly on Saturday. I very much regretted arriving after the Sultan's procession at the head of his army had left for Syria. And so that my compatriots wouldn't miss the description of the procession and to be honest, I am here quoting my friend Shaykh Muhammad Ahmad ibn Iyas, a well-known man of learning in Cairo and the author of a long history of the land of Egypt. I wish, if I have time, to introduce him to my own people. Ibn Iyas, despite his old age, watched the procession and wrote down what he saw. He has given me permission to copy what he has written. My friend, ibn Iyas says:

Then came the Sultan al-Ashraf Qansuh al-Ghuri. He was preceded by the Caliph about twenty paces in front of him. The Sultan rode a bay horse with a gold saddle and saddle-cloth, wearing a white Baalbek coat, embroidered with a wide border of gold on black silk; it was said to have in it 500 *mithqals* (weights; measures) of gold. That day was of great splendour and magnificence. The Sultan was handsome and a fine figure in processions. Then came the royal flag and behind him the Chief Mamluk, Sunbul al-Osmanli, accompanied by the armour-bearers in full uniform. He entered Cairo by Zuwayla Gate and passed through the streets in this awesome procession. All of Cairo trembled at his sight that day and the people who had all come out – nobody stayed at home – greeted him with loud prayers for his welfare, their faces visibly shaking with excitement. The women cheered him by ululating from the windows.

The Sultan marched in that cavalcade until it came out of al-Nasr Gate. It was a day to remember.

Following that the chests were brought down, containing gold, silver and monies, which were said to be equal to a thousand thousand dinars, not counting the other metals. The treasury was depleted of all the money that had been collected since the beginning of the Sultan's reign up to the day of the departure of this campaign. He also depleted all the other storehouses, including gifts of great value and magnificent weapons collected by former sultans, gold saddles, crystal and cornelian, embroidered saddle-cloths and other royal treasures. The chests were accompanied by a group of treasury clerks and officials in full uniform. The chests were loaded on fifty camels. It was said that all of these monies were deposited in the Aleppo Citadel. On Sunday, the sixteenth, the Sultan sent a herald into Cairo to proclaim that the Sultan would leave Raydaniyyah on Friday, 20 Rabi al-Akhir (of the Islamic calendar), that every soldier given his orders must be present and that no excuse whatsoever shall be accepted. When the Sultan had set himself up in the camp, he appointed a number of judges and notables to look after the people in his absence: the Judge Mahmud ibn Aja was appointed Secretary, Judge Alaa al-Din ibn al-Imam as Controller of the Privy Funds, Judge Shihab al-Din Ahmad ibn al-Ji'an as Controller of the Sultan's Bureau of Documents and Judge Zayni Barakat ibn Musa in his usual posts as *Muhtasib*, Governor of Cairo and Tax Collector for all Egypt. To his posts was added that of Overseer of the Sultan's Treasures.

'May God make this land secure.'

Strictly Confidential: no human eyes should see this.

A paper prepared on the occasion of the meeting of the convention of Chief Spies from the four corners of the world in Cairo, Mother of the World, Garden of the Universe, to exchange views and review methods being used and others newly introduced and to exchange knowledge and mutual benefits. This paper has been prepared in the Bureau of Spies of the Mamluk Sultanate and delivered by Supreme Shihab Zakariyya ibn Radi, may God forgive him and acquaint him with His methods and ways.

Cairo
Jumada al-Ula 922 AH

FIFTH PAVILION

In the Name of God, Most Gracious, Most Merciful.

God Almighty has said, 'Lo! Thy Lord is ever watchful.'

God Almighty has said, 'Verily, God is the Knower of things hidden.'

God Almighty has said, 'He utters no word but there is with him an observer, ready.'

God Almighty has spoken the truth.

The Messenger of God, God's blessings and peace be upon him, has said, 'He who believes in God and the afterlife should say good things or be silent.'

Amr ibn al-As, may God be pleased with him, has said, 'Talking is like medicine: if you take much of it, it will be detrimental and if you take a little of it, it will be beneficial.'

Now then: it has never happened before that the chiefs of our profession from all over the world have met. This is an event of great moment and significance, from which future generations will derive great benefit and learn useful lessons. They will learn that we've borne a heavy burden and paid an exorbitant price, that we've suffered in great anguish and sacrificed a lot for the sake of pleasing God Almighty. Our purpose in holding this convention is to find new methods and unknown ways to help us with our difficult tasks, which will enable us to arrive at the heart of the truth. This will make things easier for those who will come after us. May God help us.

It so happens, due to the nature of our profession and conditions surrounding it, that we find ourselves in a strange position. This requires of all of us, from the chief spy who has control over the affairs of the whole State down to the junior spy who trails a man or a woman and who reports everything that is said in a gathering, of all of them it requires intelligence and astuteness. Each has to find ways and means that enable him not only to live securely among men but also to be popular and well liked. This might appear to be difficult. How can a man who by profession must peek into people's lives and their secrets, an activity that is disliked, be well liked? How can he make people come to him for help with their problems? But first, let's establish an important point.

The spy's task, without beating about the bush, is to administer justice among the people. But he does so in a manner unacceptable to the people. Let's then observe the following facts: there is nothing in the world on which two people would agree. If, for example, we take this very hall in which we are sitting, away from the noise and hubbub of the world: we don't all see it the same way; the supreme Chief Spy of India sees me standing here while the Chief Spy of Yemen sees me from the left side; as for the honourable Chief Spy of Sudan, he sees me from another angle in a different way. Even the interpreters see me in different manners and convey to Your Excellencies my speech but not my words, just the meanings. Hence, I have more than one form and shape, even though, in reality, my posture has not changed at all and my speech has changed in the process of translation but its meaning has remained the same. Thus, what we see as justice is seen by others as injustice and as a crime.

A spy does not work for himself at all. In the first place and in the final analysis, the goal is to please God Almighty, then the Sultan, then the State. So long as the spy is a believer in God, be he a Muslim or a Christian or a Buddhist, he spares no effort to strengthen and protect the State.

No wise man will claim the existence of a single human being who is loved by all his people. Such a person has not been created yet. Wasn't the Seal of the Prophets and the Master of Mankind, Muhammad, persecuted by his people? Didn't the Jews throw stones at him from the walls of Ta'if, causing the heat to burn the bottom of his feet and his blood to flow? Didn't they conspire to kill him? Didn't they fight him? Didn't one of their women eat the liver of his uncle, Hamza, raw? And before that, didn't they hurt the head of Christ, peace be upon him, with thorns? Didn't they drive nails into his flesh and didn't they crucify him? As for our lord Joseph, it was his own brothers who threw him into the well and broke his father Jacob's heart. Even the Great Buddha's life was filled with pain and agony. That is the way it goes with the saints and the martyrs. The one moral of these stories is that no one is loved by all the people in the upper classes, no matter what miracles and distinctions he might have. Hence, the ruler of any country must, of necessity, be hated by one segment of the population. The ideal ruler is one who makes the majority like him and decreases the number of his enemies. Therefore, there must be enemies who are lurking and lying in wait to pounce on the ruler. Those enemies are either external, in other words of a different race and religion, in which case one should rally round the ruler; the spy's task in this case is sacred and no two people will differ about that. The enemies on the other hand, may be internal enemies and those are to be found among the princes, the elite, as well as among the populace.

The great lesson learned from all the different histories is that in the case of internal, civil strife the spy must be neutral. The spy works for justice alone and the symbol of justice is the very throne itself.

Should members of the elite or groups among the populace conspire against the throne, the matter should be reported to the person sitting on it. This is a must. But, let's suppose that certain conspiring members of the elite or the populace (this latter hypothesis is rare) were able to seize power. What should the spy do? To that we say that so long as someone has been able to seize power from the person sitting on the throne and to sit on that very throne, that could only indicate weakness on the part of the former. How could he establish justice if he couldn't protect himself?

A question might arise: should the new keep the old? Here, in order to preserve authority, certain conditions may be laid down, the implementation of which will depend on the skill of the spy and his ability to penetrate to the heart of that which is hidden and to everyone's secrets. And, so long as someone is aware of the existence of an eye that sees what other eyes don't, he will fear that party and show it great respect. The great Chief Spy of the State of Maghrib has related to us what happened two hundred years ago when the Chief Spy of the time was partial to the ruler in power and was so zealous in his loyalty to him that he earned the enmity of all the princes and scholars. When one of them was able to depose the ruler and take his place, the Chief Spy didn't stay neutral but openly showed hostility towards the princes, even though he was certain the ruler had been killed. This is the epitome of stupidity; he caused harm to a great many people around him. The ideal course of action would have been to keep silence and watch the populace, so that they wouldn't poke their noses into the conflict by siding with this or that side. A lot has to be taken into consideration in the case of the populace and each of us will address the issue in another session. When things settle down however, he should begin to do his job and establish justice. Let's then move on from this point to the other one with which we started: how can the spy be well liked by the people in spite of the fact that they hate his task and his job?

How does the spy become well liked by the people? Among the characteristics of a great spy, the cream of the crop, is his excellent ability to acquire the talents and skills of all people. The nature of a spy's job compels him to interact and deal with all kinds of people from different races, thousands of people who are different in temperament and predilections. No one is like another. The true spy, the real top-notch spy, is one who has been able to combine all the characteristics of all people. But this is difficult. It might appear to be impossible, but for us it is quite feasible. A spy should be a coal-trader when he talks to coal-traders, an ingenious apothecary when he talks to apothecaries, a dissident when he talks to dissidents, a hashish smoker when he finds himself in the company of hashish smokers, a sinner when he seeks the path of sinners, a contrite penitent when he prostrates himself in the midst of penitents and content with those who are content. He has to move from showing hatred to expressing love in the blinking of an eye and he must be convincing in both cases. He must master the language of the rich, be humble when he mixes with the poor, be foolish and loved by the fools. When he sits with women, he should be able to find his way to their hearts and their imperfect minds. That's what we see in a truly able spy. The most important criterion to measure the skill of a spy is how knowledgeable and conversant with people's affairs he is. The more knowledgeable a spy is, the better command he has of the foundations of learning and the different arts, the more capable he is of unveiling the secrets of the world. This, of course, is impossible for every spy to accomplish. Hence, we say it is not necessary that the spy be fully trained in all subjects; rather he should have a general idea – not a superficial one, though – of each history, each science and each art, an idea of a special nature and impressive appearance. For that purpose, I have prepared special courses in all branches of human knowledge that we teach in our schools. My men take these courses and they sharpen their skills. Wonder not then, my great spy brethren, you who are in charge of the secrets of the universe, if I tell you about a young spy – one of my men – who can debate with the most learned scholars in their narrowest fields of specialization without having any prior knowledge of what he is debating. His method hinges on a very sharp intelligence and on taking words and ideas from his interlocutor, then changing them in a certain manner and pronouncing them as if they were his own. If you like, I can bring him before you and let you and him have whatever discussions you like. One of the objectives I intend to attain before departing this world is to bring each of my spies up to a level higher than that young man's.

In addition to what we've mentioned, there is another method that we employ to penetrate to the secrets of this world, to reach the quintessential, primal truth: I have designated, for each of the classes and groups, individual spies, who are steeped in their respective customs, traditions and whatever has to do with them. I am now talking about career spies. In addition, there is another class, which is made up of 'adjunct' spies, by which is meant a class of spies made up of individuals who join us from those various groups, in the sense that if I want to gather intelligence on coppersmiths, for instance, I would recruit one of them, rather than going around in circles and sending in an outsider who needs time to become an insider. It is important to maintain total confidentiality in the case of adjunct spies and give them a good training to make their talents match our work. Adjunct spies should be chosen on the basis of utmost honesty, trustworthiness and integrity. If the chief spy succeeds in recruiting such a person, that would be a great achievement indeed. We have been told by the great Chief Spy of China how he has succeeded in recruiting the most distinguished scholars, notables and Buddhist monks: they all work with him and are part of his team. It is natural in such circles to encounter some resistance and rejection because of what people conceive to be the meanness of our tasks and their being at variance with honour and honesty. Let me, however, say in all confidence that there is no man in this world who cannot be recruited by an able spy. What you do is examine each person's particular circumstances and life and through that you can find out how you can render him more pliable and amenable, provided that that takes place quietly and without cruelty. I have now a living example, a man at the prime of his life, for whom we have been preparing for years. One of these days, I am going to write a detailed paper on the process we are putting him through. When I reach the goal I have set from the start, I am certain that he will write the part of the paper explaining what has happened to him. Previously, this man couldn't stand the mere mention of my name and cared about nothing except inciting the populace against those in charge. Here I must salute our most illustrious colleague, the Chief Spy of the Western Frankish Kingdom, for his great success in recruiting the children of the kingdom. He has inculcated the spirit of spying in their minds since the earliest sign of vocabulary acquisition; no sooner does a child hear a word from his father or his mother than he reports it. Children are the most truthful of God's creatures and they never lie in their testimony. Thus, if each of us were as successful as our most illustrious colleague, we would be able, in a few years, to convert all human beings into spies. This is a lofty goal, which conforms with every religion and creed. Our most illustrious colleague has the right to keep his secret methodology of transforming children into spies, for obviously he hasn't achieved that in the blinking of an eye but rather after the efforts of years and years. But we do hope to benefit from his experience. Please permit me to express my boundless admiration of him and his ways. Let's make the ultimate goal and guiding light of our lives the transformation of all humans into spies. What we are after is the real, incontrovertible truth and that is difficult and elusive. But, oh, how many the roads leading to it.

How do we arrive at the knowledge of the original truth? What I am reading out now, you are hearing. Upon leaving the hall, if one of you were to sit alone with a friend and try to recall what I said, would he say it in the same way? The same words? Definitely not. It's impossible. When we recall a certain sitting, a certain gathering or a trip, we can never recall exactly what we have gone through. Rather we relate it in sentences that do not even come close to what actually happened, that do not tell it exactly. When I am given a man accused of inciting the populace, he will initially deny it. How would I know the truth then? I could, of course, just kill him, for in this age of ours nobody asks us about what happens to anyone, nobody holds us accountable, no one asks for blood-money. But I am no executioner, nor am I unfair. I am just trying to arrive at the truth, and, when it is uncovered, it will reveal other things that are both more far-reaching and more precise, things that would have been lost for ever if we had just killed the person from the beginning. Knowing what happened is a difficult matter; the past does not exist in a specific place and time to which I can go and retrieve what has happened. We do not encounter yesterday or last year in the form of existents; rather we meet them up here, in our minds, in the changes and vicissitudes that befall us. In order to reach the real, original truth, it has to be uttered from the heart and the mind; it has to be convincing and be supported by evidence and proofs. In order for a person to tell the truth, I am entitled to use whatever methods I deem appropriate to induce him to tell it. Hence, all that our men do, all the methods they employ for the purpose of uncovering the truth have been permitted by all creeds. I might respectfully cite here the treatise of the Chief Spy of the Frankish Portuguese Kingdom on the new means of making men tell the truth. All of these are innovations, which have contributed dimensions that we have long awaited and longed for. Permit me now to touch upon the methods we follow here to make circumstances more amenable in the service of our mission.

Making circumstances amenable: we begin by following up a person while he is still at large, not already in our gaols. We get to him through certain chinks in his armour; we make those chinks wider; we undermine the foundations. As I have already mentioned, it is very easy to kill a thousand people, but that is not important. What matters is changing what is in the head and the heart. And *that* is difficult. But we don't shy away from difficulties. If we determine that a person has departed from the norms, that he incites the people, opens their eyes, makes them look at the high and mighty, instead of throwing such a person in the Maqshara Prison – and Maqshara, dear sirs, is one of the most horrible facilities on earth and I personally take pride in it and invite you to a tour of it in which you will be acquainted with what we have prepared for the prisoners. Nothing will be kept from you. To go back to our point, though: we begin by studying the person's life, examining all the circumstances surrounding him. Then I pour my water on the fire of agitation, taking away its sting and at a specific moment I blow, extinguishing all heat in the heart of the ashes. I use the knife of time on his mind and remove from it what makes him different from other people, so that I might not find them one day rallying around his words, stoning a prince or burning down a palace or looting a market or attacking the procession of the Sultan. As I have already said, no one is beyond changing and turning around. Your Excellencies, uncoverers of the truth, this is what we here understand, this is what we institutionalize: nobody stays the same; no flower remains in bloom; no tree stays standing tall; no woman remains young for ever; no bird just keeps flying upwards; no ecstasy stays alive; the sun rises in order to set; the day breaks to grow old and is strangled by the night; the moon does not stay full in our eyes; the river begins in order to end; after a while the pouring rain stops and a distance, no matter how long, grows shorter and comes to an end. My dear sirs, masters of the secret of the world, no man remains the same. Time alone is not the cause. We help it along. If we find in a man's soul the slightest fear in spite of his reputation for bravery, I hover from a distance like a bird flying very high, like the kites here. I do not pounce down, plunging my talons and beak. Rather, I circle round and round, then descend to a certain height, then fly away once more, disappearing only to descend again like an arrow or a meteor or lightning or a thunderbolt, pouncing like a passing flash in the mind. At that point one phase ends and another begins. Dear illustrious sirs, there is no person alive who does not have within himself holes and wounds, cracks, and dilapidated, tottering fortresses, which it is my duty to penetrate. Sometimes I get there slowly, stealthily making no sound, no breath and no hiss. Then I would set up my mangonel, fortify my positions, array my poisoned arrows, brandish my swords and then attack in one fell swoop, investing, burning, destroying, turning buildings into rubble, living-quarters into wastelands, security into despair and hope into a slaughtered failure; the harbour that once gave shelter to ships I render incapable of sheltering one leaf fallen from a tree. If there is one drop of fear in the edifice of courage, I turn that first into a pool, then an ocean. If deep down in the heart there is love for some woman, I turn it into boundless hate. If there were obstacles between the man and his beloved, which we hoped to overcome, I turn them into insurmountable barriers. I draw boundaries and set up barricades; I dig trenches and set up my ambush, causing open wounds that remain raw even after death. I leave in the soul a turbidity that never leaves it. If a man resents being poor, I sow in his soul hopes of riches and glory. I make him taste glimpses of prosperity, which he gets used to, and then I turn him into a monstrosity in the eyes of the people, incapable of going back to his own folk nor of even looking straight ahead. This way, instead of excising him while still living, I change him. He would be walking on his same old two feet, moving his arms, using his own tongue to speak, called by his own name, but in reality he would be a different person, having nothing in common with the baby that slid out of his mother's womb or the young boy who strutted among his friends. Even his manhood I turn into femininity. I change the shape of the beard and moustache; I don't shave them off, nor do I pierce his ears and put ear-rings on them or remove his organ. Everything remains intact, but he won't be there. He will think, but he will think the way I want him to. He will also incite the people, but in accordance with my goals and not as he likes. This is how we handle him while he is at large. If we move to the time that a man might spend in gaol; here I permit myself to disagree with my colleague the great Chief Spy of Portugal about certain things mentioned in his paper. He placed too much emphasis on bodily torture. It doesn't have to be that way. We have now the case to which I have already referred. What do we do to him? For example, we open the door suddenly very late at night and our man would laugh in his face in a special, deliberate manner and ask him in a tone of voice that resembles cold meat on which fat has coagulated, 'Can I be of service?' We offer him, at a specific time every day, a quarter-filled glass of water, very ordinary water, but its effect on him is more painful than burning his fingers. We were able to secure a location from which he was forced to watch his former beloved, with whom he was passionately in love and about whom he composed several poems. We made him see her stark naked with her husband on top of her – her own husband and not anyone else – and she was doing things that made his head actually turn grey. The moment of beating or torture itself does not hurt, holders of the secret of the universe. What really hurts a man is anticipating that particular moment. At the time of torture he wonders what other forms of torture await him. The main thing is to live in continual waiting for that moment. What will happen the following moment? Why hasn't it happened? What is the significance of that glass of water? Has its taste changed? Yes, it has actually changed. Maybe they've put some liquid or drug in it that would make me forget where I am or what time it is. Perhaps they wanted me to lose my virility. Maybe they are killing me slowly.

Most distinguished sirs, only a few short days ago we conducted an experiment on a man; we blindfolded him and touched his neck with a razor blade so lightly that it left a very slight skin wound, but we held a thin tube connected to a small water-skin containing warm water. The drops kept flowing as we told him, 'Tell us where your money is and we will stop the bleeding.' He actually believed that his neck was bleeding profusely and he told us all we wanted to know. He even told us more than we had bargained for. He informed on a friend of his, an emir famous for inequity and looting. He kept screaming, 'Stop the bleeding! Stop the bleeding!', as we made noises to give him the illusion that we were actually trying to stop it. The man died in a few moments, even though he hadn't bled at all but had believed the warm water to be blood and his veins to have run out of blood and dried up; and so he died. I usually blindfold the prisoner. He would walk, expecting a sudden blow, but where? When? That's what he is wondering the whole time. On one night in particular I let into his narrow, clean cell (this is a new system for gaols here, which we are implementing in total secrecy), I let into his cell one of my men as if he were a prisoner. Before long they would be fighting over the slightest things. This is what I did to that young man I told you about. I ordered my man to press against him while he was asleep. He got up in a state of fright thinking the man was going to corner him and rape him. Thus do I turn life into a hell lined with thorns, so that death becomes a cherished hope and an unattainable joy.

A plea: we were excited by the interesting paper delivered by the Chief Spy of the youthful State of Kajura in which he outlined what he wished for our jobs in the future. Please allow me a few simple elaborations on his thoughts. I have also prepared very specialized appendices about several problems facing us, which I will hand out to you, each in your own language. I say with optimism that nothing is difficult or out of God's reach; that which we think is impossible today will enter the realm of the possible tomorrow. And tomorrow, for us, is unlimited. I see a day on which a truly able spy can monitor every man's life from the moment of birth until that of death, not only on the outside but the thoughts that he keeps to himself and what he sees in his dreams. In this way we will be able to know his inclinations and his predilections in such a way that we can predict what he will do, say in the twentieth year of his life, and so step in to prevent him or help him. If a man is asked about the original truth and he denies it, the spy will be able to retrieve the whole situation from time and confront the person who denies. I see a day coming when a spy can monitor the whispers and moans of coitus between a man and his woman. If a conversation between two men on a boat on the Nile takes place, I'd be able to capture it as I sit here and intervene in the conversation at the right time and move it in a certain direction. I see a day when organs would be removed from a person's body and asked about what they have done, and they won't be able to deny it. I see a day when people will be given specific numbers so that the spy might assign numbers to the dwellers of each alley: this is number One and that number Two, in such a way that no two people would have the same number. This is a matter that we have discussed at length in one of the appendices, which I am going to hand out, and it will help us keep track of people better than those many confusing names.

Now then: what I've just said may be nothing more than fantasies now, but when they do materialize, the spies of the future will say, 'Look, our ancestors were more far-sighted and more audacious.'

God's peace and security be upon you.

Chief Spy of the Land of Egypt
Zakariyya ibn Radi

Appendix I

A paper on how to prepare prisoners' food, what their sleeping arrangements should be like and the best moments to interrupt and disturb their rest

For the Eyes of Chief Spies Only
Translated by the Translation Department at the Cairo Spies Headquarters
922 AH/AD 1516

Appendix II

A paper on proposed methods of giving people numbers instead of names and the texts of judicial decisions permitting that in all religions

For the Eyes of Chief Spies Only
Translated by the Translation Department at the Cairo Spies Headquarters
922 AH/AD 1516

Appendix III

A paper on surveillance on surveillance or how a spy should monitor another spy

Classified Confidential (for Chief Spies Only)
Translated by the Translation Department at the Headquarters of the
Markets Inspectorate of the Land of Egypt
922 AH

Appendix IV

A paper on how to convince people that what does not exist does

Classified Confidential (Chief Spies Only)
Please hand this Appendix back after reading and studying it
Translated by the Translation Department at the Headquarters of the
Markets Inspectorate of the Land of Egypt
922 AH

Kom al-Jarih

AT the same time every year the house is opened to the disciples, those who seek the truth, travelling all over the world out of love for the members of the Noble Household of the Prophet. Some of them have actually met the Prophet Ilyas, peace be upon him, who never died, because he had drunk of the spring of life and so death could not touch him. Shaykh Abu al-Su'ud has lived in the hope of meeting him, learning from his wisdom and listening to the stories of bygone generations. Shaykh Kirmani has told him a story that was undoubtedly true: in his early youth, he travelled through Persia, where people once worshipped the light and the dark and where the Magi's fires burned. When he got near the sea, he met a man in white, with a white beard, moustache and hair, walking vigorously as if he were a twenty-year-old youth. Shaykh Kirmani was about to board a boat to cross the great sea. The Shaykh, from whose eyes emanated a strange brilliance, greeted him and warned him against taking the boat, saying, 'The vortex is acting up. Whoever rides it shall perish. The beasts of this sea show no mercy to anyone whom bad luck throws their way.' Shaykh Kirmani stayed away from the boat and the white-haired man disappeared. A thought flashed in Shaykh Kirmani's mind: the man whom he had met and who had warned him was none other than al-Khidr, peace be upon him. Later on he learned that the boat had sunk. He was overcome with regret. Why hadn't he stayed with him? Why hadn't he followed him? After three months, which he spent in hopeless regret, he made up his mind, trusted in God and began his travels, hoping to meet him and accompany him. But that was impossible; no one has ever seen al-Khidr twice. And yet he never lost hope.

Shaykh Abu al-Su'ud hasn't seen al-Khidr or the Prophet Ilyas. In the cellar the sorrows are getting sharper, stabbing like a sharp-pointed sword. The two immortal prophets have deserted the land in which he lives. He has seen much, but he hasn't seen them. His heart trembled when he saw the dead after a barbaric raid, when he saw cities conquered by a plague that had left nobody alive. At such times, the eternally perplexing question would assail him: why have they died so easily? Why has man been brought to this life and lived and known pain and hope if his going hence was so simple? In the cellar he heard of the people of Egypt's trust in him. He heard of what Zayni has been doing: raising prices and arresting people. His advancement and all his posts are reasonably justified; doesn't he always say, 'Had it not been for the trust of my master and my imam, Shaykh Abu al-Su'ud al-Jarihi, I would never have accepted?' One of the disciples told him how Zayni had addressed the people in the deep South and told them that Shaykh Abu al-Su'ud was praying for them day and night and that he trusted him to look after the land and the people, that he counselled him to administer justice and do what was good. He was only following the teachings of his master.

Now, after such a long life, comes a man who uses him. If the Prophet Ilyas, who has lived in all epochs, were to come to him he would tell him, 'It is your fault; you have not known your era; you haven't delved into it to learn its secrets.' But neither the Prophet Ilyas nor al-Khidr, peace be upon him, will guide him. In the cellar he thought he heard the voice shouting at him; the voice is heard but never seen and comes only to those who are righteous. It comes either to guide them or to warn them. The Shaykh is afraid of delusions. But the voice never becomes a delusion: has it come to warn and save him or has it come to chide him? Oh, the sorrow that grips the wounded heart! How can he get to see the truth? They say, 'His master blessed him the first year.' But the people kept shouting his name and cheering him. They forgot that. Only his own role was singled out to sum up what was going on. If only he could reach the Tree of the Truth, about which the good hermits have told him; whoever ate of its fruit will never be misguided. If only he could find the truth about every issue, no matter how complex or twisted! He hasn't found the tree and will never see even its reflection. An old Southern Egyptian dervish brought him a few dates and some milk. He ate and drank. He bent over and told him, 'Master, there is a man at the door named Damarawi.'

'There are no barriers between people and me.'

Damarawi, apparently a well-off man, came in. 'I walked all the way over here, Master.'

'Where are you from?'

'Manfalut, Master.'

Zayni had gone to Manfalut after the Sultan had left for Syria. He gathered all the people of the region, great and small. At the beginning he talked about everything, about the truth behind the news and the perfidy of the Ottomans. He said among other things that he was certain that the Ottomans were moving to take Egypt, but that the soldiers of the Sultan and the knights of God would take care of them. He said Egypt was protected by the godly saints and that it would be difficult to conquer a land which had Sayyidina al-Husayn, Sidi Ahmad al-Badawi, Sidi Abd al-Rahim al-Qinawi, Sidi al-Fuli, the mighty pillar Sidi al-Disuqi, Sidi al-Rifa'i and the other major saints and my master of the miracles of light, Abu al-Su'ud.

'He caused tears to flow down people's cheeks, Master. Then he said that the Sultan's treasury was in dire need of money. He begged them to agree to paying the taxes of one year in advance, in addition to the present year. And since the times were hard and people had no money, they complained and moaned and wailed. He spoke softly to them, saying that whoever owned something should sell it. He had spared them the atrocities of the emirs and the Mamluks. Had he let them have their way, they would have gone there with their swords and then the people would have sold their sons and daughters as they would cattle. That was not strange; it had happened before several times. With every other word he would mention the counsel given him by his master, Shaykh Abu al-Su'ud. And the people, Master . . . Oh, forgive me, Master.'

Damarawi cries. Al-Khidr, peace be upon him, turns his face away. The disciples shout and the murmurs grow louder.

'After he dismissed the people, he asked me and four other people from the village to stay. He told us many things about our monies and we wondered later on how he knew those things. Then he said he was going to levy on each of us the sum of one thousand dinars. He said we must pay. What was strange, Master, was that there was no more softness in his voice; he yelled at us and showed harshness, saying that he gave us a month. If we were late, he was going to pray that his master turn against us and our homes would be ruined.'

He dismissed Damarawi. He saw the sky frowning. Now the peasants were going back to their mud houses, the Sultan's soldiers were lighting fires in the plains of Aleppo, mariners were getting lost in strange seas. Sayyidina al-Khidr guides them to safety. Now travellers lost in the desert were losing their minds as the nightfall descended like rocks and stones; no one could rescue them except the Prophet Ilyas. At a specific moment during the night, unknown to anyone, even the most pious saints, and in an unknown place to which no living creature has ever been, Sayyidina al-Khidr and Sayyidina Ilyas would meet to cast a glance at the land of Gog and Magog, lest they should break the dam and drown the world. A thought bothers the Shaykh: have some Gogites penetrated our world, disguised as humans? He is going to leave the cellar for a while. The house has been empty since Said stopped coming.

'Faraj!'

The old disciple came. He comes here only once a year at a specific time.

'Go to Zayni Barakat. Wear the red scarf of your turban. Call out his name. Tell him to come here to me. Don't let him tarry.'

Secretariat of the Head Spy of Cairo

Urgent and Important

Report submitted to the Supreme Shihab Zakariyya ibn Radi, Chief Spy of the Sultanate.

In the latter part of this night, Zayni Barakat ibn Musa, Overseer of the Sultan's Treasures, Markets Inspector of the Land of Egypt, Governor of Cairo and Tax Collector for Upper Egypt and Lower Egypt, was summoned by Shaykh Abu al-Su'ud al-Jarihi, and he went. When he entered he was made to sit down in front of the Shaykh. When he turned to him, the Shaykh paid no attention to him; rather he yelled at him and said to him, 'You, dog, why do you oppress the Muslims? Why do you steal their money? Why do you say things that you attribute to me?' Zayni was surprised and tried to leave, but the Shaykh got up and called one of his disciples (a dervish named Faraj) and ordered him to take Zayni's cloak off. The dervishes surrounded him, the Shaykh gave the orders, and he was beaten with shoes on the head until he almost expired. Then he ordered him put in irons and sent for Emir Allan and awakened him and told him to go up to inform the Viceroy Emir Tuman Bey of the matter and to tell him that that dog was doing harm to the Muslims. Emir Allan, the Chief Executive Secretary, immediately went up to the Viceroy and awakened him and told him of what had happened. Emir Tuman Bey said to let Shaykh Abu al-Su'ud do what he saw fit.

As of the time of this writing, Zayni Barakat ibn Musa is still detained at Shaykh Abu al-Su'ud's house. The Shaykh said to his disciples, 'Keep the matter secret for a day or two until I extract from him what he has stolen from the poor people, then we would expose him in disgrace on a donkey and rid the world of him.' As of this moment, the populace has no knowledge of what is happening; some people, however, have wondered why Zayni has not gone in procession to perform the dawn prayers as usual.

On our part, we have sent men and agents everywhere, especially to Kom al-Jarih.

It has come to our attention that the dervishes and disciples of the Shaykh and all leaders and members of the Sufi orders in Egypt will announce the news and agitate the people.

May you enjoy the Security of God Almighty.

Head Spy of Cairo

Secretariat of the Deputy of Supreme Shihab Zakariyya in charge of Ottoman Affairs

Great Catastrophe

After lots of conflicting reports and much hearsay and rumours, we have received, only moments ago, a true account of what had taken place. We are sending that to you right away. We are sorry that we could not come in person, as we have been busy collecting facts. A great catastrophe has taken over and overwhelmed the whole country. Its details are as follows: Sultan al-Ghuri was suddenly surprised by the troops of Selim ibn Uthman on Sunday, 25 Rajab (a day of constant ill fortune). The Sultan had performed the morning prayers, mounted and headed for Tell al-Far where it was said the tomb of Dawud, peace be upon him, was. The Sultan mounted there and arranged the troops himself. The Commander of the Faithful was to his right, surrounded by forty copies of the Quran in yellow silk cases, borne on the heads of a number of nobles; one of the copies was in the handwriting of Imam Uthman ibn Affan, may God be pleased with him. Around him also was a group of Sufis and dervishes, among whom was the successor of Sayyidi Ahmad al-Badawi, accompanied by red banners. There were also the heads of the Qadiriyya Sufi order, accompanied by green banners, the successor of Sidi Ahmad al-Rifa'i, with Khalifah banners, and Shaykh Afif al-Din, servant in the Mosque of Sayyidah Nafisah, may God be pleased with her, with black banners. On the right flank of the troops was Emir Si Bey, Viceroy of Damascus, and on the left flank Khayrbak, Viceroy of Aleppo.

It was said that the first to be engaged in the battle was Second

Commander Atabek Sudun and Malik al-Umara Si Bey, Viceroy of Damascus, and the veteran *qaranisah* Mamluks but not the newly imported *julban* Mamluks. Accompanied by some deputies, they fought valiantly, defeating the Ottoman troops, inflicting terrible losses and capturing seven standards. They also captured the guns on the carriages and the musketeers. Ibn Uthman was about to flee or to surrender, as over ten thousand of his men had been killed. The army of Egypt was victorious at first; would that it had continued so! A report reached the *qaranisah* Mamluks that the sultan had told his *julban* Mamluks not to fight but to let the *qaranisah* Mamluks fight alone, and that dampened their ardour. In the meantime, Atabek Sudun was killed in battle, as was Malik al-Umara Si Bey, Viceroy of Damascus, thus the troops in the right flank were defeated. In addition to that, Khayrbak, Viceroy of Aleppo, was defeated and fled, thus causing the left flank to be defeated. It was rumoured that Khayrbak was secretly conspiring with the enemies of the Sultan, who was standing under the flag with a small body of Mamluks and who began to shout, 'Oh, lords, now is the time for valour! Fight and I pledge to you that you will be rewarded', but no one listened to him and they began to leave him. Then he turned to the Sufis and the shaykhs around him and said, 'Pray to God Almighty for victory, for now is the time for your prayers.' But no help or succour came. The Sultan's heart became as a red-hot coal that could not be extinguished. That day was intensely hot and the dust was thick. It was a day on which God's anger against the Egyptian army was kindled. When the Sultan was certain of defeat, he was immediately stricken with paralysis, which affected his side and caused his jaw to drop. He asked for water and they brought him some in a golden cup. He drank and moved two paces, then fell off his horse, stood for a moment and then died from the shock. It was said that his gall-bladder burst and that red blood flowed from his throat. His body was not found, nor was it ever known what became of it; it was as if the earth had swallowed it up there and then.

This battle lasted from sunrise until the afternoon, ending in the way God had decreed it to end. Ibn Uthman turned from Marj Dabiq to Aleppo and took it without resistance, seizing the money and treasures of the Sultan and the weapons that he had taken out of Egypt.

This is a summary of what happened in Syria. We pray to God to protect us from disasters yet to come. We shall keep you informed as soon as we learn anything.

God's security be upon you.

Deputy of the Supreme Shihab in charge of Ottoman Affairs.

Amr ibn al-Adawi

WHY has he sent for him? Has he been found out, exposed? Or was it the defeat of the army, the approaching troops, the rumours and the general confusion? Even the house of ibnat al-Khubbaiza, he cannot go to. He has no money now after having had so much before. His place in the *riwaq* is gone; he stays at the house of someone from his village for a day or two, then moves on to confront eyes with the same glances. He doesn't know what the Head Spy of Cairo will say, but would he pay any attention to him in the midst of all these worries and confusion? He doesn't know. He is now crossing the alley of al-Utuf, afraid of being seen by any of the scholars. Even those who had cultivated his friendship in the past out of fear were openly hostile to him on the night he found himself lost. He was met outside the *riwaq* by all who slept next to him, near him, his classmates, Syrians, Maghribis, Afghanis, all watching what was happening. They bundled up his clothes and threw the bundle down at his feet. Shaykh Hamza, the oldest and most senior student in the *riwaq* said, 'Leave us, Shaykh Amr. Don't show us your face again!' It was as if a hand of stone had fallen on top of him. He almost yelled at them, 'Do you know to whom you are speaking? At whom you are yelling?' At that very moment he saw himself sitting before the Head Spy of Cairo. He used to feel proud when he sat with the merchants or the scholars, as he recalled what the Head Spy had told him. He also felt sorry that he couldn't tell them about it. He felt proud whenever he saw anyone. He can send anyone to Maqshara Prison. Have they forgotten that? Sweat poured profusely all over him, wetting his clothes.

'What happened, Shaykh Hamza?'

Anger gleamed in the eyes; Shaykh Salah, the Southern Egyptian said, 'Get out of here! May God ruin your house as you have ruined people's houses!'

Shaykh Baha al-Haqq approached and took off his shoe.

Shaykh Hamza stopped him. 'You have harmed us and counted our every breath and reported everything we did; the wrong done to Shaykh Said and Shaykh Mabruk is on your head.'

It was a day for which he was not prepared. What happened to him? They went to the Rector and said about him what they had never said before. He ordered him thrown out of the *riwaq*, the classes, al-Azhar. He ordered that he be exposed. He looks at the entrance of the *riwaq*: will he never cross that threshold again? Is he never going to listen to their breathing, to the hallucinations of their dreams? What is he going to write in his reports, then? Oh, the man will not show him any mercy. He has failed and lost his cover and that, for a spy, means death. Where will he go? Faraway days look him in the face; days when he went door to door begging a few dirhams by reciting the Quran. He wouldn't dare enter any of these houses now. His clothes are in a bundle, where will he go? Should he go back to them, beg for forgiveness, tell them about his mother whose present whereabouts he doesn't know? Years have passed since she left. He doesn't know where she is. She hasn't found him. Maybe she will reach the *riwaq*, but now she will not find him there. She will go round the mosque, a blind cripple with a broken heart. If he told them about her, they might have pity on him. He realized that he had forgotten his mother's face, what she looked like. If he were to meet her, he wouldn't recognize her, if she were alive – for she had died in his heart years ago.

He carried his clothes and fled. The roads were filled with grief, as if the blood shed at Marj Dabiq had flown and covered the dust of Cairo. People's wounds were raw; there was mourning in every home. As for his own wound, it had penetrated to the very marrow. He cursed Shaykh Hamza and the scholars and secretly cursed the spies. Who knows? Maybe they exposed him for purposes of their own; maybe the Head Spy of Cairo spread the word himself, supervised his disgracing. Once he heard Shaykh Hamza cursing the Chief Spy of the Sultanate and neglected to report it. Was it laziness? Now he wished Shaykh Hamza had known what he had done. He trembled and stood still. He heard a strange, mysterious cry coming from deep inside al-Utuf. A man may get killed: what value does one human life have? Many a head has rolled in Marj Dabiq! If they caught him now, they would think he was a spy corresponding with the Ottomans. Being stoned to death would be a welcome destiny. Not even Zakariyya himself would be able to save him. Maybe the Head Spy of Cairo is hatching this scheme to get rid of him completely: some spies would arrest him now and shout, 'A spy for the Ottomans!' He should hurry up, then. Everything was receding now; it was as if he had never gone to ibnat al-Khubbaiza, never slept with sweet Latifa, never listened to delightful Haifa, never studied and never memorized *hadith*. If only he had stayed in the village, with his mother, a peasant with a wife and children!

The gate makes a heavy squeaking sound as it opens; the huge bolt hurts him. The same corridor he has crossed many times. He trembles; is he going to cross it going out tonight? He doesn't know what they will do to him. In the first room he met the Deputy Head Spy of Cairo.

'Sit.'

His back didn't touch the back of the chair. He saw himself in the man's eyes, realized how thin he was and how pale his face.

'You've exposed yourself and exposed us.'

He was tongue-tied. What are they going to do to him? When the messenger reached him at Fustat, he prepared a long speech that he was going to deliver: all he wanted was a roof over his head; he could work as a servant, cleaning mattresses and washing dishes; hasn't he exerted his utmost effort in his service? Has a single report that he prepared ever missed the mark? Hasn't he uncovered tens of agitators? Now he cannot find a single word beyond what he had prepared. The Deputy Head Spy of Cairo got up. Amr noticed that he was tired; he wished he could tell him, 'Take it easy; don't exhaust yourself.' He wished he could make small talk with him.

'You will cause us trouble.'

Amr's heart trembles like a wet dove; he is beginning to sense what has been decided in his case from the words and movements of the man; as he walked back and forth in the room, he hit the palm of his left hand with his right fist.

'You will stay with us for some time until your situation is resolved.'

'Here?'

Amr saw eternal night ahead. A baffled female apparition hovered around him; he didn't know to whom it belonged. He wished he could get close to the Deputy and whisper gently, 'Take care of yourself; look after your health', whereupon the Deputy would say, 'May God keep and preserve you, Amr.'

Said al-Juhayni

WITH an old, torn rag, Hamza ibn al-Eid al-Saghir began to wipe the usual place on the bench. 'We missed you, Shaykh Said. More than two years? How could you stay away from your friends for so long?'

Said narrowed his eyes, which had grown tired and had a hard time distinguishing nearby objects. Is Hamza telling the truth? Or is he just pretending? Did he really not know the truth of what happened? Hasn't he heard? If he was pretending not to know, then something must have warranted that. Hasn't he chanced to hear conversation among some of his Azhar patrons? Hamza is rubbing his hands together; there is unmistakable sincerity in his welcome. Have they advised him to fake it? Is there anything in his glances that should make him suspect him?

'It hasn't been that long, Master Hamza . . .'

In a few words he answered him so that Hamza or any other spy standing near him, hiding in the shop or in any other place that he couldn't see, would understand that he wasn't complaining about what had happened. Said knew that they had him under surveillance; that somewhere in a very real, specific spot there was a man monitoring his words, keeping track of people he met and the conversations he had with them. Whatever he said was reported and subjected to very close analysis. There was nothing, no matter how vague or mysterious, that they didn't understand. And no matter how many years passed, even if he had only one day left in his life, they would arrest him and take him to task. They are capable of inflicting on him in one day pain and suffering that no one can experience in a hundred years. They are trying hard to straighten him up and discipline him; doesn't a father beat and harshly discipline his children? He watches the road. The winter leaves a sorrow in the heart. A burst of blood in the veins brings back to him the sound of approaching footsteps in long, endless corridors. Faces are looking at him calmly, coldly, with eyes that penetrate to the very fabric of his dreams. They had to work very hard on him for a long time, telling him about the few stray words that he said in his sleep at the *riwaq*. Some time ago a friend of his had told him about it; many people talk in their sleep in unintelligible words. As for him, he only said one or two words at a time: 'the first', 'the last', 'yesterday', 'tomorrow', 'the dual', 'the singular'. They kept asking him about the meaning of these words for a whole month, and he kept swearing that he didn't know. They were merciful and believed him; they were kind, very kind to him and they believed that he was telling the truth. At other times they retrieved conversations that he had with others on different occasions at infrequent intervals. The questions kept coming about the meanings of words; they kept trying to explicate, analyse, match letters, prepositions, question marks; things that were like riddles to him, they were able to decode, even though he thought that would be quite impossible. They penetrated the tiniest holes, blocked up openings and filled in corridors and halls.

He came to suddenly: how could he think of what they have done to him? What if they caught up with him and knew what he was thinking about, understood that he was trying to distort their work, that he was attributing to them atrocities that never took place? Yes, they never took place. Never. Not once. If only there was a drug that prevented one from thinking about specific matters! Echoes of anonymous screams were coming to him: humans suffering, throats incapable of discharging their full load of pain, the stagnant air in closed rooms, the feel of chains. He shook his head, banishing the thoughts, stamping out the ideas. What he went through were bad dreams. Yes, dreams.

'Prayers on the Prophet! God protect us!'

Hamza ibn al-Eid al-Saghir was smiling; his words sounded kind, the friendliness was in his eyes; he didn't know what was behind it all. In this very spot he had seen Samah a thousand thousand times. Her memory makes the blood rush into the arteries and the veins. Samah? How had he loved her one day? Why did he suffer what he suffered? He pronounced the name loudly from the gap. He heard and saw enough to bring shining stars tumbling down from on high, enough to cause a proud spirit to fall. Rottenness got to his very essence. He had thought no one could touch her. Ruin got to the pretty face; the land lay fallow; the plague killed off all the hopes. One day he had thought he was going to cross the oceans, walk across the world's waste quarter, climb the mountain of Qaf and go to Waq Waq, land on totally deserted islands, eat iron and drink fire, if only she would accompany him! Now he was wondering how. How had he ever loved her? He didn't know where she was, whether she was in Cairo or had left for the countryside with those who had gone in recent days. She must have given birth to a child who called her husband 'Father' and called her 'Mother'. Her features must have changed; her hands must have become coarse. It was as if he were remembering a stranger living overseas whom he knew one day. It was as if there were a turbidity in the soul, a drop of black ambergris that refused to go away.

He didn't know why he suddenly remembered a man whom the whole of Cairo had known years ago. That man had spent years without touching a woman. Then, with the money that he had spent all his life saving up, he bought a sweet young slave girl. She cried out for help and enlisted the aid of Zayni. Zayni saved her from the man who then lost his mind and kept roaming the streets, puzzled, confused and insane. Oh! Samah was like a spear stuck in his heart, and he didn't know that it was there. He had even shed tears for her. Now he says, 'Thank God that I didn't marry her', as if someone else had told him the story of what happened. He brought the mug of fenugreek closer to his mouth. The taste is different. Has he forgotten the taste? If he had craved fenugreek there, they would have brought him some.

'God shield us and protect us!' At the beginning he approached him with warmth, but the secret sorrow on the face, and the invisible aloofness in his eyes, which dug long, thin lines around them, as if he had just awoken, as if he were suffering a grievous loss or had just stopped after crying for a long time, made Hamza ibn al-Eid al-Saghir see a barrier rising between the two of them. 'We are honoured, Shaykh Said.'

There is a seething tension in the air. He walks along the pavement surrounding the open main courtyard of the mosque behind the columns, looking at them. He doesn't go near the circles, except at class times; even then, he keeps to himself. He is not going to give conjectures or suspicions a chance. He sees the eyes gleaming and tens of men going to the outskirts of Cairo, carrying loads of dirt, digging emplacements for the cannons that Sultan Tuman Bey had worked hard to have made. Snatches of conversations come to his ears.

'Had Tuman Bey gone out and confronted them at Salihiyya, he would have surprised them when they were tired and without food. But they are rested now and moving towards Raydaniyya.'

'I think that Tuman Bey should go out and circle round in the desert and surprise them at Bilbays. To dig in at Raydaniyya and wait for them does not bode well.'

'Perhaps the emirs had convinced him of that for reasons of their own.'

'Did any one of us suspect Khayrbak before?'

'There is a rottenness in the air, shaykhs!'

When somebody asks him anything he answers with a meaningless nod. His abbreviated smile brings conversations to an abrupt end. He knows that his friends have pity for him, that they have guessed what had happened to him. He doesn't care what they say. He hopes they won't provoke him with what they say; any word that is said and lost in the air doesn't matter to them. He crosses the long corridor tiled with old marble, his hands behind his back, going to and fro, inexplicably afraid of going out into the open space, as if he might lose his balance if he were to walk in a straight line and fall, arms outstretched, face trembling, crying for help that will never arrive and hopeless succour that has been intercepted. If he walked a lot, a thousand thousand eyes would see him, each two eyes belonging to one person. If only he could select the people among whom he moves! At night, as the Shaykh of the *riwaq* is about to close the door, he gets up, breathing fast and hard, almost uttering a plea buried in his chest not to close the door, as if it would never open again. Sleep doesn't come until he is dizzy, short of breath, unconscious. He doesn't sleep; he faints.

'There are fifty thousand bedouins in Giza.'

The scholars come and go. Some of the new ones are younger; they came after he had gone on the 'trip', as he called it to himself. There is a lump as hard as a hazelnut in his throat. If only what was happening now had happened two years ago! Two years? It was more like tens of years, a whole lifetime. Is he going to stand like that, avoiding the discussion groups? What is leaving a bitter taste in his mouth, what is puzzling him, is what he is hearing now: the Ottoman troops are getting closer, almost touching Raydaniyya; their horses are trampling the land of Egypt, their swords slaughtering the people of Sharqiyya and Bilbays. They may have overrun a town or a village in which Samah had taken refuge with her husband; maybe they have ravished her in the courtyard of an old mosque, soiling her honour, which he had kept intact in his fantasies until he saw it trampled under the offspring of emirs one unbearably oppressive day. Said is tossing and turning on a mat of thorns. How long the distance and far away the travel between the time when he was shaken by a simple act of injustice, such as a man being beaten in the middle of the street. His sorrow and perplexity multiply: how come he is not moved by what is happening? The Syrians and Maghribis, people from near and far, have been stirred and shaken; the women – and even the little children – shout prayers for Tuman Bey. Perhaps he is afraid that his zeal might be misinterpreted. Perhaps they would be annoyed if he shouted or prayed loudly; they want him calm and quiet. If he shouted in support of Tuman Bey, how would he know if his shouts would be heard in his own words? He saw the poor women of Jamaliyya, of al-Utuf al-Juwwaniyya, al-Rum and Batiniyya standing in front of the tomb of Sayyidah Nafisa, exhausted with grief, raising their voices in prayer to God to grant victory to Tuman Bey and the troops of Egypt, the army of Islam. Inside the mosque are men in turbans in continual prayer, reading al-Bukhari; young men, whom he once faulted for their indifference and reluctance to confront the oppression of the emirs, were now showing zeal, and he didn't know where it came from. Did he really fault them? Anyway, there is no mistaking the defeat on the faces. He can see the signs of alienation, even in the buildings in the alleys.

The moment of sunset is the embodiment of death; sorrow is overflowing and serenity is an unattainable delusion. The call to prayers is sad; it adds a hundred years to one's life, intensifying the sense of alienation of those without home or wife or hope. It is as if the faraway countryside has been erased from space and time. The sails do not lead the boats to a safe harbour. A woman clad in yellow silk goes by; even fantasy cannot undress a woman any more. If Bilqis the Queen of Sheba herself were to come and dance for him in a closed, faraway room, the hairs on his head would not move in the slightest.

A tiny child, with tears in the eyes and fingers in the mouth; the puzzlement of the beginning of life, looking for his father, looking for his mother? Said doesn't know. The childhood impaled in his eyes stirred a hidden fear in his heart, made it overflow with compassion. He stopped to watch the child, then realized the gravity of what he had just done. How was he going to explain his sudden stopping before the crying child? He saw himself stretched out on an old mattress, around him children crying and women striking their faces with their hands in lamentation. If a person could have his wake while still alive, he would have set it up and brought the professional wailing women from all over! If only he could crucify himself on Zuwayla Gate and expire as tears came pouring down his face like that idol standing on an island, which he never saw in the middle of the ocean and which shed tears profusely whenever anyone approached it. The market-place was empty; the traffic had died down on the streets, which looked like empty arteries of the heart. He looked over his shoulder. The crying child was in the middle of the road, his legs thin as a reed pen hardly able to support his body. Every move he made embodied the misery of the beginning of life; he didn't know where to go. In his mind's eye he saw a woman who had fallen down among the baskets in the lime market, stricken with paralysis, laid on her back unaware of what was around her, her mouth spraying saliva, while a baby crawled to her breast seeking the life flowing from it. When did he see that sight? When? He got depressed.

With great care he sought out news about him. Undoubtedly he learned that he had been released. In the *riwaq* it occurred to him to sneak out under the cover of darkness to call on him. But that would be the surest way to be found out. Every day that passed without his going to Kom al-Jarih made him realize that the distance was growing longer, that perhaps he would never set foot in the house again and would not breathe its air suffused with rose-water. A few years ago it never crossed his mind that a day like that might ever come. He didn't go to Kom al-Jarih, but cautiously kept making inquiries about his master. He learned that when the emirs offered Emir Tuman Bey the post of Sultan, he refused and turned it down, and they couldn't find anybody to convince Tuman Bey to become Sultan, except Shaykh Abu al-Su'ud. Said sees his serene face; perhaps he is reluctant, not forgetting his siding with Zayni Barakat and his subsequent disappointment. No, he wasn't disappointed. After he came back from the 'trip', a man whom he had met there and who had sat with him for long periods of time came to him and asked him to go to Hamza's shop as usual, and, if the name of Zayni was mentioned while he was there, if people wondered about Zayni's disappearance, he should say (the man had asked him in a very polite manner) that Zayni was somewhere near by, making preparations and raising money and arms. Said did not object; what harm could come of that? The people at the shop wondered about Zayni's disappearance, and he said, 'He is sending his followers throughout Egypt to call upon the bedouin chiefs to send their men to Cairo.' He remembered that day that a Frankish man appeared to be listening attentively to everything that was said and he was suspicious of him. After a few days, the people learned the truth. Shaykh Abu al-Su'ud himself had arrested Zayni and detained him in his house. Said was ashamed of himself; he diverged from something that his master had done, but he had an excuse: he didn't know. Besides, the man had asked him in a very polite manner, a simple request; no harm done. The Shaykh sent to the emirs telling them not to betray their master nor intrigue against him but to support him in his stand against the Ottomans who were determined to take Egypt. Said knew that many disciples had arrived from various towns and villages. They wore red and green scarves once worn by Sayyidi Ahmad al-Badawi, who had miraculously reached out his hand and, without stirring from his place, brought the Muslim prisoners from the lands of the infidels. Shaykh Abu al-Su'ud goes out every day to the open country, carrying sandbags with the soldiers. The people cried when they saw how energetic he was despite his grey beard and grey hair and they cheered and praised God. If his master saw him he would forgive him. He is burning with longing to see him, but he is not sure of their reaction. They let him go, but they also left him without a course of action.

Said ordered his usual mug of fenugreek. Hamza was grinding it, adding to it chopped hazelnuts and, if the customer wanted, he would brown it in purified butter, which would make it a delightful breakfast, more delicious than boiled fava beansprouts at Maraghi's restaurant in front of the Chapel of the Blind. The troops were crossing the street now. Something heavy fell near by. Said had not begun to drink his fenugreek. A stranger whom he had never seen before approached.

'Shaykh Said?'

'Yes?'

'Please, come with me for a few moments.'

The winds are favourable; is he going on another trip? Should he run? Where to? Where?

'It's nothing, really. The Head Spy of Cairo has sent for you. I am not supposed to tell, but I sympathize with you. I know how sensitive you are and what you must be thinking.'

Hamza looks in. 'You haven't touched your fenugreek, Shaykh Said. You didn't drink the fenugreek! There is no might or strength except from God.'

Announcement

People of Egypt! People of Egypt!
  Inhabitants of Egypt!
  Jihad! Jihad! Jihad!
  Victory comes from God alone.

Zakariyya ibn Radi

HE didn't stop for one moment from Muqattam to Birkat al-Ratli. The alleys were closed; people were scurrying in no particular direction. Early in the morning a rumour spread in the city like fire in dry grass: some people swore that they saw the Ottoman troops coming from the direction of Fustat and attacking Tuman Bey from behind. The people were terrified and their hearts trembled. Zakariyya was all by himself, except for Mabruk, who walked beside him. The darkness mixed with the light and the shouts of the passing troops embodied for Zakariyya something mysterious. He realized that he was witnessing events of great import that didn't happen often in world history. Before, a sultan would go and another would take his place, but they were both from the same group. As for now the whole group is in danger, threatened by others, by strangers whom nobody could stop. He pities Tuman Bey; he knows what a difficult situation he is facing. He is somewhat pessimistic and he is the only person in Egypt who knows what is really in store. He is not comfortable about Janbirdi al-Ghazali's siding with Tuman Bey and he has evidence and proof. The Ottomans are a plague that is coming at the wrong time, a plague that has no relation to how low the rise of the Nile is: an evil scourge. Their troops are barbarians; Zakariyya knows about them. They are animals with no discipline. He hurries his pace, trying to escape a consequence that he sees as imminent. That is what he is going to discuss in a little while with Zayni, that man who came into his life, his thoughts, his soul and changed things round. When Zayni was arrested, he was surprised, even afraid. For long years he has been intriguing against Zayni; there was a time, during the lamps incident, when he turned the whole population against him. Nothing will ever make him forget that Zayni planted Wasila, the Turkish slave girl, in his house; it was also Zayni who caused her to be killed, her crystalline body to be buried in the desolate grave. Months ago he realized that Zayni had never created a special team of spies to gather its own information; not a single spy worked for him. It was just the regular *Muhtasib* staff. Zakariyya has been working very hard all these years, leaving no stone unturned to find a single spy working for Zayni. His men couldn't. He was certain that Zayni's men were unparalleled when it came to camouflage and he held them in the highest esteem. Then Zakariyya realized he had been duped in the worst way. Zakariyya wished that there actually were a spy team working for Zayni; as it was, he had to admit that the whole matter was nothing but a rumour started by Zayni. He built a whole system in the air; he created it and didn't create it. For days Zakariyya suffered the bitterness of being duped, but deep down in his heart he was filled with secret admiration for Zayni. For Zakariyya to live in an age by himself was an ordinary occurrence; but for the two of them to complement each other like that! Zayni's presence was good for Zakariyya; he made him a likeable person after he had been hated and disliked; Zakariyya had to develop and upgrade his methods and techniques to face Zayni's tricks and deception. Besides, there are the direct benefits that Zayni has contributed on a number of occasions, his good ideas about developing spy practices and procedures. Zakariyya smiles. Zayni presented everything as if it were part of the procedure followed by his own team of spies. Everyone in Egypt now knew that there were two groups of spies, one following Zakariyya and the other Zayni. But that is all an illusion created by Zayni.

However, the situation might change if the Ottoman plague were to overrun Egypt. That is what Zakariyya is going to discuss with Zayni. There isn't a single scrap of paper in his house in Muqattam now; Shihab al-Halabi and his secretariat are all at Zayni's secret headquarters in Helwan. Also, there are the registers and the records in which can be found everyone alive in Egypt. He is going to need these in the next few days. A long time ago, when they arrested Ali ibn Abi al-Jud and Zayni took over, he got rid of his papers and killed the Sultan's beloved boy. To this day he hasn't figured out the secret of that relationship; the boy is dead and the Sultan is dead. How distant that time seems now, many long years, during every day of which he reiterated his determination to kill

Zayni off. Many opportunities presented themselves. When Shaykh Abu al-Su'ud sent for Zayni and humiliated him and worked him over, his hair stood on end. This must be handled quickly and firmly; it was no joking matter. Here was Zayni in the hands of a good, pious man who was respected by the emirs, great and small. Zakariyya could deploy his aides everywhere and agitate the people against Zayni, make public his secrets; he could send long lists detailing the monies hoarded by Zayni: the pearls, the Balkhash stones, the rubies, the turquoise and the heaps of gold. A brief message would tell our master that these were the places where Zayni has hidden his monies. He was overcome with perplexity.

He once read in the histories of the Ismaili sect about a *fedawi* sent to assassinate a prince or a notable and how, in carrying out his task, he faces certain moments when decisiveness is a must: it didn't matter whether the decision was right or wrong. What mattered was making the decision. Hesitation might cost the *fedawi* his very life. That was the old lesson that Zakariyya read and that very night he decided: Zayni's life must not be wasted. He sent for Ibrahim ibn al-Sukkar wa al-Limun and ibn Kifuh and deployed his ears and eyes everywhere to talk to the populace very intelligently and in any way they saw fit about Zayni's fairness, goodness and piety and remind the people of what he had done for them. Then they were to talk about what Shaykh Abu al-Su'ud al-Jarihi was doing. True, the Shaykh was a man of God, a blessed saint, but what were shaykhs doing in matters of the State? What were hermits doing with affairs of this world? If they preoccupied themselves with matters of dinars, they would be deviating from the right path. When Shaykh Abu al-Su'ud ordered Zayni Barakat exposed in disgrace by making him ride a donkey backwards through the streets and Emir Allan, the Chief Executive Secretary, decided to hang him on the door of his relative who monopolized the fava bean trade in Egypt at Fustat, Zakariyya sent an urgent message to Tuman Bey about large sums of money that Zayni had, which had to be returned to the treasury. If he were hanged, the money would be lost when the country was in dire need of it. Besides, there were very important matters of a confidential nature in which he was still involved. His death would result in great harm befalling the emirs, the populace and the Sultanate itself, especially in these critical moments. With the message he sent a short letter, suggesting that Tuman Bey reduce the number of his public appearances so that his prestige might not diminish among the populace and so that they might not get used to seeing him.

Zakariyya knows quite well that Zayni would rather be hanged than saved by Zakariyya. Men like Zayni accept what Zakariyya has done arrogantly. When Zayni was returned to Shaykh Abu al-Su'ud and they changed their minds about hanging him, Zakariyya was relieved. Who knows? Maybe Zakariyya would find himself in a similar situation out of which only Zayni could extricate him. These were turbulent times in which nobody was assured of his safety or of that of his family, especially people like Zakariyya.

He was now approaching Birkat al-Ratli. Naturally he didn't go down to the city or tour its bazaars; his deputies sent him reports all the time, even from places overrun by the Ottomans. Some of his deputies were martyred. He never imagined that he would see such ruin and desolation among the people. The minarets were like letters frozen in the air. His son, Yasin, and his harem were in the deep South. He is haunted by the same feeling that he is living at a time that is witnessing great, rare events. Finally he sees Zayni's house. In a short while, they will be talking, the second time since Zayni had been released. Wasn't he stupid when he thought, thousands of times, of getting rid of him? There is a secret smile on his lips. Did he really think of that? Did he, really?

Announcement/Announcement

People of Egypt! The Supreme Hünkar informs you, therefore listen and be warned: whoever hides a Mamluk will be hanged; whoever hides the money of a Mamluk will be hanged. Listen and be warned.

Announcement/Announcement

People of Egypt! People of Egypt! Whoever informs about the whereabouts of Tuman Bey will receive a thousand dinars! Whoever brings him, dead or alive, will receive a thousand dinars from the

Protector of the Two Sacred Cities and the Seas, Selim Shah, the Supreme Hünkar.

Announcement/Announcement

People of Egypt! People of Egypt! Whoever sees Shaykh Abu al-Su'ud al-Jarihi, whoever sees any of the dervishes of Shaykh Abu al-Su'ud who are causing sedition and attacking the troops should bring them to the Camp of the Hünkar. It will be greatly appreciated! It will be greatly appreciated!

Announcement/Announcement

People of Egypt! People of Egypt! Whoever hides the slave girls and women of the Mamluks shall be hanged without further ado.

Announcement/Announcement

People of Egypt! People of Egypt! Nobody should go out after sunset! Nobody wear a veil!

Whoever is caught shall be hanged. People of Egypt! People of Egypt! Be quiet, be quiet!

Violators shall be hanged.

SIXTH PAVILION

Kom al-Jarih

Said al-Juhayni

THE grave has an embrace that no one escapes; it presses the ribs
of the faithful and the infidel, erases the first and the last, makes the
dual singular, disperses the plural, equates the manifest with the
hidden. Every soul will know what it has done and the body organs
will talk, telling what sins they committed. Said knows the hard
way to Kom al-Jarih. His heart is gripped by anguish, a target for
arrows and spears that do not miss, a field for battle and combat.
Since his return, he has been wishing to see his master for just one
moment, and then nothing else – before or after – will matter; to
hear his voice, to know what thoughts are going on in his master's
mind about him, his own person. The time has come when a son
does not know his father, when a brother will be asked about his
brother and will deny him, even while he is standing next to him;
the day when all pregnant women will miscarry; when people look
drunk, even though they are not drunk. The air is stagnant: is it
the calamity? Ah, what will convey unto you what the calamity is!
There is a stillness in the air: is it the smoke that appears before the
Hour of Resurrection? The alien troops are deflowering the virgins
at the door of al-Mu'ayyad Mosque, at the dome where he bent
over, many, many times, took off his shoes and entered the solemn
mosque, filled with humility.

What is left then? Perhaps the Antichrist will appear, come down
from Muqattam, come out of the alleys of Husayniyya, appear to
the people suddenly from the Khalij, the city canal, from the Nile
before the time of the annual inundation, or from the Roda Island,
from the Great Pyramid riding his beast, which spies out and conveys to him the news of the world. The night will be long; people
will wake up and find nothing but continuous darkness. The first
rays of light will turn the heads: here is the sun rising from the
west, not a disc of gold but a limp, black pie. What is left then?

Appear, Sufyani, accursed conqueror, blow the horn: once, twice, three times, everybody dies and total ruin ensues for forty thousand years. The pangs in the chest: what disease have the days spawned? What is there to fear when the soul is a ruined site; when the houses fear those dwelling in them? What is left?

'We know, Said, that you wish to see your master. This is your right, of course. And need I remind you "He who taught me one letter makes me his slave"? You said his name several times in your sleep. Sha'lan, what name did Said repeat in his sleep when he was our guest for some time?'

'Shaykh Abu al-Su'ud. He mentioned no other.'

'See? Go to him. Don't be afraid. On the contrary, we want you to resume your relationship with him exactly as it was before. We want you to enjoy his confidence. Don't alienate him. Go to him, prostrate yourself at his feet. Cry. Shed real tears. He will ask you, "Where have you been since your return?" Tell him, "They forbade me, but I don't care about that any more. I have disobeyed them and come to you." Curse us; curse our grandfathers! Pray God to ruin us! Say whatever you want to, Said. You must revive his confidence in you. You are the son that he didn't beget and yet begat.'

He walked round Bab al-Wazir, the tomb of Sayyida Fatima al-Nabawiyya. His feet are hurrying up; he hasn't seen these houses for quite some time. The glow of hopes, the desire for travel, running, rushing, loving, touching a kindly hand, a pleasant meal after an ancient winter sunset. No, none of that came to him. Rather he had old, impaled images: little holes in the walls; he saw human beings. 'Do you know this one? He was a great and mighty emir. He has been in gaol for thirty-four years. He passes water here, eats here. He has forgotten his own name. Really forgotten his name. He forgot words, letters and sounds.' Another hole housed a young prisoner who has never seen the light or what it might look like. In his eyes there is a blue gleam, like cats' eyes in the dark. He is twenty years old and he has spent the twenty years here. His going out into the world might appear to him as your going to gaol appeared to you. Among the rocks lives wither away, die out; among the rocks or in the frightening, narrow, clean rooms where his friend Mansur is stretching out now. What is left then?

'What we ask of you, what we want, is to benefit from his learning and his wisdom, to learn the precious words that he says; what he thinks of people, what he intends to do as far as Tuman Bey is concerned. Since the Hünkar came into the city we know that he's staying at home . . . But there are disciples who go to him. Who are they? Where do they go? There are some who claim that the Shaykh intends to go out to join Tuman Bey. But would you believe that? Would it enter your mind that Shaykh Abu al-Su'ud, the good, kindly, pious, God-fearing man could bear arms and kill somebody? You are the one who knows him best: if that were indeed his intention, then it is a change about which we must learn. For no reason really, except to benefit from the knowledge: how old age can stand fighting, attacking and retreating. Of course, you are not going to tell him what we want. This way you would be disseminating his teachings and wisdom to all the people, through us. Then there is a secondary issue . . .'

The house is quiet and peaceful. He spent the best time of his life here; it passed like a chant, a sweet song. He crosses the threshold of the house. How is he going to face him; with what meaning left in the eyes?

'We know you can do it. Otherwise, we wouldn't have come to you. We are asking for your help, Said. You are close to us; you are one of us. You are ours.'

'You are one of us. You are ours.'

'As for that other matter. Come over here, closer. Sha'lan, go out. Go out for a few moments, because what I am going to say is very highly confidential and only Said will hear it.

'Of course, neither you nor any good Muslim is happy with what the Ottomans have done to us. Hence, Zayni Barakat – and, by the way, he sends his greetings and apologizes to you. He would love to see you, but the eyes of the Ottomans are all around his house. Anyway, Zayni has made up his mind and trusted in God to form a group to work underground, not openly, a group of strong warriors for the cause of God, like you, to irritate the Hünkar, to eliminate treason. What we ask of you is easy: submit to us the names of able-bodied young men who would not hesitate to sacrifice themselves. Give us the names and we will find them and convince them to join us in this jihad.

'Do you understand me, Said? Do you understand? Well, then, tell me. What do I want?'

Is that where he came to look around again? Here he had knelt before his master. This floor has been wet from the water in which the dried dates were washed. Here he pronounced her name. There is not a single sound in the house. The cellar is destroyed. Where did his master go? What is left then? If only he could catch one glimpse of him! He would tell all, divulge the secrets, air the rottenness, open his wound to heal if he were to catch just one glimpse of him! After that, let the world end. He knows that he would be met with a loving word and a serene look; he would relate his nightmares to his master and rebuild that which has been destroyed. It never occurred to him that he would come here one day and not meet him. What is left then? If he saw him now he would tell all, the old and the new. Oh, there is no turning back. In his mind's eyes he sees his master. Is he still his master? He sees him travelling in the countryside, calling upon the people to fight. Who would take him to him? Who would tell him where he could find him? His master is gone. What, then, is left?

Said al-Juhayni

OH! they ruined me and destroyed my fortresses!

OUTSIDE THE PAVILIONS

One last excerpt from the diary of the Venetian traveller Visconti Gianti (923 AH)

In my long travels, I haven't seen a city so devastated. After a long time I ventured out into the streets. Death, cold and heavy, hung over the air of the city. The Ottoman troops roamed the streets, stormed into houses. Walls have no value here, doors have been eliminated; security is lost and no prayer or supplication will do any good. No one is certain that they will see another day. In a narrow alley I saw a woman who has been slaughtered and her breast cut off. I looked around me: floor tiles and dust in a faraway house; a child cries; I do not know whose child it is. At a charitable public drinking-water fountain near Zuwayla Gate, I saw human beings whose lives had been ended in diabolical ways: inserting a red-hot skewer into the ribs and pushing it to come out from the other side. Someone's tongue is sticking out as if it were an idiotic question mark. Why did what happened happen? The eyes look like rotten plums. The heralds do not have a moment's peace, day or night. The search for Tuman Bey, the Sultan of the country, who is in hiding, is growing more feverish by the minute, especially after his sudden appearance at Shaykhun Mosque and the people rallying around him, then his attack against the Ottomans in Bulaq. I heard that, as soon as he appeared anywhere, the people would gather around him as if they knew when he would come. I also heard that large numbers of dervishes (religious men) have joined him and have been attacking those Ottoman soldiers who walked in outlying alleys and roads, killing as many of them as they could. This has frightened the invaders, who were told to take precautions and walk only in large groups.

This morning I went up on the roof; I saw sorrow hanging, like a thick roof, over the city, as if the houses themselves have been shedding tears. I saw the face of my friend Shaykh Muhammad Ahmad ibn Iyas one day before the Ottomans entered the city. His features prophesied the coming defeat; he was broken. I haven't seen him since that night. I heard from someone I trusted that Tuman Bey had appeared in Southern Egypt and that he had gathered thousands of armed bedouins around him. It was said that a Muslim saint who used to live in Cairo had left his house and gone to the countryside lighting a strong fire there and rousing the people. The person who told me also told me that that saint was one hundred years old, or even older, and that he was very brave, that he had drunk of the water of the fountain of life and that whoever drank from the fountain of life never died and never was defeated. Indeed, hundreds of youths and men and women, most of whom had never seen him while he stayed in Cairo, have gone to follow him. He also told me that that saint had a mighty banner called 'The Prophet's Banner' and that as soon as he unfurled it the whole Egyptian nation from one end to the other would rise and fight the invaders until it finished them off. I expressed scepticism to my interlocutor and asked him, 'Why hasn't he unfurled the banner now?' He answered confidently that that would happen only when He orders it (he pointed to heaven). The man, an Azhar shaykh, cried and said that according to the ancient books, 'Egypt is God's favourite land; whoever wants to harm it, God will cut him into two halves.'

Today, finally, it was announced that it was safe to go out, so I decided to come out to find out what was happening. I realized the risk I was taking as the invaders were not to be trusted to keep their word: they would announce that it was safe, then simply disregard what they announced. I found the house of my friend, Shaykh Rihan, burned and destroyed and nobody could tell me where I could find him. I heard that the man about whom I talked so much during my second trip, Zayni Barakat, had appeared. Some shaykhs said that he was trying to recruit young men to fight against the Ottomans, but one of them raised questions about Zayni's intentions, especially since he had gone up to the Citadel several times and met with Khayrbak for a long time. I learned that Khayrbak (I mentioned him earlier) had indicated that he was pleased with Zayni, for when the invaders came into Egypt, Zayni was sitting at home in disfavour with the former Sultan Tuman Bey, stripped of all his posts. One of his former deputies, Abd al-Azim al-Sayrafi had replaced him in his most important post. Before the end of the day the news was confirmed. In the late afternoon I heard the herald beating a drum. I stood waiting and saw three black horses with three riders carrying a scale, weights and a flag with the emblem of the *Muhtasib*: a brandished sword. Behind them came a white horse on which rode Zayni Barakat ibn Musa and behind him a fat man whom I didn't know. The street is empty: desolateness rampant. All the shops are closed. Around the little procession was a stench of rottenness. A few passers-by looked on, listened to the drumbeats, shook their heads and didn't stop. When the procession came close to me I saw Zayni and noticed that he had a veil on. I didn't remember what he looked like, for I had met him only once. I must meet him again. The herald announced that Khayrbak ordered that Zayni Barakat ibn Musa be appointed *Muhtasib* of Cairo, that whoever had a complaint should go to him. The herald then paused and proclaimed an order from Zayni himself. I listened; he was explaining the new Ottoman currency that had replaced the old Mamluk currency. I followed the small procession, which was moving towards Bab al-Futuh Gate. At the bend it disappeared and the faint announcement moved away in the sallow air.

FOR THE BEST IN PAPERBACKS, LOOK FOR THE

In every corner of the world, on every subject under the sun, Penguin represents quality and variety – the very best in publishing today.

For complete information about books available from Penguin – including Pelicans, Puffins, Peregrines and Penguin Classics – and how to order them, write to us at the appropriate address below. Please note that for copyright reasons the selection of books varies from country to country.

In the United Kingdom: Please write to *Dept E.P., Penguin Books Ltd, Harmondsworth, Middlesex, UB7 0DA*

If you have any difficulty in obtaining a title, please send your order with the correct money, plus ten per cent for postage and packaging, to *PO Box No 11, West Drayton, Middlesex*

In the United States: Please write to *Dept BA, Penguin, 299 Murray Hill Parkway, East Rutherford, New Jersey 07073*

In Canada: Please write to *Penguin Books Canada Ltd, 2801 John Street, Markham, Ontario L3R 1B4*

In Australia: Please write to the *Marketing Department, Penguin Books Australia Ltd, P.O. Box 257, Ringwood, Victoria 3134*

In New Zealand: Please write to the *Marketing Department, Penguin Books (NZ) Ltd, Private Bag, Takapuna, Auckland 9*

In India: Please write to *Penguin Overseas Ltd, 706 Eros Apartments, 56 Nehru Place, New Delhi, 110019*

In Holland: Please write to *Penguin Books Nederland B.V., Postbus 195, NL–1380AD Weesp, Netherlands*

In Germany: Please write to *Penguin Books Ltd, Friedrichstrasse 10–12, D–6000 Frankfurt Main 1, Federal Republic of Germany*

In Spain: Please write to *Longman Penguin España, Calle San Nicolas 15, E–28013 Madrid, Spain*

In France: Please write to *Penguin Books Ltd, 39 Rue de Montmorency, F-75003, Paris, France*

In Japan: Please write to *Longman Penguin Japan Co Ltd, Yamaguchi Building, 2–12–9 Kanda Jimbocho, Chiyoda-Ku, Tokyo 101, Japan*

A CHOICE OF PENGUIN FICTION

Maia   Richard Adams

The heroic romance of love and war in an ancient empire from one of our greatest storytellers. 'Enormous and powerful' – *Financial Times*

The Warning Bell   Lynne Reid Banks

A wonderfully involving, truthful novel about the choices a woman must make in her life – and the price she must pay for ignoring the counsel of her own heart. 'Lynne Reid Banks knows how to get to her reader: this novel grips like Super Glue' – *Observer*

Doctor Slaughter   Paul Theroux

Provocative and menacing – a brilliant dissection of lust, ambition and betrayal in 'civilized' London. 'Witty, chilly, exuberant, graphic' – *The Times Literary Supplement*

Wise Virgin   A. N. Wilson

Giles Fox's work on the Pottle manuscript, a little-known thirteenth-century tract on virginity, leads him to some innovative research on the subject that takes even his breath away. 'A most elegant and chilling comedy' – *Observer* Books of the Year

Gone to Soldiers   Marge Piercy

Until now, the passions, brutality and devastation of the Second World War have only been written about by men. Here for the first time, one of America's major writers brings a woman's depth and intensity to the panorama of world war. 'A victory' – *Newsweek*

Trade Wind   M. M. Kaye

An enthralling blend of history, adventure and romance from the author of the bestselling *The Far Pavilions*

A CHOICE OF PENGUIN FICTION

Stanley and the Women   Kingsley Amis

Just when Stanley Duke thinks it safe to sink into middle age, his son goes insane – and Stanley finds himself beset on all sides by women, each of whom seems to have an intimate acquaintance with madness. 'Very good, very powerful . . . beautifully written' – Anthony Burgess in the *Observer*

The Girls of Slender Means   Muriel Spark

A world and a war are winding up with a bang, and in what is left of London, all the nice people are poor – and about to discover how different the new world will be. 'Britain's finest post-war novelist' – *The Times*

Him with His Foot in His Mouth   Saul Bellow

A collection of first-class short stories. 'If there is a better living writer of fiction, I'd very much like to know who he or she is' – *The Times*

Mother's Helper   Maureen Freely

A superbly biting and breathtakingly fluent attack on certain libertarian views, blending laughter, delight, rage and amazement, this is a novel you won't forget. 'A winner' – *The Times Literary Supplement*

Decline and Fall   Evelyn Waugh

A comic yet curiously touching account of an innocent plunged into the sham, brittle world of high society. Evelyn Waugh's first novel brought him immediate public acclaim and is still a classic of its kind.

Stars and Bars   William Boyd

Well-dressed, quite handsome, unfailingly polite and charming, who would guess that Henderson Dores, the innocent Englishman abroad in wicked America, has a guilty secret? 'Without doubt his best book so far . . . made me laugh out loud' – *The Times*

A CHOICE OF PENGUIN FICTION

The Ghost Writer Philip Roth

Philip Roth's celebrated novel about a young writer who meets and falls in love with Anne Frank in New England – or so he thinks. 'Brilliant, witty and extremely elegant' – *Guardian*

Small World David Lodge

Shortlisted for the 1984 Booker Prize, *Small World* brings back Philip Swallow and Maurice Zapp for a jet-propelled journey into hilarity. 'The most brilliant and also the funniest novel that he has written' – *London Review of Books*

Moon Tiger Penelope Lively

Winner of the 1987 Booker Prize, *Moon Tiger* is Penelope Lively's 'most ambitious book to date' – *The Times* 'A complex tapestry of great subtlety . . . Penelope Lively writes so well, savouring the words as she goes' – *Daily Telegraph* 'A very clever book: it is evocative, thought-provoking and hangs curiously on the edges of the mind long after it is finished' – *Literary Review*

Absolute Beginners Colin MacInnes

The first 'teenage' novel, the classic of youth and disenchantment, *Absolute Beginners* is part of MacInnes's famous London trilogy – and now a brilliant film. 'MacInnes caught it first – and best' – *Harpers and Queen*

July's People Nadine Gordimer

Set in South Africa, this novel gives us an unforgettable look at the terrifying, tacit understandings and misunderstandings between blacks and whites. 'This is the best novel that Miss Gordimer has ever written' – Alan Paton in the *Saturday Review*

The Ice Age Margaret Drabble

'A continuously readable, continuously surprising book . . . here is a novelist who is not only popular and successful but formidably growing towards real stature' – *Observer*

FOR THE BEST IN PAPERBACKS, LOOK FOR THE 🐧

PENGUIN INTERNATIONAL WRITERS

Titles already published or in preparation

Gamal Al-Ghitany	**Zayni Barakat**
Isabel Allende	**Eva Luna**
Wang Anyi	**Baotown**
Joseph Brodsky	**Marbles: A Play in Three Acts**
Doris Dorrie	**Love, Pain and the Whole Damn Thing**
Shusaku Endo	**Scandal**
	Wonderful Fool
Ida Fink	**A Scrap of Time**
Daniele Del Giudice	**Lines of Light**
Miklos Haraszti	**The Velvet Prison**
Ivan Klima	**My First Loves**
	A Summer Affair
Jean Levi	**The Chinese Emperor**
Harry Mulisch	**Last Call**
Cees Nooteboom	**The Dutch Mountains**
	A Song of Truth and Semblance
Milorad Pavic	**Dictionary of the Khazars (Male)**
	Dictionary of the Khazars (Female)
Luise Rinser	**Prison Journal**
A. Solzhenitsyn	**Matryona's House and Other Stories**
	One Day in the Life of Ivan Denisovich
Tatyana Tolstoya	**On the Golden Porch and Other Stories**
Elie Wiesel	**Twilight**
Zhang Xianliang	**Half of Man is Woman**